GANGLAND CARTEL

Romell Tukes

Lock Down Publications and Ca$h
Presents

GANGLAND CARTEL

A Novel by *Romell Tukes*

Romell Tukes

Lock Down Publications
P.O. Box 944
Stockbridge, Ga 30281
www.lockdownpublications.com

Copyright 2020 Romell Tukes
Gangland Cartel

Lock Down Publications
Like our page on Facebook: Lock Down Publications @
www.facebook.com/lockdownpublications.ldp
Cover design and layout by: **Dynasty Cover Me**
Book interior design by: **Shawn Walker**
Edited by: **Cassandra Sims**

Stay Connected with Us!

Text **LOCKDOWN** to 22828 to stay up-to-date with new releases,
sneak peaks, contests and more…
Thank you!

Submission Guideline.

Submit the first three chapters of your completed manuscript to ldpsubmissions@gmail.com, subject line: Your book's title. The manuscript must be in a .doc file and sent as an attachment. Document should be in Times New Roman, double spaced and in size 12 font. Also, provide your synopsis and full contact information. If sending multiple submissions, they must each be in a separate email.

Have a story but no way to send it electronically? You can still submit to LDP/Ca$h Presents. Send in the first three chapters, written or typed, of your completed manuscript to:

LDP: Submissions Dept
P.O. Box 944
Stockbridge, Ga 30281

DO NOT send original manuscript. Must be a duplicate.

Provide your synopsis and a cover letter containing your full contact information.

Thanks for considering LDP and Ca$h Presents.

Gangland Cartel

ACKNOWLEDGEMENTS

First, and Foremost, All Praises are Due to Allah. Shout-out to my Parents, Family, and Readers. Peace and Respect to: All my Muslim Brothers out there on the deen.

Shout-out to my Yankees in Peekskill and NY Fam: Smoke Black, love ya, bro. Fresh, CB, YB Spayhoe, and Lingo. Bk-OG Chuck, Tom Dog, all of Flatbush, and my guy, Skrap Fort Green.

My B-more Team: Roc, Stucky, and Tay. My NJ Fam: Blue, B.G., Beast, Rugar, and Trouble from East Orange. My N.A. and Atlanta Niggas. My Philly Brothers: OG Musa and Big C.

To the Readers: Put Allah first, stay focused, and surround yourselves with good energy only. I'm only dropping street lit shit and every book is going to be a movie. So, stay tuned and thanks for support.

Big shout-out to Ca$h and LDP: We in the building.
The Game is Ours!

Romell Tukes

CHAPTER 1
HARLEM, NEW YORK

"Brazy, please, I swear I ain't do it, fam. I swear on my momma and daughter life I ain't have nothing to do with that robbery," Bing cried out. Helplessly, he pleaded for mercy as he sat tied to a chair by his wrists and ankles.

"Bing, you too old not to take full responsibility for your actions," Brazy said, with his back facing Bing as he fumbled with something on the table. His crew surrounded and stared at Bing, who was nearly naked, in just a pair of boxers.

"It was Moe Joe and Blu Boy. You know I would never cross you like that! We grew up in the sandbox together," "Bing said, looking through two swollen eyes and with a busted lip.

Brazy and Bing had been close friends since the first grade. The two did dirt together and they had always remained loyal to one another. That is, until Bing teamed up with a nigga from another rival hood to rob Brazy's stash house for $125,000 and seventeen keys of coke.

Brazy didn't have a clue as to who the culprit was. But when Bing started telling niggas he had a new plug in Philly, and selling keys in the hood for the low, he knew something wasn't right. Since Bing was known for nickel and dime hustling, it wasn't hard to put two and two together.

"Why, Bing? You know I would of gave you anything," Brazy said. "Who held you down when you did your seven-year bid?"

"You, but—"

"Nah, *but* nothing. When your kids needed school clothes who gave it to you?" Brazy asked.

"Brazy, man," he moaned out through tears.

"When the Lincoln niggas tried to kill you who saved you?" he asked angrily.

"You, fam, I'm sorry. I was high off dust, but I give you my word, I can get you your money back," Bing said remorsefully, as he sat stripped of his manhood in an old rundown storage warehouse, near a metro train station. He regretted ever letting his girlfriend, Ashely, talk him into robbing his childhood friend, especially since Brazy was a well-known drug lord and vicious gangsta.

"Nah, blood, it's too late. Hold that nigga's hands down," Brazy ordered his crew. The four men did as they were told. His little brother, Rugar, stood off to the side watching the entire scene unfold. The busted window made the atmosphere even colder.

"Come on, man," Bing yelled, right before they filled his mouth with dirty socks and taped it together with gorilla tape to muffle his screams.

"Rugar, come here, bro. See, this what happens when a real nigga turns bitch and violates the G-code of the streets. They let greed take over mentally and emotionally," Brazy said. Then, he lifted a razor-sharp saw blade and slammed it into Bing's fingers and started sawing them off. He worked the saw back and forth as if he were cutting down a tree, causing Bing's fingers to drop to the floor and roll.

Rugar's eyes grew wider as he watched and listened to his brother. Like a madman, Brazy continued talking to his crew while cutting off the other fingers, as if it were nothing. Today was Rugar's first day of training with his brother and he hadn't been expecting this.

Bing finally passed out due to the amount of blood he'd lost, but that didn't stop Brazy and he continued to mutilate him. He cut off both of Bing's hands and shot him in the head seventeen times, as if he'd been a stranger off the streets.

"Let this be a lesson to you all, even you Rugar—never cross the ones who never crossed you," Brazy said. He tossed the bloody saw on the floor before walking out with his little brother behind him. The goons were left to clean up his mess.

***

Two days later, Rugar woke up in a cold sweat. It was five o'clock in the morning and he'd been having a nightmare about seeing the nigga's fingers and hands get chopped off. It was dark in his room so he hadn't even seen the shadow sitting in the chair in the corner.

"Get dressed and hurry," Brazy said, in a low pitched voice. He scared Rugar so badly, he rolled out of his bed causing Brazy to laugh.

"What the fuck, son?" Rugar said, getting up from the floor, rubbing his now-bruised knee.

"Shhh, before you wake up Uncle P and China. Here." Brazy tossed him an all-black Champion sweat suit. He had been in his little brother's room for about an hour, watching him talk and yell out in his sleep. He knew he was having a nightmare as a result of what he'd seen two days prior, but since he wanted to be in the game so bad he had to take everything that came with it. Seeing he was fully awake, he left his brother alone so he could get himself together.

Rugar brushed his teeth, washed his face, and got dressed. He made sure to grab his pistol.

Minutes later, the two were driving down the dark Harlem streets. Since it was just nearing dawn the sun hadn't come up yet, and even with the streetlights on, it was still dark out. The black Challenger with tinted windows made them look like detectives as they creep down the block. It wasn't long before they pulled up to 116th and Morningside St., across from the park.

"What we doing here, bro?" Rugar asked when Brazy parked.

"Sometimes it's just best to watch and listen instead of asking questions. That's what you got eyes for," Brazy told him, as he watched a blue van parked across the street.

"Facts." Rugar took heed and watched the seven cars parked on the opposite of the road.

"Today is gonna be a big step for you. But let me ask you a question," Brazy said and continued, "if your own blood ever crossed you, what would you do?" he asked seriously. Just as the question left his lips, a black Benz AMG truck pulled up behind the blue van.

"Treat them like the OPP, the enemy. 'Cause when they cross that line the love and loyalty is crossed with it," Rugar said sternly, wondering what his big brother was getting at.

"Good stand on that," Brazy said. They looked as a black guy dressed in a suit hopped out of the AMG to meet two big white boys who looked like policemen.

Rugar wondered why the dude in the suit looked so familiar, but it was too dark to see who him clearly. "Damn, that nigga snitching," he said. He saw the dude in the suit hand the two cops a stack of photos and shake their hands, before jumping back in his Benz and pulling off.

After the blue van pulled off and was out of sight, Brazy pulled off on a mission to tail the Benz, even though he knew where it was headed to. He'd been watching the black dude, whose name was Ronny, for about a month. Every Tuesday and Friday mornings, Ronny would snitch to the police and give them information on Brazy's operations. Luckily, Brazy had the NYPD on his payroll so they didn't fuck with anybody from the Empire. Plus, they were the most vicious crew to ever come out of New York and he was the team's captain.

Twenty minutes later, after seeming as though he'd been driving in circles, the Benz came to a full stop at a big church. Ronny parked in his regular spot and proceeded to open the church doors. Ironically, he was the Pastor of the church on Lenox Ave.

"Can't be," Rugar said in a baffled tone. Seeing the church he'd grown up in fucked him up, but when he got a closer look at the man's face his heart stopped. It was Ronny, his first blood cousin.

"Yep," Brazy said, shaking his head.

Ronny walked inside the church, sat down in the front row, and opened up his Bible.

***

Ronny was a thirty-six-year-old handsome man with a beautiful wife, who was also affiliated with the church. He'd grown up in

Lincoln Projects where he was one of the most ruthless niggas to come out the jets. He had caught a body when he was eighteen years old, and ended up doing a fifteen-year prison bid, in the cold mountains up north. That was where he became a devoted Christian and gave his life to Jesus.

He knew Brazy had a big drug ring. He wanted him, and any other drug dealer putting poison in the Harlem streets, off the streets. Though he'd had many talks with Brazy urging him to stop, each time, Brazy would just brush him off. So, Ronny chose to take matters into his own hands. He went to the NYPD narcotic division and dropped a dime on him.

"Hope I'm not disturbing you, fam," Brazy said, as Rugar followed his footsteps. From the look on Ronny's face, it was clear they'd scared him. Rugar

"Jamel, what's going on?" Ronny greeted, calling Rugar by his real name. He couldn't help but notice the gun at his side.

"You know what's goin' on, Ronny," Brazy snapped.

Ronny could sense he knew something so he just cut the acting.

"Marlo," Ronny said, calling Brazy by his government.

"It's *Brazy* to you, rat-ass nigga!"

"Look what you out here doing to our people. Anybody can be a killer and drug dealer, but it takes a real man to build up his people instead of destroying them. I came home and became a pastor, now you got Jamel out here toting guns, gangbanging, and selling poison. How can you do that to your own blood?" Ronny shouted.

"How the fuck can you snitch on *your* own? I know our pops is turning over in his grave, but Rugar made his own choice, and I'ma always support my family good or bad," Brazy said.

"You goin' to hell," Ronny shouted.

"I know, but you gonna beat me there." Brazy looked at his brother and nodded his head.

When his brother gave him the signal, Rugar didn't hesitate, and he shot Ronny in his face ten times, and left him dead with blood all over his Bible. With that out of the way, the two brothers exited the church.

With no remorse, they hurried to the vehicle just as the blue skies hid behind the sun, letting them know it was morning and time for breakfast.

***

In the diner, they ordered the same meal every time they went there for breakfast, which was chocolate chip pancakes, waffles, eggs, and sausage.

"Ever since mommy and daddy got killed and Uncle P took us in, all of us have basically been left to raise ourselves. I'm twenty-four now, bro. I had a rough life in the streets. But even if mommy and daddy *were* still here, how could they raise us properly living the life of bank robbers, Blood?" Brazy asked. His mother, Chilli, was Cuban, and his father, Big Joe, had been a football player until he'd torn his ACL. Once his football career ended, he became a bank robber with his high school sweetheart, Chilli, on some Bonnie and Clyde shit.

"I feel you," Rugar stated, as he sipped on some fresh-squeezed orange juice. As they sat talking, people finally started to enter the small sized diner.

"I don't want you in this street shit. It's bad enough you already Blood and pumping under my hood. I always wanted better for you and China, bro. That's why I chose the streets even though Uncle P already a made nigga," Brazy said. Their uncle was a retired kingpin who owned many businesses.

"This is my life and I want the power and respect. When I dropped out of school and got my GED, I was done with that shit. My heart always been in the streets," Rugar said.

"That's cool and all, bro, but this shit ain't meant to be a career. There ain't no lucky gold treasures at the end of the tunnel, only prison or death. When you get enough money, go legit. Own you some homes, businesses, or properties," Brazy said, schooling him, "you gotta hustle for a reason not because you fiending, Blood," he said with a mouth full of food. Rugar

"OK," Rugar said as he listened attentively.

"Feed your wolves or you'll become wolf meat. It's a cold game and sometimes the hunter becomes the hunted. If anything ever happens to me, you'll be given my position within the Empire, and you'll become the man," Brazy continued. "Stay next to Naya. She's the realest bitch you'll ever meet. She's a different kinda breed, trust me, son," he said, stamping Naya as official. She was the closest woman to his heart, but due to their lifestyles, their relationship was complicated.

"Copy that, but nothing will happen," Rugar said, eyeing the cute waitress who walked past him smiling. Looking at him, she assumed he was older than he really was.

Rugar was light-brown skinned with wavy hair and hazel-brown chinky eyes just like his sister, who looked foreign. He had thick eyebrows and stood six feet even. His arms and chest were tatted, and his body was chiseled and lean. He had a nice smile with deep dimples on both of his high cheek bones.

Brazy was a little darker and taller, standing six feet, three inches tall. His waves matched his brother's and his burly physique made him look as though he stayed in the gym. His entire body was inked up, and his chipped tooth seemed to enhance his cocky attitude. He was a big homie for his own Blood set and he was the head of the Empire, an organization filled with the highest ranking Blood members in New York, and the biggest drug ring in NY and NJ.

The two men talked over breakfast for an hour before leaving the diner. Afterwards, they headed over to one of Brazy's traps so he could teach Rugar how to cook coke and dope, and then weight it.

Training day was in and Rugar was loving every bit of it, especially the power behind pulling the trigger. The more he thought about the killing he'd just done, the more he thought about killing again. He was already loving the street life.

Romell Tukes

CHAPTER 2
YONKERS, NEW YORK

"You sure this is it, cuz?" Lil C asked. He looked through the tints of the steel-gray Buick Regal TourX Essence, the four-door, hatchback model.

"Yeah, cuz, I already told you that, son," Loco said. His tone indicated his frustration because his big homie and best friend doubted him.

"Nigga, you saying that to say what? You know what happened last time, son." Lil C was referring to the last robbery they'd done in Brooklyn. They had robbed and killed the wrong nigga and came up with nothing.

"My bad, but shit happens in the field, son. That's a fact. But you think it's time?" Loco asked, as he watched the clock hit 1 a.m. They had parked on the block and hid between a row of cars on Palisade Ave on top of a hill.

Waiting on their victim to come back from Harlem as he did every night, Lil C watched the five-floor complex brick building.

Lil C was a Crip from Harlem, born and raised in 155th Polo Grounds Projects. He was one of the best boxers in the city and he'd won four Golden Gloves fights. He was "that nigga", and he had a crew of Crips under him ready to shoot and die for the big homie. With a bright career in boxing, he tried his best to stay behind the scenes. He let Loco run the gang, get money, and feed his crew. But when they had big licks, he would go with him, then feed his projects and soldiers.

Both of his parents were from Kingston, which made him a true Jamaican. His father, Big C, was serving a life-sentence in the feds for trafficking drugs, and his mother, Michelle, worked at the Harlem Hospital. He trained with his trainer, Jumbo, six days a week, so at seventeen his body was well developed. He had long dreads, a high-yellow complexion, and green eyes. Women loved him and considered him a pretty boy but he was loyal to his wifey, Mena.

Loco was a hoodrat who stayed in trouble and always ended up on Rikers Island. He had dark skin, wore his hair in braids, and had a stocky build. Though girls considered him handsome, he was loud and disrespectful. The two had been best friends since the 3rd grade. When he was just three years old, his pops got killed by a store owner after robbing him for twenty-six dollars. His mom Desaray was a crackhead who caught a sixty-year bid when he was ten. She killed another crackhead for stealing her crackpipe and a dime piece of crack. He'd been living with his grandmother ever since.

"Right on time, son," Lil C said. From the driver's seat he noticed a candy-red BMW i8 Roadster Coupe droptop that cost at least one hundred fifty thousand.

***

Playboy pulled into his apartment complex in Yonkers, just thirty minutes away from Harlem. He'd been raised in Uptown Harlem and he was a big player in the dope game. He had a big family known for getting money with heroin, coke, dust (PCP), and weed.

He was pushing forty and he'd been in the game nearly twenty years. He had never spent time inside of a prison and there were two main reasons why. One, because he ran a smart operation. And two, because the time he'd gotten caught with five keys in his truck, he ended up snitching on his Dominican plug and found a new connect. It had been ten years since he'd brought the feds to his connect's doorsteps to save himself. As a result, his old connect got deported and sentenced to eighty years. Now, years later, he was a big supplier in Harlem and his only competition was Brazy, Blu, King Chulu, and Lost, an old head from St. Nick.

Playboy had to get out of Harlem. He didn't believe in sleeping where he kept his shit at, especially since that had been the reason for the downfall of a lot of good men he knew.

After hustling keys in Harlem and running four projects, he would creep off to Yonkers until the next morning. Even though he lived in the nice part of Yonkers, it was just four blocks away from the hood which was just like a little Iraq in Yonkers. The Elm St., GMG, and Creechy Gang niggas were vicious crews nobody wanted to face. Y.O. was off the chain and it was the home of DMX, Mary J Blige, and the LOX, but they'd left out how deadly the small city was in their songs.

Like he did every night, he entered his building and peeked his surroundings to make sure the block was as quiet as it usually was. Nothing seemed out of place.

Once inside his crib, he locked the door and left the top latch unlocked like always. The pad was nice with two bedrooms, two bathrooms, and a nice view of Yonkers. It was decked out in Gucci rugs, Gucci drapes, and Gucci couches. He had a big walk-in closet filled with two million seven hundred thousand dollars' worth of jewelry and designer clothes.

Next, he went to undress and take a long shower.

Forty-five minutes later, Playboy was walking out of his hallway bathroom in a Hermes robe and slippers.

"Get the fuck on your knees," Loco said in his deep voice, as he shoved the Draco in Playboy's face. He dropped to his knees in fear at the sight of the two young niggas because he knew the Draco was powerful enough to break a bear in half.

"Please, just don't kill me, young brother. You can have whatever you want," Playboy said, knowing the routine. He'd been robbed many times in his life, but this was the first time he'd been robbed by two barefaced kids. His pull was so strong he knew he would have both of them dead before they could even spend a dime of whatever they took.

"Nigga, shut up where the shit, cuz?" Lil C asked, looking the man in his eyes. Playboy tried to get a good look at every detail of Lil C's facial and physical features so he could put a bag on his head.

"Check the mattress, under the bed flood. Lift the rug up and you'll see a small latch," Playboy stated sadly.

Lil C wasted no time and he went to work. Loco held Playboy at gunpoint and the two stared each other down.

Minutes later, Lil C come back with a black Hefty garbage bag filled with drugs, money, and jewelry. He had a big smile on his face. He knew there was more somewhere but for now he was good with what he had.

"Y'all took everything, but I never saw y'all and y'all never saw me," Playboy said, making both gunmen laugh. Lil C placed a silencer on his Draco.

"What's that for?" Playboy asked realizing the light skin kid had attached a muffler to his gun.

"Playboy, we from Harlem. You remember how Rico did Mitch, son," Lil C said before he shot Playboy in the chest. The impact of the powerful weapon blew his chest out through his back.

Lil C and Loco left quickly. Since the gun fired was muzzled by the silencer, they knew nobody had heard the commotion so they made their exit from the building.

Days later in Harlem

Lil C was in Jumbo's gym in the boxing ring sparing with another fighter. The fighter was nowhere near his skill's level but he was getting off on him.

"Left hook, right jab, move," his trainer Jumbo yelled from outside of the ring. Lil C's foot movement was stiff today and he had a big fight soon so he had to get him sharp.

Jumbo was an older Spanish man who was well-respected and powerful in Harlem. He ran the boxing club in an effort to keep kids off the streets and out of trouble.

Back in the day Jumbo had been one of the best fighters but never went pro due to being in the streets. He knew Lil C could be the next big thing. He had never met a kid like him before—not to mention he held a 19 win, 7 KO's, and a 0-loss status.

"Stop," Jumbo shouted. Lil C was on the ropes with his guards up blocking a couple of power punches. He saw Jumbo go upstairs to his office and knew he only did that when he was upset.

Sweating profusely, he spit his mouthpiece out and took off his boxing gloves.

"He gonna make everybody do 1000 burpees and a couple of hours on the rope," one of the fighters said, knowing how Jumbo got when one of the good fighters' performance was bad.

"I'ma go holla at him," Lil C said, and headed up the stairs.

The gym was big upstairs and downstairs. It was equipped with two large boxing rings, five punching bags, weights, treadmills, pull up and dip bars, and a juice bar.

"Jumbo, can I holla at you?" Lil C asked from the opened door.

"Sit down. What's your problem today?" Jumbo asked. You taking easy hits, moving slow, and you moving like Ali before he got knocked out. We got a big fight that's gonna spark your career. Shit, you already got agents watching you," he said, brushing his long slick hair back.

"I just got school problems. I'ma tighten up, trust me," Lil C said, lying with a straight face.

"No, *trust yourself*," he told him, "and that school shit you talking is bullshit 'cause you make straight A's Chris. Don't play me, play lotto. But I'ma let you slide today, but tomorrow be on your P's and Q's," Jumbo said.

"Okay," Lil C said as he stood to his feet.

"Make sure you and everybody else do burpees for an hour and the rope for an hour. Then er'body can leave," Jumbo said reading the New York times.

"A'ight," Lil C said. He went back downstairs to tell the other thirteen boxers what they had to do. Most of them was pissed because they wanted to enjoy their Friday night, and it was already 6 p.m.

Polo Grand

Lil C walked through his hood dressed in an Adidas tracksuit, carrying a bookbag. He saw his crew sitting in front of building 67.

21

Polo Grand had over twenty tall skyscraper buildings in the projects. There was a big basketball court in the back where big basketball tournaments were held in the summertime.

"Yo', six, what's cracking?" Poo Bear said in his loud voice. He was drinking on Cîroc.

"What cracking wit' the Locs?" Lil C asked, dapping up everybody as each one threw up the Crip gang sign.

"Where you been at?" Turf asked, as he continued rolling the blunt. At sixteen years old, he was the youngest of the crew but he was live.

"Training."

"Okay, Mike Tyson," Loco said. He stepped out of the building looking fly, dressed in an all blue Louis Vuitton outfit as if he were about to walk the runway of a fashion extravaganza.

"Whatever, but where y'all going?" he asked. "Everybody looking all clean," Lil C said, knowing he wasn't really the partying type.

"We going to *Zipcode*," Big Porky said. His deep voice matched his big six-five, three hundred nine pounds frame. At twenty years old, he had diabetes and other health issues but he was still a gun dapper.

"Ain' goin', cuz. Y'all go 'head and enjoy yourselves. I gotta train in the morning but I'ma go holla at Mona tonight." He always chilled with Mona on Friday nights because her mom and pops would be working late hours.

"Cool. We'll hit you on the way back but Cole and JD looking for you," Loco said. He already knew they'd just come home from the Island and needed to get on their feet.

"Hit the Crip's hands so they can get on their feet but tell JD to leave that wet alone," Lil C said.

"Man, you know he love that dust," Turf stated. Everybody laughed.

"A'ight," Loco said.

"I'm out, cuz," Lil C said. He headed to his building in the back of the projects.

Since the Playboy lick, Lil C's goons had all been eating. They had scored twenty keys and sixty thousand dollars in cash. The jewelry they'd stolen from the lick totaled another twenty-five thousand dollars after they'd pawned it all. Lil C had to feed his hood. Plus, he looked out for the Crips all over Harlem, and the niggas up north in prison. However, most of them had no idea how he got his money.

Romell Tukes

CHAPTER 3

Brazy and Blood Hound rode through the night Harlem streets in an all red Lexus LS500 with custom made seats, sitting on 22-inch rims.

"How the little homie coming along, Skrap?" Blood Hound asked in his low pitched voice, over the Chinx drug album blasting through the system.

Blood Hound was a super Blood. Everywhere he went he was dressed in all red with red flags hanging from his pockets. He looked like a hound dog in the face which was how he'd gotten his name. Plus, he had two long scars on his face that he'd gotten during a gang riot up top—the scars made him look even rougher.

"He got a lot more training to do but he got a lot of potential. I just want Rugar to understand how serious this shit can get," Brazy said, swerving around the potholes, trying not to fuck his rims up.

"You know he could be hard-headed sometimes, especially when he with my little cousin, Mantenta," Blood Hound stated. He shook his head.

"Facts," Brazy said and busted a sharp left.

"Them two niggas shot up the whole Wagner Basketball Tournament in broad daylight," Blood Hound said. He paused as he reminisced on the shooting that occurred the prior year. The chaos started because a nigga was staring at Rugar's watch.

"You gave them the guns, nigga. Luckily, they ain't kill or hit nothing," Brazy said. He looked around and noticed how lit it was uptown. Niggas were hustling on every corner in front of the corner stores, females were half naked trying to sell pussy, Muslims were out trying sell oils, soaps, and bean pies, and bootleggers were trying to sell bootleg DVDs and CDs.

"Them other niggas hand guns," Blood Hound reminded him.

"Bro, you gave them little niggas the OK with the drum," Brazy added. He stopped at a red light when he saw some hoodrats eyeing the Lexus as if they knew him. The females crossed the street four-deep, all in heels and shorts skirts, dressed as if they were on their way out.

"Yo', I gave Munchy and Big O them twenty keys and the cash was right too," Blood Hound said, changing the subject. Brazy pulled off from the light and headed to pick up some money from Maverick, one of his workers.

"A'ight. Oh, I almost forgot, son. I need you to holla at your boy King and his crew. I heard them niggas on a bunch of bullshit robbin' rappers and fiends. I got too much going on with the Empire, all the Bloods in the five boroughs and up top, to babysit a little nigga," Brazy said being honest.

"A'ight, Blood I got you," Blood Hound said, laughing because King Hound was under him. He was two years younger than Blood Hound but he stood six feet, seven inches tall, and he weighed two hundred ninety pounds, nothing but solid muscle from lifting weights while in Attica prison and Auburn. During his incarceration he was the big homie because he was putting in so much work, so Blood Hound gave him some status.

King Hound was a real standup dude, but he was hot headed and quick to play the role of a crash dummy. The two met years prior on Rikers Island. Blood Hound had the place on lock before he went up north to do five years.

"Yeah, laugh now, nigga. But we don't need no more heat on us. Money and violence don't mix, son," Brazy said. He stopped on 144 St. and Drew Hamilton. He checked the time because he had to shoot out to Queens to see Bullet who was a member of the Empire.

Boom! Boom! Boom! Boom!

Brazy ducked as his windows shattered and the sounds of cannons ripped through the Lexus from different sides of the car. Both men hopped out quickly and began busting back like they were in a shoot-out in the wild-wild west. When a group of nearby civilians ran to take cover, Brazy shot one of them in the face when he popped up from the side of his car and ducked back down quickly.

Blood Hound was shooting wildly until he caught four hollow tips to the chest, causing his body to collapse in the middle of the street.

Brazy saw what happened and popped up shooting fearlessly. Walking fast toward the other two gunmen, he caught one of them in his neck three times. The last shooter looked scared shitless as he took off running. As Brazy licked off five more shots in his direction, the big man's steps seemed to pause as if he was running in slow motion. Sirens could be heard from the distance, snapping him out his zone. He rushed to Blood Hound to see his best friend since 5th grade gone, no longer breathing. He heard pedestrians yelling as they looked on in horror at the two innocent teenage-girls laid out in the street, dead from the stray bullets. He hopped in the Lexus, which had been shot up and filled with bullet holes, and pulled off. The witnesses stared at him and watched him speed off.

All he could think about was the fat gunmen who he knew all too well. Baby Blue was his name. He and Brazy had become enemies in middle school over a bitch Brazy was fucking whom Blue had been trying to wife.

The two crossed paths a lot but it had never led to gun fire because Baby Blue knew his Crips were no match for Brazy and his army. But tonight was the start of a new war.

**

Brazy rushed to Naya's crib and parked a block away just in case the police was looking for his shot-up Lexus. He used his own key to get inside her apartment.

"Oh shit, big homie, what's poppin'," the twins Mark and Marcus said. The two were sitting on the living room couch playing Xbox for money. Two fully-loaded Dracos lay at their sides. The twins were under Naya who was under Brazy, of course. They were from Newark, NJ, and they were her personal security and hitmen whose body count was crazy. Brazy said nothing as he rushed to the back to see Naya. There were visible blood stains all over his all white GIVENCHY outfit.

Naya was in her room on her king sized bed. Wearing nothing except a tank top, and booty shorts which displayed her shaven camel toe print, her body was nicely toned and curvy. She was watching *Get Rich or Die Trying* with Rapper 50 Cent, one of her favorite movies.

Naya was beautifully mixed with Arabian and Indian but she looked Spanish. Her skin was a golden tan and her jet-black, long slick hair looked good against her complexion. Her exotic looking eyes were a bright gray and greenish color. At five, five, one hundred twenty-five pounds, her round ass, was just the right size for her petite frame. A nice set of perky C-cup breasts made her package complete.

When Brazy burst through her door she grabbed her Colt .45 pistol with the extended 30-round clip from underneath her pillow.

"Oh shit," she said, realizing she was close to shooting him

"Get rid of this shit and my Lexus around the corner," Brazy told her as he came out of his clothes in a hurry. He looked in her closet where he kept a change of clothes and grabbed something to put on.

"What happened?" She looked him up and down with wide eyes. Why the fuck you got blood everywhere?" she asked, watching him pace in a panic.

"Break this gun down and get rid of it as soon as I leave," he said, ignoring her questions.

"Blood, slow down. Talk to me, babe," she said. She walked over to him and stood directly in front of him.

Naya was a model as a kid, but later in life she chose to become a Blood. She eventually became part of the Empire and began running the streets of Jersey.

"I had a shoot-out with Baby Blu and they just killed Hound. I got two of theirs but two little girls got caught in the crossfire," he said. He grabbed two duffle bags from her top shelf.

"Fuck! Now what?" Naya asked. "Just chill here. Or we could go to Newark to my hood," she said. She began throwing on her clothes without waiting for answer.

"Nah, I need you out here," Brazy said, stopping her movements. "I'ma go up to Albany, but just make sure you holla at Rugar and give him my position in the Empire. Teach him whatever he's missing," he ordered Naya. Her eyes became misty and blurred, and before she knew what was happening she was crying, something she hardly ever did. For some reason, she felt like this would be there last encounter.

"Okay, I'll do anything you need me to," she said wiping her tears. Brazy had been her first lover and the only man she'd ever been with. Their relationship had always been complicated and built on the gangsta lifestyle they lived. It was more or less some ride or die friendship type shit since they were in the streets heavy.

"Do the right thing, ma. I love you. Always hold shit down. I'm call you when I get up top," Brazy said. He left her room and called a cab on his way out. She told him she loved him too once the door closed.

Back in the room, the twins had turned the game off and started watching the 8 p.m. news. They were shocked to see Harlem on the breaking news as the reporter began her segment:

"Good Evening. Reporting to you live, I'm Sandra Williams back with a breaking news report live from 144th St. in Harlem. A messy crime scene has left five dead, two of which were teenaged girls. The police believe it was a gang or turf war over drugs; however they are still in the early stages of the investigation. Oh... hold on, I'm just hearing there is live video of a man believed to be the suspect," the reporter said, as she played a quick video of Brazy shooting in the middle of the street.

"OK, Merriam, back to you." Just like that, the story switched to other news.

The twins knew who the shooter was. Shit, almost every gangsta in New York did by now.

"Take care of Naya," Brazy said sternly. Without looking back, he exited the neat apartment.

Manhattanville

After the cab dropped Brazy off at his stash house, he sent Rugar a text before breaking his phone into pieces. He grabbed two large military duffle bags and filled each with money he had stashed inside his hallway closet. Next, he poured himself a couple of shots of Henny. He had always lived by his own code and he'd rather be carried by six of his own than judged by twelve crackers. So, being the gangsta he was, he planned to hold courts in the streets because he was married to the streets until death did them part. With that thought in mind, he downed his last shot, grabbed the keys to his GMC Yukon truck off the wall, grabbed two loaded pistols with the extendos, then he exited his pad.

Minutes later, Brazy was doing the 25 speed limit down Douglas 105 and Columbus Ave, a very busy street. He made a left turn and picked up speed, rushing toward the exit so he could get the fuck outta Harlem. He glanced in his rearview and within a matter of seconds, he saw the red and blue lights tailing him.

"Fuck!" he shouted, "ain't this about a bitch!" He hit the steering wheel with his fists. He pushed the peddle to the gas hitting 80 mph as the big truck dipped in and out of the night traffic.

More police fell in line behind him and cops seemed to be coming from almost every side getting in on the chase. One of the NYPD officers rammed into the back bumper of the Yukon which caused Brazy to lose control of it and slam into a corner street pole.

The impact was so hard, Brazy was dazed and almost flew out of the front window—fortunately, he was wearing his seatbelt. His Tom Ford suit had blood all over it. As his vision began to clear up, he looked in his rearview and realized he was surrounded by over thirty NYPD cop cars.

"Get the fuck outta the car with your hands up," the police announced on the loudspeaker. Pedestrians watched the scene from across the street—some recorded it to post on Instagram and others on YouTube.

Brazy placed his two pistols in his lap and said a quick prayer. Seconds later, he hopped out shooting like he was in a gangsta movie. The loud *pop!* of Gun fire sounded off like fireworks on the 4th of July. He was able to hold his own for a minute and thirty seconds before he fell down and slumped over in the door panel of the truck. NYPD had filled him with forty-six rounds.

During the melee, three officers were left dead in the street, two African American males, and one white male. Four other officers were wounded and seriously injured.

Romell Tukes

CHAPTER 4
FOSTA PROJECTS, HARLEM

Uncle P was parked and sitting in all black tinted Audi A7 four-door hatchback with two touchscreen dashboard equipped with an audio system, camera view, climate control, map display, Google, radio selection, phone, and contacts. "Uhm, shit, girl," Uncle P moaned, as he looked at the beautiful woman who lived downstairs in his building. She bopped her head up and down in his lap, twisting her head as she slobbed on his dick, deep throating him with no hands.

Darya was a beautiful single mother who worked at Footlocker to provide for her son. Her child's father was doing a ten-year prison bid up top so she'd been left to raise him on her own. She was thirty years old, slim with brown skin, cute, and she had a Lupita Nyong'o model-like look about her. Uncle P had ridden by her and offered her a ride. Considering she'd had a crush on him forever, one thing lead to another and she started rubbing his manhood almost as soon as she'd closed her door. Next thing he knew, it was in her mouth and she was sucking as if she were a newborn baby on a titty for the first time.

"I'm cum-m-m-in-gg," Uncle P said, groaning as he released a thick wad of cum inside her mouth. Like a pro, she didn't flinch an inch but swallowed every drop like a good girl.

"So you gonna call me later?" Draya asked, smiling as she fixing her loose weave and grabbed her fake Gucci purse.

"Yeah," he replied, pushing his dick back in his slacks. He had seen the girl plenty of times but he never would've thought her head game was on some Pinky shit.

Draya leaned in to kiss him but decided to give him a hug instead before exiting his car. She headed to her building and walked past crowds of young men who all knew her.

Pete was in his early forties but looked as if he were in college. He had no gray hairs in the waves he sported, and his face was clean cut aside from the goatee. He was fit, tall, brown-skinned, and sexy—the women loved him. He used to be one of the biggest drug dealers in Harlem before he took in his brother, Big Jay's three kids after Big Jay and his wife, Chili, were both murdered during a bank robbery.

With so much money, he invested every cent into multiple businesses. He owned a car lot. He was the CEO of a law firm. He ran his own hair salon and barber shop, all with the help of a couple of his side chicks.

Uncle P saw his phone ringing on the TV monitor in the dashboard but the number displayed was private. He knew it was too late for anybody to be playing phone games so he answered.

"Holla," he answered seeing how late it was.

"P, this is Anna from building nine," the old lady said. It was the lady who used to baby sit him when he was a kid.

"Hi, Anna, how are you doing?" he greeted and asked politely. "How did you get my number?" he asked. While he waited for her to reply, he noticed Draya had left a fake gold earrings on his floor, obviously trying to get him jammed up. He was far from worried about childish shit like that since all his bitches knew how he got down.

"Oh Lord, you didn't see the news?" Anna asked. Her voice trembled and her tone was laced with worry.

"Anna what are you talking about"

"Brazy was gunned down by the police a few minutes ago and it's all over the news. Says he killed a couple of them. I'm so sorry," she said before she heard the dial tone.

After Anna's call had come in, P's phone started ringing off the hook with back-to-back calls. He turned the phone off and shed a tear for his nephew. He had shown him the game at a young age.

Shaking off his emotional state, Pete knew he had to tighten up. He knew the hardest part would be breaking the news to Rugar and China. He said a quick prayer and summoned the strength to exit his car.

***

China and Rugar were lounging in their Polo pajamas. They were watching Martin reruns on the living room couch eating their favorite cereal, Lucky Charms.

"Turn the TV off," their Uncle P said as they laughed at Martin Lawrence acting a fool.

"Damn, Uncle P, what's up," Rugar said. He sensed something was very wrong. P's expression reflected his sadness which wasn't his style since he was always smiling.

"Your brother was gunned down by the police tonight," he said, allowing the words to escape his mouth quickly. I'm—"

Before he could finish explaining what he'd heard so far, China screamed and ran to her room in tears. She figured something was wrong when she saw some chick post on Facebook 'Damn Brazy, you went out like a real nigga.' China thought the female had been talking about another Brazy since she'd just spoken to her brother a few hours prior.

"I'm sorry, Rugar, but this is what the streets give us in return besides jail. I'ma go check on China," Uncle P said, and headed to China's room.

Rugar sat on the couch and noticed he had thirty-five missed calls. He didn't bother checking who they were from or what they wanted. He went to his room with his head hung low and looked at all the photos of him and his brother. He knew he had to put on his joker's face, hold his family up, and carry on his big brother's legacy. He lay down and cried himself to sleep, promising himself this would be the only night he'd shed a tear. He could hear Brazy's words in his head, *'there is no room for weakness in the game'*.

Newark, NJ

"I'ma ask you again because I'm sympathetic when it comes to old bitches. Now where is he," Naya asked. She held a gun in her palms and the twins stood behind her in Ant's mother's living room. She was dressed in a black Dolce & Gabbana dress with black six-inch heels. She always dressed sexy but today was Brazy's funeral but she just had to make the pit stop.

Mrs. Taylor stood shaking and crying and not because of her shady son. Besides, she had never let him in her home near Prince Street because she knew he was caught up in street dealings. She cried because her husband had tried to fight off the gunmen, now he was lying dead in the hallway.

"I swear to Jesus I don't know where he is! If I did I would send you to that no good piece of shit," Mrs. Taylor said, crying so hard she begin to choke.

Ant owed Naya a lot of money for the key she'd given him on consignment. He had been ducking her and she was determined to find him.

"Well, you raised the piece of shit," Naya replied. Without another word, she shot Mrs. Taylor seven times in her chest hoping Ant would get the message and show his face.

Once she was outside the house she climbed in the back of an all-black Land Rover truck that had been parked in the driveway. The twins got in the front and they drove off, down the block. Two black Lincoln Aviator's filled with Naya's goons pulled out of the parking lot to follow them.

The morning sky always calmed her nerves so she looked out of the window thinking of all the good times she'd shared with Brazy. Never in a million years did she think he would get killed. He had so much power and he was smart. He was the epitome of a born leader.

Naya knew she had to stay focused on business and the Empire because that's what Brazy would want. Even though she was the Godmother of the Blood set, there still needed to be a Godfather. The crown had already passed down to Rugar, now she only hoped he accepted the position and was ready for the crazy life that came with it.

Brooklyn, NY

Lil C and Loco arrived in Brooklyn. They walk upstairs from the subway and got off the four train to meet Uncle Lo, the plug. Lil C needed more work because he was almost out. The only person he knew was his man's brother who was deep in the game.

"You put that new crew on Lincoln and Madison? Since Puff and them niggas got booked that shit been a goldmine," Lil C asked, waiting on Lo to pull up.

"Yeah, cuz. Lil Jay and Smoke over their Crip and they got that shit on lock," Loco said, eyeing a thick chick.

"A'ight copy."

"You ready for your big fight?" Loco asked. He knew how sick his homie's hand game was and he'd seen him knock out plenty of niggas.

"That's a fact, son. You know how I give it, but I just wanted to make sure y'all was good," Lil C stated honestly.

"Bro, we good. If it wasn't for you a lot of Locs would be out here starving 'cause we feeding over sixty Crips out here. The crazy shit is you don't even have to do this shit. You used your prize-fighting money to put niggas on their feet," Loco said. He laughed but he was dead serious. Lil C did a lot for his homies and he didn't even sell drugs. He let Loco handle the business while he boxed and kept the money flowing.

"I guess it's the Crippin' in me, cuz," Lil C said and chuckled. Just then, a sky-blue CLS450 pulled up blasting lyrics by Fabolous.

Him and Loco hopped in the Benz and sped into traffic. With the windows down, they headed to Flatbush and Lincoln.

The ride was quite because Lo never talked in cars due to the FEDs having been on his line for years. They tried hard but had never been able to get him indicted. Knowing how they bugged niggas cars by placing wires up in the steering wheel and dashboards, he'd rather be safe than sorry.

There were over a hundred Crips posted up on the block, enjoying the beautiful summer day. Lil C and Loco embraced everybody. They had all heard of Lil C in the Crip field because he had the whole Harlem under his rolling thirties set.

"Come holla at me, man," Lo said in his strong Jamaican voice.

They walked between two buildings in an alley that led into a basement full of tables used for gambling since it was their gambling spot.

There were Jamaicans sitting on carts smoking big blunts of weed, women in short jean skirts, and even though it was only 12 p.m., there was Jamaican rum everywhere. Normally, it would be packed but it was still early. When nightfall set in, the spot would be so deep, the cops would have to shut it down.

Flatbush was mostly filled with Crips and West Indians so this was Lil C's and Loco's second home since both were Jamaican rude boys.

Lo and Lil C went into a small room and talked business in Jamaican for an hour. Then he had Loco bring him his bookbag and he gave him his Fendi backpack—both bags were full of re-up money.

Lo had everything except coke, but his righthand man had the keys for the low so he called him.

An hour later, Lil C and Loco were riding in a Mazda truck with two young women. The women were being used as mules to carry twenty-eight pounds of weed, thirty keys of coke, fifty thousand pills, and fifteen keys of dope, back to Harlem to flood the streets again.

CHAPTER 5

The sky was bright, the sun was shining and the temperature was 89°, hot and muggy. The funeral was packed more than a club serving free drinks all night. There were gangbangers, drug lords, OGs, hoodrats, friends, and family out to show their final respect to Brazy. Of course, the bitches were dressed to impress hoping to catch a big dick baller nigga.

He lay in his casket dressed to the nines in a Dior suit and red flag tied around his right wrist. The service had lasted two hours. Now they were leaving the graveyard as Brazy's casket was lowered six feet underground.

Rugar saw China hugging friends and family members. She had on an all-black high-slit strapless Prada dress with a pair of Prada sunglasses hiding her puffy eyes. Rugar wore an all-black Michael Kors suit with shoes to match, and his AP bust down watch shined every time the sunlight hit it just right.

"You good, nephew?" Uncle P asked. He walked up on the side of him, as he stood posted under a treeRugar watching the scene.

"Yeah, I'm good," Rugar said. Then Montonta walked up to him dress in a red Gucci suit.

"A'ight, let me go finish tending to our guests," Uncle P said. He walked off looking dapper in a black Ralph Lauren custom-made suit straight from Italy.

"Yooo, what's poppin', blood? This shit got me fucked up Skrap. First my cuzzin' Blood Hound now the big bro," Montonta said. He posted up on the tree with his best friend.

The two had been close forever. They fucked the same bitches, wore each other's clothes, and spent nights at each other's homes. Both had become Bloods under Brazy on the same day and they knew each other better than anybody.

Montonta was Nas' twin. At eighteen years old, Nas could pass for his father since the two looked so much alike. Montonta was tall, handsome, had the gift of gab, and he was a known shooter through Harlem. All he knew was the streets. His mom was a fiend and he had never met his father.

"I miss that nigga already, blood," Rugar said. He saw Naya and a crew of Bloods following her.

"Damn, Skrap," Montonta said as he saw Naya approaching them. She had put a red flag around the bun in her hair and she had on very little make up.

"You remember the last time she wilded out on you for looking at her too long? You know you got them creepy looking eyes," Rugar said causing both men to laugh.

"Little bro, what's poppin'?" she said as she leaned in and hugged Rugar tightly.

"How are you?" he asked.

"All is well, I guess. Sorry about our loss," she said, trying to sound tough and hide her true emotions. Naya had known known Rugar since he was a little kid and she was basically family to he and China.

"More or less just staying strong," he replied. Her goons posted up, ice-grilling the guests because the New Jersey niggas weren't too heavy on the New York niggas. It was like a low-key hatred between the states.

"Do you have a second?" she asked.

"Yeah," he told her.

"In private," she said, looking at Montonta and acting as if he wasn't even there. He knew Naya's name was bigger than the Pope's in Roman, and she was known for getting a nigga's shit pushed all the way back.

"I'ma go check on the gang, I'll be over there by China," Montonta told Rugar. He ice-grilled the twins then smirked at them on some cocky New York shit.

Naya and Rugar walked off until they got on the rocky path. The place was just starting to clear out.

"Seems like I haven't seen you in forever. You've got so big and handsome just like—" She stopped herself midsentence not wanting to bring Brazy's name up considering his death was still fresh on her soul.

'I know, and it's okay. But what's shaking? I can tell you got shit on your mind," he said. They came to a stop as she played with the long red manicured nails she'd gotten done at her shop in Jersey.

"It's that obvious, huh?" She laughed. "Listen, that night the police killed him, he gave me a direct order and told me to give you his status in the gang along his position within the Empire. This is very big. I'm sure you know he was the highest Blood ranking member on the East Coast and down south," she said

"I know," he said. He recalled what his brother had told him weeks prior at breakfast... *'if anything was to happen to me you'll be in charge of the Empire'*.

"I know he was showing you the game but if you need assistance I'm here for you. Oh, and before I forget, this is for you," she said. She dug in her purse and pulled out a piece of paper with an address on it. She handed it to Rugar.

"What's this?"

"Rugar, it's a cold game and we all play for keeps. But at the end of the day, it's a dog-eat-dog game. Your brother could of went to UCONN, Texas A&M, and UCLA to play football but he chose the streets. We all have a choices, bro. And so do you, Blood. Either way, you're family, regardless. That paper is something to hold you and China down. It's from me and Brazy but I'ma give you seventy-two hours to get back at me with your decision," she said walking off like the boss bitch she was.

"I don't need three days, I'm in," he called out behind her. "I'ma continue what he started and let niggas know there's a new Don in town. I also plan to call an Empire meeting. Get back at me," he said. He walked off and left her standing in place with a smirk etched on her face. Rugar and China climbed into a limo. There was seven cars full of niggas from the hood, ready to pull off and tail them.

Naya was the last to leave. She had stayed at Brazy's gravesite twenty extra minutes talking to him as if he were right there in front of her.

Once she was done, she and her crew left the graveyard. She was in the second truck which had gotten cut off at the bottom of the hill by a black Ford Expedition with tinted windows.

"Stupid ass niggas," Mark said. He blew the horn to get the truck to move. Seconds later, the door of the truck flew open and two gunmen jumped out shooting two AR-15s high-power assault rifles.

"Duck!" Marcus yelled as he grabbed the Draco from underneath the seat and climbed out. He and Naya started letting off shots.

The goons in the truck in front of them had all slumped over dead in the Lincoln truck.

Naya gave one of the shooters a headshot while Mark caught a shot to the arm. His twin Draco caught the last shooter twice in his legs taking him out, as the Ford Expedition pulled off at full speed.

Naya and her shooters ran after the truck shooting at it. She saw the second gunmen crying in pain, still alive. His legs had been blown halfway off down to his thigh bones.

"Help," he moaned. Naya walked up to him, and without mercy, she kicked him in his legs causing him to scream so loud it echoed.

"Who sent you?" she asked. Twin pulled off with his brother to get him medical attention because he'd been shot. He knew he had to take him somewhere other than a hospital. Going there right now could possibly link them to the shooting and nobody from Jersey wanted to go to Riker's Island jail.

"Baby Blue," the wounded man said. "He told us to get Brazy's wifey," he said about to pass out.

"Okay, well I'm his wifey. Tell him I miss him when you see him," she said and blew his brains out. Afterward she jumped back in the truck and burned rubber, heading back to Jersey. All she could do now was hope her soldiers were okay.

She knew Baby Blue and he was a nobody. However, he was the reason Brazy was dead and he had just put an attempt on her life. As far as she was concerned, he was as good as dead.

***

Rugar had just walked in his crib from having a big meeting in the project's recreation center. Sixty or more Bloods from his projects, and the Tarf project's across the street, had all been in attendance. He had given orders to niggas and let them know he was the new HNIC and they were all about to eat. Everybody was gassed up and ready to take over the city.

"Damn, Unc, what the fuck you burning Rugar said smelling burnt chicken. He frowned up his nose and smirked because he knew his Uncle P was a bad cook.

"Trying to make a meal but I'm glad you here," P said. "Come here and let me holla at you for a minute." Fanning the smoke in the air, he walked from the kitchen and into the dining room.

"What's up, old head?" Rugar asked. He sat down in a chair at the table. His voice was nearly gone from shouting at the meeting.

"I saw your little pow-wow so it's not hard to put two and two together," P told him. "I guess you taking your brother's spot which are some hard shoes to fill. The game is eighty-five percent mental and fifteen percent physical. Remember that," he said, schooling his young nephew.

"That's real," Rugar said. He listened attentively, making sure he absorbed all the wisdom his uncle gave him.

"There's no honor amongst men no more. Everybody ratttin' nowadays," P said. "Back in my day when I was in the game, it was different. Now it's watered down. Learn the difference between power and respect, son. One is earned and one is given," Uncle P stated. He looked into his nephew's brown eyes and saw the look of a boss. He always knew Rugar had the swag and presence of a leader.

"I got you."

"Good. You got a meeting tomorrow with a very important man and close friend of mine. Be sure to go alone and know that you're in a grown man's game now," he said, passing his nephew a piece of paper with an address written on it. Just as he had turned to go back to the kitchen to finish cooking, China came in from work.

"Hey, what's goody, y'all," she asked. She had on a pair of tight jeans that hugged her fat ass and she was wearing her work shirt.

"How was work?" Uncle P asked.

"Busy. I was so happy when Chulu came and picked me up. Oh my God, but why it smell like that in here? What you burning?" China asked, peeping inside the kitchen.

"Chill, son. Just sit down and get ready to eat," Uncle P said.

"When I was coming in the building there was like thirty niggas downstairs tryna open the doors for me. Niggas was treating me with OG respect and it fucked me up 'cause I was just cursing one of them bum niggas out the other day," China said as she sat down.

China was stunningly beautiful. She was red bone who looked Spanish with Chinese eyes. Her body was thick with the measurements 36-24-42. Standing five feet, five inches tall, she was a showstopper everywhere she went.

"You're the queen of the hood what you expect?" Rugar said trying to gas her up, but she caught on to what he was doing.

"Boy, please," she said and waved him off. Uncle P brought the food out. He had cooked baked chicken, corn, greens, wild rice, peas, and apple pie for dessert. The three of them ate and enjoyed the food as they talked for hours, all trying to block out thoughts of Brazy not being there.

CHAPTER 6
HARLEM

Rugar and Montonta had been locked in Montonta's room for one full hour counting money non-stop. The room was small and hot. The only thing keeping them a little cool was the ten dollar fan from Dollar Tree that sat on the dresser..

A few hours earlier, Rugar had gone to the address Naya had given him at his brother's funeral. When he went inside the apartment located at the address, he had found two duffle bags on the kitchen floor filled with blue faces.

"Damn, son! I ain't never even seen this much money on TV," Montonta said, as he sat Indian style in a pair of basketball shorts and a tank top. They had counted so much money his fingertips had begun hurting.

"Me neither, but we gotta hurry, my nigga. I got a meeting in an hour and a half," Rugar said, counting the money as fast as he could and placing the blue-faced bills in stacks. Luckily, math had been their favorite subject before they both decided to drop out in the 11th grade.

Minutes later they were done, and both were sweating as if they had just played one-on-one full court basketball.

"How much you got, Blood?" Rugar looked at Montonta's stack.

"Four hundred fifty thousand on the nose, boy," Montonta said, smiling. He wondered how many guns he could buy with that much money.

"I got the same so that's nine hundred thousand! Damn, that's close to a mil," Rugar said, looking at both stacks stacked up like two small mountains.

"What now, bro? All the homies wanna know what's poppin'. Since Brazy been gone half of Harlem world been dry," Montonta said, wondering what Rugar's plan were. But regardless of what he decided, he knew his friend was a mastermind.

"Patience, my friend. Put the money up and don't let nobody know where it's at, especially your mom," Rugar said, as he stood up to leave.

"I got it, fam. I'm not leaving this crib until you come back," he replied, knowing how vicious his mom was. She would steal from him all the time to get high off crack.

When Rugar left, Montonta locked his room door and turned on his stereo to listen to an old Jay-Z album. He tossed all the money on his queen sized bed and dived in it to take a nap, feeling like a boss.

One Hour Later

Rugar walked into the classy high-scale restaurant lobby dressed in a gray Brook Brother's suit and tie with a pair of gray and white Stacy Adams on his feet. He had taken a Uber cab to the lower Eastside of Manhattan. He beat the heavy traffic on the expressway by taking the city streets, which was why he was ten minutes early.

"Excuse me, sir, how can I help you?" a pretty young white women asked. Dressed in a black blazer and slacks while standing at the lobby podium, she held a clipboard in her hands.

"Yes, I have a meeting with someone. This may sound crazy, but I don't know the person's name," Rugar said, as the waitress looked at him as if he were crazy.

"Okay, sir. Just give me one second," she said. She typed something into the computer, checking the guest list and appointments scheduled for the day. "Is your name Rugar?" the young lady asked, wondering who would name their child that.

"Yes," he said.

"Good. Follow me. The boss awaits you in the private booth area in the back," she said, giving him a warm fake smile. She led him through the restaurant, strutting the fat wide ass that didn't seem to fit her skinny waist and legs.

The restaurant was topnotch with its marble floor, dim lights, expensive silverware, designer tablecloths, paintings, high ceilings, private booth areas, and a view of the Hudson river—the food service appeared to good as well.

On his way to the back, Rugar saw the Governor of New York having lunch with company laughing and smiling.

***

Jumbo was sitting in his booth drinking a glass of water. Dressed in a Valentino suit, he was looking over one of the restaurants he owned when he saw a young man in a suit approaching his section with Harley.

"Hi, I'm Rugar. It's nice to meet you," Rugar said, extending his hand to the Spanish man with the silk hair.

"Nice to meet you, kid. Have a seat, get comfortable. You hungry or thirsty?" Jumbo asked, as Harley walked off the take some orders.

"No, sir."

"Oh, please don't hit me with that sir stuff," Jumbo said with a chuckle.

Jumbo was Cuban but he was raised in the roughest parts of Harlem. He was a Cuban drug lord who ran the Cuban Cartel family which had been passed down to him a long time ago. He was raised with Pete, Big Jay, Big Smooth, and Lucci. He was their supplier back in the day but Uncle Pete and Rugar's pop were close family to him. He was also a very successful businessman with a diplomatic politician background which brought him close to powerful people.

With property all over the world, he didn't have to sell drugs. Only a few people knew he was a major supplier for other cartel families within the world's biggest organization known as the Cartel Commission. The Commission consisted of leaders of the biggest cartel families who had come together to get money.

"You a sharp dresser just like your brother and father," Jumbo said, smiling. His comment caught Rugar off guard.

"Excuse me? You know my father?"

"Yes, I know your whole family. If I didn't I wouldn't have never called this meeting, but that's not all, Jamal," he said, calling him by his real name.

"Huh?"

"I'm your Godfather. I was there the night you were born. Me and your father were as thick as wolves at night, kid," Jumbo said, thinking about back in the day.

"Wow." Rugar was shocked. "Why am I just now meeting you?" he asked.

"To be honest, bad timing. I was suppling Brazy before he was killed. And considering the lifestyle I'm into, I'd rather keep family at a distance. I'm sure you'll understand one day," Jumbo said. He nodded his head toward the big investor who was leaving with his mistress.

"I still don't fully understand"

"I'm sure you do. I'm one of the biggest drug dealers in the states," he said.

Rugar almost choked as he took a sip of water. "This is crazy," he said.

"From my understanding, you'll be taking over your brother's position. So I'm here to help. All I ask in return is that you give me your loyalty," Jumbo said sternly.

"Of course. I wouldn't have it no other way. That's already been embedded in me," Rugar replied.

"Good. So let's get down to business. I'm going to make you a millionaire in a matter of weeks, kid. Just listen and follow my lead," Jumbo said. Rugar nodded his head. He and Jumbo talked about drop offs and pickups for close to two hours.

CHAPTER 7
POLO GROUNDS

Lil C stood in the middle of the projects' park. It was late at night and he was surrounded by thirty something young men, all dressed in navy blue and Crippin' hard.

"Now tell me this shit again, and yu bettah bloodclot get it straigh, ten," Lil C shouted, highly pissed off. As the Jamaican in him started to come out, he looked at Poo Bear and Turf, analyzing what he'd just heard from Tommy.

"The homies Turf and Lil Jay saw Smooth Loc coming out of the stash house during the shift change carrying a duffle bag. And since it was shift change they thought nothing of it," Loco said, telling Lil C the story that had been told to him.

"Yeah, and when we went upstairs, cuz, everything was gone—the money *and* drugs. His name Smooth Loc for a reason, cuz," Tommy said, trying to be funny at the wrong time.

"How the fuck is it your shift, Tommy, and you see the man coming out with a duffle bag knowing pickups and drop-offs are on Sundays, and you didn't think nothing of it?" Lil C asked. Tommy just shrugged his frail shoulders.

"Find Smooth. Hunt the nigga down," Loco said. He noticed Lil C place a potato on the barrel of a pistol with a weird smirk on his face.

Seconds later, Lil C shot Tommy in his head four times and his body fell on the park slide. The potato muffled the loud gunfire so nobody in the neighborhood heard or saw anything expect the ones in the park. Lil C walked off. He called a Uber to take him to Mona's crib so he could spend some time with her since she was going through a lot.

Her father was one of the police officers shot and killed last month by the notorious gang leader and kingpin drug dealer, Brazy.

Upper Westside

King Chulu was in the bedroom of his condo with Selena's smooth toned legs jacked up in the air over his shoulders. He lay on top of her slaughtering her tight and wet little peach pussy. She was his side bitch but she really liked the gangsta, and his cocky swag turned her on. Her home was in the South Bronx where she was raised and attended college. She danced at clubs and sometimes bartended when she needed the extra money.

One hundred percent Panamanian, Selena was sexy with long jet-black hair that flowed down to her lower back. She was light skinned with dimples, and long eyelashes that brought out her blue eyes. Her lips were thin and her ass was nice and round. Her B-cup breasts sat up plump and firm over a flat, six-pack abdomen. Just five feet, three inches tall, she was a real dime piece.

Chulu was a Puerto Rican pretty boy with long hair and the kind of swag women loved. He was tall at six-two, had green eyes, and he was tattooed up from his feet to his neck.

"Yess, ohh, umm! Fuck, papi, yess, fuck me harder," she moaned. His hand was around her neck choking her and he thrust deep inside her pussy trying to paralyze her.

"Take this dick," he said through clenched teeth. She gripped his waist trying to hold on for dear life. She felt herself about to climax again for the third time in forty minutes.

"Oh my God! I'm cum-m-m-ing, daddy," she screamed and began squirting on his dick.

He commenced to pounding her pussy like an angry caveman. When he finally released inside her, it looked like the Nile River all over his Balmain sheets. He turned her around and bent her over on all fours. Seeing her fat plump pussy staring back at him, he slowly worked the tip of his erect dick into her tight pussy walls.

"Damn, is this what you want?" King Chulu yelled. Pulling her long ponytail forced her ass into his long massive dick.

"I can't take it!" Hearing her cry out caused him to pick up speed.

"Oh, shit, Chulu, please stop. I'm cum-m-ming, papi, ohhh!" Selena yelled. She bit her bottom lip so hard, the dry skin came off. When she started to cum again, he came with her. Her body trembled and shook like the holy ghost had gotten into her. Selena attacked Chulu's dick with her mouth and sucked on the tip. Her mouth was warm and she used her tongue to lick the leftover juices. She bopped her head up and down on his ten-inch dick trying to deep throat him as much as she could. He was so big, she started to choke and almost vomited when he shot a thick load down her throat. With watery eyes, she swallowed every drop feeling as though the cum was about to pour out through her nose.

When he was done, King Chulu stood to his feet and put on his Versace robe. He looked at Selena awkwardly.

"Bitch clean this shit up and change my fucking sheets," he said. Then he turned to go to his bathroom to take a shower before leaving to pick China up.

Selena did as she was told and took the soaked sheets off the bed. Afterwards, she put a new pair on knowing his next move was to kick her out. She got dressed in her Yves Saint Laurent minidress and slipped on her Jimmy Choo heels.

King Chulu stepped out of the shower and wrapped a towel around his chiseled waist. She stared at his bare chest in awe and he walked around showing his eight pack and well-defined upper torso.

"Este fin de semana?" she asked, hoping to see him again the upcoming weekend for some more bomb ass dick.

"Quizás," he said which meant maybe or perhaps in Spanish. He removed the towel and began to dress putting on a Balenciaga outfit with the shoes to match.

"The money is on the living room table for you," he said, when Selena stood to leave. He picked up his phone and placed a call just as she walked out.

She walked down the hall to a large, clean living room where she saw a stack of bills lying on the table. She grabbed the money and counted thirty-five hundred dollars. She wasn't a gold digger

51

but she refused to fuck with a broke nigga. She smiled and stuffed the money in her pocketbook.

***

Driving the all yellow BMW M5 with tints, King Chulu made his way down the highway headed to pick up China from work like he normally did.

Originally from the Southside of Chicago where the Latin Kings were first thought of, he was the head leader of the Latin Kings in New York. Before he was murdered by a rival gang member in Chi-Town, his father was one of the original LK's.

King Chulu and his little brother, King Ed, were raised by their mother and uncle. They lived in the Bronx and Washington Heights where King Chulu had made a name for himself.

He fell in love with China after a year of meeting her. She was three years younger than him but that wasn't an issue because he loved her.

She was still a virgin which was of unheard of nowadays. She was also different from most of the women he came across. So, he was pleased with that. Even though he stepped out on her with other women, she was still number one. He had even gotten her name tattooed on him.

***

China walked around Joyce Designer's clothing store picking up the clothes customers had tossed around as if they had no sense. She just so happened to look toward the front of the store to check the time. Just as she did, she noticed Yondy stealing money from the cash register and stuffing it inside her bra.

"Broke bitch," China mumbled. She went to the back and grabbed her purse to leave since it was time for her to punch out.

She had been working in the mall clothing store for a year now. She had gotten the job through Brazy since Naya was the owner, though Naya was never there.

"Aye yo , ma," a tall light skinned pretty boy nigga yelled. He saw how bad she was so had to get her attention.

"Sorry, I'm taken," China said, rushing through the mall. She was trying to get to the garage where Chulu sat waiting for her.

Once she'd made it to the garage, she heard the loud Nick Jan reggaeton playing. When she saw the new clean yellow BMW pull up she smiled, happy to see her boo.

"Hey, daddy, how you doing?" she asked. She leaned in and kissed his lips after she'd gotten inside the car. She inhaled deeply loving the smell of the Balenciaga cologne he was wearing.

"I'm good, babe. How about you? Diner and a movie?" Chulu asked. pulling off with his tints up.

"Sure. Did you miss me?" she asked. She rubbed his dick making it grow hard from her soft touch.

"Hell yeah. I always miss you," he said.

"I missed you too," she said. She pulled out his manhood and kissed up and down its length. Then she ran her long tongue down the middle. Not one for teasing, she engulfed his whole ten-inch dick with her thick juicy lips.

"Shiitt, fuckk, umm," he moaned, as she went to work, bopping on his dick. She slurped and spit his pre-cum back on the head while sucking it slowly. He moaned louder, and within seconds her mouth was full of cum. As he shot out every drop, she made sure to slurp it all up.

She rolled down the window and spit it out. His legs were still shaking from the powerful nut as he drove down the highway. China liked oral sex but she still wasn't ready for fucking yet. Either way, the two loved each other and they always enjoyed their nights out with one another.

CHAPTER 8
HARLEM

It was dark when Smooth Loc walked out of the barbershop on Lenox Ave. He had a fresh cut and he was dressed in a blue Calvin Klein sweat suit.

He hoped in the new white Porsche Panamera Turbo he'd recently bought from his cousin's dealership in the Bronx on Gun Hill Road.

Since robbing Lil C and them niggas a month ago, his life had changed for better. He was fucking bad models, poppin' bottles he couldn't pronounce the name of, and stunting on his exes.

Smooth wasn't dumb either, so he moved to Newbury, NY with his aunty upstate until shit cooled down. He knew how Lil C and Loco got down. Word was, they had a price tag on his head. He knew they had found out he was the one who had robbed them for everything, especially since he knew where everything was in the stash house. But that night when he'd seen all the money and thousands of dollars' worth of drugs, he just couldn't help himself. Not to mention, his cousin, Baby Blue, had been in his ear about coming to work for him and switch sets.

Smooth was only in town to pick up some money from his man in the St. Nick projects—he had a friend of his pushing the drugs he'd stolen from Lil C and he was on his way there.

Once in front of the building of the projects, he double parked the Porsche and left the hazard lights blinking while he ran inside the first building.

Minutes later, he stepped out of the building with an extra cool bop in his step. He had a Prada bookbag hanging over his shoulder. It was around ten p.m. and the hood was dead which was why he loved going down there after the sun went down.

As soon as he stepped off the curb and walked between two random vans, he saw a shadow creep up behind him.

Smooth Loc looked back to see who was playing games with him. He was caught off guard and cracked in the skull four times with the butt of Lil Jay's pistol. He was hit repeatedly until he finally passed out. Once he was out cold, Lil Jay and Turk dragged his body inside the Chrysler Pacifica minivan then pulled off.

The two had been watching his every move for the past four hours and they had even watched him go inside his sister's crib on 114th. They knew it was now are never so they busted the move so they could clear their faces because they didn't want to end up like Tommy.

30 Minutes Later

Lil C, Big Porky, Lil Jay, and Turk stood in a cold, dark, rat infested basement in an alley near 123rd St.

"Look who finally decided to join us, cuz. Where the fuck my money at 'cause that shit in that backpack ain't nowhere close to being my shit," Lil C said, as Smooth slowly opened his eyes. Once his vision became clearer, he realized he was tied to a chair from his chest to ankles, with thick, itchy wool rope.

"I'm sorry, cuz. I was high off the dust that day and I got robbed. Some bloods took everything the next day," Smooth cried, hoping they believed his story.

"Nigga please! You don't even smoke wet. And I bet you wasn't high when you copped that new white Porsche, or when you was in the gambling spot uptown the other night," Lil C said, staring at the shocked look on his face.

Smooth's mind was racing so fast he got stuck. He knew he was trapped.

"Come on, Crip, man. We grew up together we—"

Before he could finish pleading his case, Lil C shoved his gun so far in Smooth's mouth, it nearly touched his throat.

"Nigga, you ain't Crippin' no more! Fuck-nigga who sent you? I know you ain't smart enough to pull some shit like this on yo' own," Lil C said. He knew Smooth had been in the Special Ed classes from preschool through 12th grade.

"Baby Blu," Smooth said. He started crying like a baby.

"Well thank your big cousin for making you lose your life."

Boom! Boom! Boom! Boom! And just like that, Lil C's let his Desert Eagle fill his body with hollow tips. Without hesitation, everybody else in the room followed suit and filled Smooth's body and face up with hot bullets, leaving no chance for an open casket.

"Cut this nigga's head off and put it in his mother's car in driver's seat, then send his body up the river," Lil C said. Then he turned to walk up the stairs and out of the basement. Everybody looked at each other, wondering who was going to cut the bloody head off.

"Man, I'm not with that demonic shit," Turf said.

"Rock, paper, scissors?" Big Porky said, looking around.

"Fuck it, I got it. Who got a pocketknife?" Lil Jay asked.

"Nigga, you can't cut that nigga's head off with no damn pocketknife. Here," Turf said, grabbing the axe off the hook on the wall.

Lil Jay started swinging the axe at Smooth's neck but he wasn't able to get it off on the first couple of tries. Using all his power, sweat poured down his forehead as he worked the dull axe like a lumberjack. Finally, the head rolled off.

Mount Vernon, NY

Club Sue's was a gentlemen's club with high-end dancers. Only the rich and famous and celebrities hung out there.

The club had four VIP sections, shiny black and purple lacquer floors, beveled glass mirrors throughout, two stages, and decorated bars with expensive glass shelves filled with enough liquor to knock out a tribe of elephants.

Rugar and his crew took over two of the VIP sections while some Bronx and Yonkers niggas controlled the other two sections.

Rugar wasn't much of a party goer but tonight Montonta had dragged him out to live life and shit was going good, fast. He was wearing a pair of red Amiri pants with a red Ferragamo shirt that matched his Giuseppe Zanotti shoes. Montonta wore a white Balenciaga outfit with the shoes to match and a new rose gold Audemar Piguet watch.

"This shit litty, bro," Montonta said. He and his crew had just come back from tossing 20k on the dancers. Rugar was sipping out of an Ace of Spade's bottle.

"It's a'ight, son, but I'm focused on the meeting I got coming up with the plug. I feel like I got something more to offer other than judging me based off who my brother was. You feel me, blood?" Rugar said over the loud club music.

"Fact, bratty, no stress, son," Montonta said, assuring his friend everything would go good.

"Who the fuck is these niggas?" Rugar asked. At the same time he clutched his pistol when he saw the crew twenty-deep approaching his VIP section. All his goons made their way over there as well.

The DJ got a little nervous as he watched the whole scene from his booth. Lil Durk's song, *This Ain't What You Want*, blared through the club's speakers

Once the unknown crew made it to Rugar's VIP, the two crews seemed to have a standoff. There was forty of Rugar's niggas and twenty of whoever the other crew was.

"Rugar, a female voice called out, as she parted the crew. She walked straight into the VIP. A red Dundas dress draped her curvy frame and the high heels made her legs look sexy. She held a Celina purse in her hand and she looked like a model. All the guys stared and lusted for her, even the dancers.

"Naya, what's poppin', love?" he asked and bent down to greet her with tight hug. After the embrace, she sat down next to him and crossed her legs. Rugar gave his goons a look letting them knew she was family. They nodded their heads and turned to continue partying.

"I'm chilling. I was in town and I heard from the Macks you was over here in VIP," she said pointing at the Bronx Macks.

"Okay," Rugar said.

"Hey, Montonta," Naya said. He almost choked on the bottle of D'Usse he was sipping on because he was surprised she knew his name.

Montonta gave her a head nod and went to toss some money after he stopped himself from staring at her sexy legs while trying to get a look at her panties—if she had any on.

"Weirdo, but you need some new friends," she said and smirked.

"He good. He one of the goons and he trustworthy," he said and nodded his head.

"You ready for the meeting?" she asked. She looked up and noticed one of the dancer's eyeing her, but she wasn't into women.

"I guess. I just want them to see me for me, and not Brazy's little brother. I'm tryna take this shit to another level, five," he explained. She understood.

"Respect is earned. I had it rough being a female, and a bad bitch at that. So I had to put it down viciously and pave my own way," she said honestly.

"I be knowing," he said.

The two chilled the rest of the night, tippin' dancers and bartenders while enjoying the night with their crews.

Romell Tukes

CHAPTER 9
HARLEM

Like hawks, Lil C, Loco, and Lil Jay watched Baby Blu's every move from behind the tints of the Toyota Avalon Sedan. They saw a man approach Baby Blu and his crew in front of the corner store. Then they went inside and it looked as if they were discussing business. Lil C had taken the night off from training just so he could handle this fat Big Pun look alike once and for all.

"Y'all ready, cuz?" Lil C asked? All three men cocked guns with thirty round glizzy's attached to the end. No one said a word.

***

Baby Blu was selling drugs out of the corner store but he only sold weight. Since Brazy's death, the city had been an open free-for-all. He'd heard some young nigga from uptown was on the rise in Fosta. And then there was Lil C. But from what he'd heard, Smooth robbed the little nigga for everything he had so he was out of the race.

"Listen, nigga, I ain't got all day, cuz. Here go three hundred jars of wet and five keys. Where the money at though?" Baby Blue asked, Gangsta, a drug dealer from the BX.

"A'ight, my nigga. I'ma trust you this time," Gangsta said and handed him two envelopes filled with cash. The men were in the back of a dirty storage room that was dirty with a strong odor. Before he could even count the money, some niggas busted up in the spot.

"Put your fucking hands up!" Lil C said, as Gangsta tried to reach for his piece. He was too slow though because Loco shot him four times in the heart and he fell backwards on some old boxes, dying slowing.

"Damn, cuz, what's going on?" Baby Blu asked. He recognized Loco's face but he had never seen Lil C before, so he had no clue who he was.

"You know what's crackin', cuz. Where the shit at?" Lil C asked.

"It's all in the cooler," Baby Blu said, looking at his AK-47 six feet away from him but closer to Loco.

"Yeah, thanks. *Bloc! Bloc! Bloc! Bloc! Bloc!*

Lil C gave him all headshots as he and Loco rushed the cooler and saw four duffle bags laying in there. They took two apiece and walked up front. A middle-aged Muslim man with a scared look on his face stood frozen in place.

"You good, ock. Just clean up the spot for me. This our block now and we got you, Lil C said. He reached into one of the duffle bags and pulled out a wad of money. Then he placed it in the sliding box underneath the bulletproof window.

Once they were back outside, Lil C and Loco saw two of Baby Blu's men dead on the side of the store. Lil Jay paced back and forth praying NYPD wouldn't drive up.

"You couldn't wait?" Lil C asked.

"I heard shots," Lil Jay said. Loco laughed on his way to the car knowing they had just hit a sweet lick.

Plainfield, NJ

The Empire meeting was being held in New Jersey and everybody was dressed to impressed. All the men wore suits and Naya wore a red classy Christian Louboutin cropped off-the-shoulder dress with the Louboutin heels. Her little sister, PYT, who was also part of the Empire, was dressed in an open-back Julien Macdonald, red and gold slit dress with Valentino high heels.

Everybody was seated in the old lined factory. Naya had the keys to it because she owned it. She was going to use it as a storage place but she changed her mind.

"Where this nigga at?" Bloody said. His long dreads hung in a ponytail.

"Facts," Bullet said, checking his bust down diamond Rolex Day-Date watch.

"RIP to the homie. But this nigga ain't nothing like Brazy. He got us Dom P to sip on. Brazy would'a had a nigga in this bitch thirsty," Big Smokey said in a deep voice that matched his six-six frame. Everybody laughed except Naya who ice-grilled him.

"This nigga got you roses," PYT said, looking at the flowers sitting in front of her and Naya. She was impressed to say the least.

"Who the fuck is this Romeo?" Big Smokey asked, making everybody laugh again, even Naya. Nobody knew Brazy had a brother until now, so it was new to them all except Naya.

"I could never be Romeo blood, more like Napoleon before he let shawty trick him," Rugar said seriously. He walked in from the back letting them know he was there before they all pulled off in their foreign cars.

"Good to see you," Naya said. She looked at him, admiring his fit—a red and white Emporio Armani, custom made from Paris during fashion week in Milan.

"This is Montonta, my capo & general. His seat will be amongst me. But thank you all for coming out ladies and gentlemen," he said, looking at PYT's grayish eyes which made her look foreign. He focused his attention elsewhere because he knew he had to win everybody at the table over.

"I'm Rugar aka Rugar Brim from Harlem, Fosta Projects. To be correct, Brazy was my older brother, but I'm here to carry on the torch. But let me know who's who," Rugarhe said. Everybody introduced themselves and said where they was from.

Red Hot and PYT had the Bronx, Big Smokey had Staten and Long Island, Bullet had Queens on lock, Bloody had the whole upstate on lock, Bam had Brooklyn on lock, and Naya had New Jersey.

"Now that we all know each other, let's get down to business. First, I'm not here to fill no man's shoes. I'm my own man and I'ma stand on this shit until I die. If a nigga don't like that I'm part of the Empire and here to help build something bigger and better, then kill me now," he said. "I'll give you the gun, skrap," he added. He looked around especially at Bloody who was grilling him because he disliked city niggas anyway since he was from Rochester.

"I know Brazy was suppling keys at twenty-seven but I'ma have 'em for twenty-two and the product is purer. I got whatever you need for a good price. I got my own army, money, and frame of mind. I'm young but very advanced for my age. I've done my full research on everybody in this room. There's only one way we can all succeed and remain at large," he said and paused briefly, "and that's by putting loyalty before royalty," Rugar said.

"I feel you, youngsta. But how we know the work you got any good because I ain't been able to get a key for twenty-two since the late 90's, son," Bam Bam said with his Brooklyn accent.

"He got a point, skrap," Red Hot said in agreement. He knew something wasn't adding up because it sounded too good to be true.

"True that's why I have keys for all of you in bags near the exit door. I'll let y'all be the judge," Rugar said.

What they didn't know was Jumbo was able to lower his prices and he'd found a new way to make his coke more pure since Brazy's death.

"Thank y'all for your time. Pardon me," Rugar said, excusing himself away from the table. He walked into the back with Montonta on his heels.

Now he had to win the votes of the most powerful gang leaders in New York to continue sitting at the head of the Empire, a billionaire organization.

"What everybody think?" Naya asked, once Rugar was gone. She knew Rugar needed the most votes to win and be seated at the head of the table. If not, he would just be another member of the Empire like the rest of them.

"He just a kid, blood, so I don't know," Bloody said.

"Age don't matter. He carries himself like a man, and if he can help us succeed why not put your pride to the side," PYT stated.

"I like his demeanor," Big Smokey said.

"So what's the votes? I'ma start and I say *yes* because I know he got what it takes. He already bringing shit to the table. Who else is?" Naya asked.

"I agree, and I say *yes* too. I like the young nigga," Big Smokey stated, sipping his Dom P.

"He just jumped off the porch. I don't think he got enough experience. Anybody can have a plug but can they run an Empire? So I say *no*. It's nothing against him. I like him but it's about business," Bullet said.

"I say *yes*. This nigga trippin' and he too old to be hatin'," Bam Bam said. He was referring to Bullet.

"Man, that little nigga fakin', son. I bet that work been cut a hundred times. Nobody don't even know that nigga or where he came from. I vote *hell no*," Bloody spit out. He was pissed they even said yes.

"Listen, son on his shit. I respect his mind but I have to vote *no* because I don't know his resume. All I know is he the big homie brother and he got all his status on account of Brazy. So my vote is *no*," Red Hot said. He looked like Kid Ink's twin.

Everybody looked at PYT who was now the tie breaker. "I hate being in this position but I'ma stand on what I believe in and what's right. Me and my sister live by the law of this blood shit and I can tell he official. I owe this shit to Brazy, we all do. So I vote *yes*," PYT stated.

"Well that's it. He's in now. And whoever goes against that goes against blood. And whoever goes against blood goes against us all," Naya said. She walked off to get Rugar. Her heels clicked against the cement floor.

When Rugar come back he was all smiles. He went around and shook everybody's hand and embraced his new family. Once the place cleared it Rugar, Naya, Montonta, and PYT were the last ones left.

"You made it. I'm happy for you. Oh yeah, this is my real sister, PYT," Naya said, correctly introducing the two.

"Thank you for the flowers," PYT said smiling. Rugar was amazed by her beautiful smile.

"No issue," he said.

"Call me Jasmine," she said, blushing. He blushed too.

PYT was mixed with African and Indian but she looked Latino. She was light skinned with gray and green eyes, a curvaceous body, and long, dark silky hair. A set of nice B-cup perky breasts sat upright and firm and she her stomach was a flat six pack. She was nineteen soon to be twenty.

Naya felt the vibes as the two stared at one another.

"Damn, blood, ask for her number," Montonta said breaking the crazy lustful stare.

"Nigga shut up," Rugar said. He felt a little embarrassed now that Montonta had put him on blast. Now he was scared to ask her for her math.

"Here," she said. She pulled a piece of paper and a pen out of her purse and wrote down her number for him.

"Thank you."

"No, *thank* you," PYT said with that same beautiful smile. "Call me sometimes. Come on, Naya, I got a class tonight," she said. She had rode with her sister and left her Audi at Naya's place in Newark, but her college was in New York.

"Damn, bro. She look better then Naya and she on your lines. She bad, son. Word to mother," Montonta said. The place was now empty.

"Yeah, come on. We gotta head uptown," Rugar said, walking out. His mind was on PYT.

CHAPTER 10
A WEEK LATER

In one week, Rugar had sold nearly one hundred bricks to the members within the Empire. They were very pleased and impressed with the quality of the coke and heroin he was moving. He had no clue the dope was ten times purer then what the China White fiends were already overdosing on throughout the city.

RugarThanks to Montonta muscling his way into other niggas' hoods and taking over, he had a lot of hoods in Harlem under his control.

The previous day, he'd met a cute brown skinned chick at a soul food spot. She let him know she liked his ice and style. Unfortunately for her, he told her he wasn't into relationships, but the two still had a cool conversation. He found out her name was Ashely and she was a single mother struggling trying to get her life together. She was a cool chick. He couldn't help but feel sympathetic to her situation, so he ended up giving her twenty-five hundred dollars. He also gave her Montonta's number and told her to call if she needed a job. He let her know he was about to open a computer and clothing store.

With a suitcase full of money, Rugar rode in the Uber to a car dealership. Luckily, the car was ready, and because it was Uncle P's dealership, he'd gotten a good price on it.

Hearing his cell chime Rugar answered, "Hello," Rugaras the Uber swerved through potholes in the Harlem streets.

"What's poppin'?" a female voice said through the speaker.

"Us, never them. What's the word?" he replied.

"I heard the crew loving you," Naya said.

"Sometimes. But love is a dangerous game," Rugar told her. He looked out of the window and noticed how nice the weather was. Women were dressed in little skirts and tank tops, sucking on ice cream cones, while niggas roamed the Harlem streets for hoes, money, or drugs.

"Speaking of love, has Jasmine hit you up?" Naya asked

"Nah, why? Have you spoken to her about me?" he asked.

"Boy, no, call her. Trust me, she's different from most women her age. She's focused on college and she's a big help to us. She's our financial secretary. She handles anything dealing with business but she's also well grounded. You can do the math," Naya said, letting him know she was also a pretty gangsta.

"I'ma call her soon, but where you at?" he asked as the African driver almost hit two civilians.

"I'm on my way to Patterson to holla at Nap and B.G. Them niggas out there wilding again," she said. "Oh shit, I forgot Bam Bam told me to tell you to meet him at Club Honey in Brooklyn at 11 tonight," she said.

"A'ight, I gotta go. I'ma hit you later," Rugar said and hung up. He climbed out of the cab and saw that his car was in the lot, ready, and the tags were already on it thanks to P.

When he saw the all-red Mercedes AMG E63 S4 Matic his dick got hard. He tossed the salesman the suitcase full of money and told him to keep the change. Then he got the keys and pulled off the lot.

That night at the club in Brooklyn was cool. Bam Bam showed Rugar and his crew a good time. Brooklyn niggas treated Bam Bam like he was Jay-Z.

Bam Bam gave Rugar the run down on everybody in the Empire but told Rugarhim to be sure to watch out for PYT because she was dangerous and deadly. He'd seen her kill many people. But the craziest shit he'd seen her do was when she killed her ex-boyfriend *and* the bitch he'd cheated on her with. Word on the street was she was still a virgin.

The night was fun and young but they still did a little business. Bam Bam's main purpose for calling him out was to see if they could strike a deal on one hundred sixty keys in two days—they did.

***

Today was a special day at St. John High School gym. Over one hundred fifty students were graduating, and China was one of them. She looked beautiful in her purple Max Mara dress that showed her thick curves—her ass poked out like two basketballs. She wore a little make-up and her hair was all done up. A pair of Bulgari shades covered her chinky eyes. Hands down, she was the baddest bitch in the gym.

After all the students had given their speeches and received their diplomas, everybody went with their respective family and friends.

"Hey, baby! Oh my God you came," China said. She hugged her man and nodded at his two yes-sir niggas.

"You ready for college? I'm proud of you, ma," Chulu said. He was drippin' down in Versace gear.

"Of course I am," she said. She was happy ready for the new chapter that was about to begin in her life.

"I got a surprise for you later," Chulu told her, referring to the Tiffany & Co. necklace he'd coped her. As the two stood conversing, Rugar approached them.

"Yo', what's poppin', bro?" Rugar asked. Montonta and five other goons stood behind him.

"Ain't shit, five. Just chilling, showing a little support," Chulu said. The two had a mutual respect for one another.

Rugar didn't mind his twin sister fucking with Chulu even though he was a couple of years older than her. If China was happy then so was he—unlike Brazy and uncle P who disliked the nigga—they had always said he should find a bitch his own age.

"A'ight, that's what's up. China, can you come outside real quick?" Rugarhe asked his sister. He led the way through the crowd and out the door towards the parking lot.

When they got outside Rugar leaned against a Pink CLA 250 Benz he had ordered the week before her big day. There was a big bow tied on the grill of the car.

"Oh my fucking God! No way," China yelled. She covered her mouth in awe when Rugar handed her a set of keys with the BMW emblem on them. Some of her friends approached, all wearing fake smiles of envy.

Uncle P and his main bitch, Tiff, played the background. P was happy for his niece but he would continue to watch Chulu closely.

Chulu was surprised. The Benz was killing his little gift since he'd only spent twenty-two thousand for it. He was still happy for her. Besides, now he didn't have to be her personal cab.

China went for a test drive with her friends and never came back. They took a detour and went shopping at the mall.

Meanwhile Across Town

Lil C's graduation had just ended and high school kids were running all over the place, yelling and ready to turn up. All of them were proud they had made it.

Mona facetimed him from her high school graduation in Queens, a private school for girls.

After facetiming her, he walked over to his mom who stood next to Jumbo. Jumbo was decked out in a two-piece Tallia suit. Lil C had worn a Michael Kors suit he'd just copped the day before. His money was flowing like water thanks to the Baby Blu robbery.

"I'm so proud of you," Michelle said. She hugged him. She was still dressed in her blue work uniform and scrubs.

"I'm proud of you too kid. Now you can focus more on your career," Jumbo said. Michelle gave him a look.

"If he wants that," she said. She checked her watch realizing she had to go to work so she wouldn't be late. "I have to go. I love you and I'll see you later," Michelle said, running off.

"She works hard but I gotta go too kid. I'ma see you later," Jumbo said. He walked off headed to the meeting he had to attend. He only hoped his old broken down Honda could make it on time.

Lil C walked out of the school and saw a beautiful black and Dominican chick whose name was La La. She called out his name.

"What La La?" he answered in a snappy tone.

"Damn, it's like that," she said, catching up to him. She was dressed in a sexy black mini Chanel dress with heels. Her big ass sat on her back and she was definitely eye candy material.

"You drove up here, CB? My ride left me," La La asked with puppy dog eyes. She stared at his designer suit. She had been calling him Chris Brown since their freshman year because he looked like CB with dreads.

"Where your man at? And I told your ratchet ass to stop calling me CB," he said, walking past the other students speeding out of the lot. He yelled and cheered out loud happy to be done with school.

"Sorry, but his broke ass as at home. That nigga don't even got bus fare," she said, talking about the school's football team's quarterback.

"Come on," he said, as he walked towards a sky blue drop top BMW. He stopped at the driver's door.

"Lil C get away from them white people's car before they call the police," La La yelled. She stopped walking thinking he was about to hijack the fly ass car.

Lil C shook his head and placed his key in his door. Then he climbed inside and dropped the top to feel the hot summer heat.

"Ain't no way you ballin' like this," she said, with a shocked look on her face. She climbed in the soft peanut butter seats. Damn boy, I wish I would'a known you was doing it big," she said. She licked her thick glossy lips letting him know what she was trying to do.

"You talk too much. Just sit back before your dirty ass be walking," he said. He pulled out of the parking lot and turned up a Meek Mill and Drake song. Bitches in the street started dancing and twerkin'.

La La crossed her arms. She was pissed he wasn't trying to give her no play. Then she remembered the time she had dissed him in the 4th grade.

After he dropped her off, he went to pick up Mona so they could spend the rest of the day together. Soon it would be time for him to train.

CHAPTER 11

Rugar was going through his walk-in closet searching through his designer clothes. He had everything from Gucci, Prada, Fendi, Dior, Celina, Rag & Bone, G-Star, Balmain, Versace, and Hermes—you name it, he had it. He had gotten his style from his brother and uncle.

Today was a big day because he and China were turning eighteen. The two were twins and she'd been born just a few seconds earlier than him. Every year, Uncle P would throw a block party for them. The whole city would come out, including rappers, gangstas, and the basketball players who played the six-on-six tournaments.

After picking a white Balmain outfit with the shoes to match, he was ready. He heard his phone ringing on his way to the shower. When he saw Jasmine aka PYT's name he got butterflies.

"Happy birthday," PYT said in her sweet soft voice.

"Thanks. How did you know?" he asked, as he lay back on his bed smiling.

"Naya put me on game but I heard you was having a block party. Damn, I don't get a call, a text, an invitation, or nothing," she asked.

"My bad, blood. I figured that nigga had you tied up but I would love for you to come."

"Sorry, I'm single, love. But I'll be there with Naya so keep your little hoochy thots in line," she said. She laughed even though she was serious.

"I don't got those issues. But listen, I'ma hop in the shower right quick but I'll see you there," he said. She said bye and they ended the call. He took a long shower and thought about PYT the whole time.

Hours Later

It was 92° degree outside and the block party was popping. There was free food, free alcohol, and free school supplies. The hottest DJ in the city was playing the hottest rap music, and the biggest basketball tournament in the city in Fosta projects where niggas played five-on-five basketball.

China was wearing a short off-white mini-dress with Jimmy Choo pumps. She was chilling with Chulu and his crew on the basketball court. They were watching the games everyone was betting on.

"You made me lose 20K, bro," Rugar told Montonta and Turf. Both were sweating in their basketball jerseys, fresh off the court.

"Nigga you'll be a'ight. I played four games," Montonta said. He was sitting on the bleachers when he saw Ashely and a group of bitches walk up, all looking good.

"Happy birthday, Rugar," Ashely said. Wearing Prada jeans, a blouse, and heels, her wide hips and phat ass looked good.

"Thanks. How you like the store?" he asked. He turned his attention to the red Maybach that had just pulled in front of the projects. Everybody else was looking too.

"I like it a lot and I love computers," she said. She was just about to sit down when he stood up.

"Excuse me. Y'all enjoy yourself," Rugarhe said. He realized who it was that had pulled up stunting in his hood.

"Where you going, ma? Come sit down. There's enough room," Turf said patting his lap. "Boy please! You shaped like a Newport 100," one of Ashely friends said, making everyone laugh.

"What? Bitch that's why you shaped like Precious and look like Whoopi Goldberg in the face," Turf shouted.

Half the court started laughing at the plus-size women in attendance.

The chauffeur of the Maybach hopped out in a red suit. He opened the door for Naya and PYT who were sitting in the back.

"I got it, homie. They family," Rugar told the chauffeur. All eyes were on the candy-red Maybach.

Naya stepped out first in a pink Celine dress that hugged her perfect toned frame. Her hair was in eight long corn rolled braids hanging to the middle of her back.

PYT climbed out behind her. She was wearing a red and white velvet Oscar de la Renta slip dress with red bottom six-inch heels on her feet. She wore a little make-up and her hair was styled in a bun which made her look exotic.

"Happy birthday," Naya said. Rugar was zoned out staring at PYT's cleavage and curves—she was the baddest bitch on the block but everyone was staring at both of them.

"Nigga you heard me," Naya said, pushing him playfully.

"Yeah? What you say?" Rugar asked. He hadn't heard a word she'd said because he couldn't take his eyes off PYT. PYT blushed from all the attention he was giving her.

"This shit is packed! I remember when I came out here two years ago with Brazy and it was litty," Naya said, looking around. There were crowds of people on the basketball court and all over the block which had been closed off on both ends.

"We both got a gift for you," PYT said. She leaned inside the backseat and grabbed two boxes from the Maybach.

Rugar looked at the two boxes from Tiffany & Co. He opened both boxes—one had a gold rope chain in it, and inside the other box was a Yacht Master Rolex worth one hundred fifty thousand dollars.

"Damn," he said, as he put the jewelry.

"The watch is from me," PYT said in a low tone.

"Thank you," he told her sincerely. Then he heard someone calling out his name. PYT and Naya looked back to see who it was.

"Rugar, damn you deaf," China said, approaching him. She eyed his new chain and watch.

When PYT saw the beautiful woman, a twinge of jealousy surged through her. She assumed it was his girlfriend and it made her feel like a dummy.

"Hey, Naya. Nice Maybach," China said. When she placed her brother's arms around her neck she noticed PYT grilling her. She could feel the heat coming off of her. She stared at China and Rugar as if they were a happy couple.

"Oh shit, China, happy birthday," Naya said, hugging her. Now PYT was confused.

"Jasmine, this is my twin sister, China," Rugar explained, seeing the crazy look on her face.

"Oh, oh, okay," PYT said. She tried to play if off and she really felt stupid for thinking the two were a couple.

"Happy birthday and you look amazing," PYT told China.

"Shit, you killing it too! Everybody on your line, but I gotta go where my boo at before one of these bum-ass bitches try they hand," China said before turning to leave.

"Let's walk around," Rugar said. He took the ladies around and showed them his hood. He also took them over to where his Uncle P was. Naya had known him for years but he wanted to introduce Jasmine.

They enjoyed the block party until it was over. Thankfully, no one was shot or stabbed, so it was a good day.

Later that Night

King Chulu and China had just come back from the club with Rugar and his crew. It had been a crazy night but their night was just beginning.

"Yo', this shit is so fuckin' fly," China said, looking around the penthouse suite of the fancy expensive hotel they were staying at.

There were candles and rose paddles everywhere. There was a plush white carpet, white leather furniture, an inside bar, and pool. The living room had pool tables and there was a huge jacuzzi near the window, overseeing the city right lights. The penthouse was so lavish there was an upstairs and downstairs.

"Happy birthday, love," Chulu told China. Getting comfortable, he took off his Burberry bottom-up shirt showing his off his tatts and muscles. He had a tank top on underneath the shirt.

"Thank you, babe. Look, I'ma go shower and freshen up so meet me in the bedroom." China kissed him and rubbed his semi-hard dick before strutting off.

King Chulu went to the dimly lit bedroom and put on some Keith Sweat to set the vibe. Even though he was Spanish, he still enjoyed the smooth sounds of old school R&B. He didn't want to kill the vibe by playing Plan B or Bad Bunny.

Twenty minutes later, China stepped in the room wrapped in a long towel. Her hair was wet so she let it hang freely as she sashayed around in a pair of Fendi heels.

Chulu got naked. His dick was so hard he felt a blood rush. Showing her thick thighs, China dropped her towel in front of him. Her flat stomach was perfect, and her fat pussy was pierced with a small ring right in her clit. Her pussy lips were so close together they looked closed.

Giving him a good look at her wide big ass, China turned around, bent over, and spread her pussy lips apart. Then she began playing with her pussy. She started twerking her ass like a stripper while looking back at her ass make clapping sounds.

"You like, papi? I bet I can do it better on the dick," she said. She climbed between his legs and came face-to-face with his ten inches. The feel of her breath against his pole caused it to stand at attention. "I want to suck this dick," she said. She sucked the tip slowly and used her tongue to play with the head.

"Ohh shiiitt, suck that shit," he moaned. She started to go deeper, sucking harder. She deep throat his whole dick and left no skin showing.

"Umm," she moaned. She slurped his precum while coating his dick with her saliva. She was going crazy on his dick, sucking it as if it were her last.

"Im-m cum-m-m-in-ggg," he yelled as his toes curled up like a bitch. When he bust his nut China didn't give up and she swallowed everything, letting his dick touch the back of her tonsils until every drop was out.

"Shit, babe. My turn," he said. He flipped her on her back and spread her legs apart, exposing her pretty, fat, shaved-bald pussy.

Chulu fingered her tight wet pussy with one finger. He could feel her muscles tighten. Then he licked her clit for five minutes straight and she started cumming like a waterfall.

"Ugghh fuck," she screamed, as she squirted in his face like a water gun being shot.

"Fuck me, papi. Please, go slow 'cause you're my first, papi," she said. Her legs trembled as she took in the sight of his massive dick.

Chulu entered her tight pussy slowly but only managed to get the tip in, because it was extra tight.

"Ohh," she moaned. Her body tensed up when she could feel him going deeper and deeper causing her walls to stretch. "Ugghh, harder, papi," she moaned louder. Slowly, she began to grind against his hips as she caught the rhythm. Her body felt as though she was in ecstasy.

"Mhhmmmm," Chulu moaned while gritting his teeth. Feeling her walls grip his dick almost made him nut too soon but he held himself back. *Her shit too damn good*, he thought.

Minutes later, they both released body-shaking orgasms. They changed positions and she bent over. Chulu got behind her and spread her wide fat ass. He slowly entered her and she moved in a slow motion, throwing her ass back on his dick, taking every inch.

"Uggghh, my God, yesss! Fuck that pussy," she yelled like a freak, as he worked his dick in and out of her. Hitting her G-spot, she exploded on his dick a second time.

When he released again he pulled out and shot it on her ass while she bounced it up and down making it jiggle. China wanted to ride so she got on top and buckled down on his dick. Arching her back, she rode like a seasoned cowgirl until she nutted back to back.

Once she was done, she saw red dots and she was embarrassed. He had just burst her cherry but Chulu found it funny. The two cleaned the sheets and fucked raw for two more hours before going to sleep.

***

Mona and Lil C just got done having rough sex for three hours in Mona mom house both of them was out of breath.

Laying on her man's six pack, Mona wore a pair of red La Perla thongs and a matching bra that held her double-D breasts in place.

A mixture of black and white, her complexion was high yellow and her skin was smooth and flawless. She had a thick body and hazel eyes. Her cheeks were embedded with deep dimples and her hair was long, dark, and silky. She was always told she resembled the beautiful actress, Lauren London.

"You fuck me good and treat me even better. If I ever catch you cheating, I'ma kill that dusty bitch and paralyze you from your waist down. You'll never be able to use this again," she said, grabbing his dick.

"Damn, chill girl," he said. He laughed as he grabbed her hands playfully and held her by her wrists.

"Yesterday I was out with Emma, and her friend was talking about niggas in Harlem who fine and shit and getting money too. Then she described you—the pretty nigga who boxes and looks like Christ Brown from Polo. I wanted to kill that bitch but I knew she didn't know you. But still," Mona said.

"Fuck her, boo. You know it's forever us. I don't be worried about no other bitch and neither should you," he said.

"You right, babe." She leaned in for a kiss.

Mona was planning to go off to college in Texas soon so she wanted to spend quality time with her man. Ever since her father had been killed on duty by Brazy, she had been dealing with anxiety and depression, except for when Lil C was around.

"I love you and nothing can separate that, not even distance," he said

"I love you more, daddy. But I want some more of this dick," she said, pulling his dick out. She stuck her head underneath the covers and began sucking it. She put it deep in her throat because she didn't have gag reflex. She sucked his dick for thirty minutes until her jaws locked. Then, she wanted to try anal sex for the first time.

After five minutes into it, her tiny asshole couldn't take it. She tapped out and fucked him the vaginal way for another hour. That is, until her mom caught them in action.

CHAPTER 12
NEW ROCHELLE, NY

PYT was on her lunchbreak at a Subway restaurant, eating a six-inch veggie sandwich, while texting Rugar. She attended an Ivy League college majoring in business and accounting. She was borderline genius and her college was just ten minutes away.

Since it was hot outside, she'd worn a sky-blue Christian Dior sundress and sandals that showed of her pretty manicured feet.

Within seconds, she received a text from Rugar asking her to go on a date with him the upcoming weekend. She wanted to scream so bad but there were too many noisy white people around her.

She was delighted to reply *yes*. She gave him the time and an address where he could pick her from. The address was one of Naya's spots near Harlem because she lived in the Bronx.

As she sat thinking she began to reflect on her crazy life. When people looked at her, normally all they saw was a pretty face. They didn't know what was behind the mask.

***

PYT was born and raised in Zimbabwe, Southern Africa, where her given tribal name was Zeema. Her father, King Omen, was a tribal leader. He had trained PYT to be an assassin. He'd taught her how to kill, disarm enemies, fight, sword fight, shoot bow and arrows, martial arts, and how to move like a ninja.

PYT and Naya had the same mother but different fathers. Naya's father was a wealthy Arabian man who was killed by an unknown hitman. PYT's mom and father met on a trip while her mother was on a vacation—that's where she met King Omen and got pregnant.

They both agreed to let PYT stay in Africa until she was old enough to go to the states to live with her mother, sister, and Naya in New Jersey.

PYT came to the states in her early teens. Naya took her little sister under her wing and helped her get an education. She didn't know how vicious of a killer she was until the night she'd gotten ambushed in Newark outside of a club. It was PYT who saved her life.

When Naya told Brazy about her crazy skills and how smart she was, Brazy brought her into the Empire for all the business proposals. She took out a couple of powerful drug lords which gave him more room to build his Empire.

Ever since then, she'd been finding her way in life. Shit had been great and she was proud of herself.

Washington Height

Loco and Big Pork had been following King Chulu around all day. They were in a GMC black truck with tints. Sick of watching him make pickups and drops-off all day, it was now dark out.

"Yo', son you farted again?" Loco said, looking at the three hundred pound young man.

"Maybach, it was that Taco Bell, cuz," Big Porky said, watching King Chulu come out of a building on Post and Academy.

"You starting to piss me off, but did you see what he just did?" Loco asked, referring to the two big trash bags King Chulu had tossed into the backseat of a green BMW X5 truck.

"Hell yeah," Big Porky said. He was lying since he was really looking at the hotdog stand on the corner because it smelled delicious to him.

Loco had been watching King Chulu for months. He knew his status and knew it would be hard to get close to him. But today was his lucky day because he only had one nigga with him.

"Follow him, cuz," Loco said when he saw the truck pull off.

"A'ight," Big Porky said. He made sure to keep a good distance. In less than ten minutes later, King Chulu pulled into an alley behind a couple of stores. One was his homie's pizza shop that he co-owned, and the other was where he stashed money at.

King Chulu saw the GMC truck with tints pass by him. It was going toward the back of the alley as if the truck was one of the store owners entering through the back.

Paying the truck no mind, Chulu continued having a conversation with King Ike about a situation in Queens he needed him to handle.

Tat, Tat, Tat, Bloc! Bloc! Tat, Tat, Bloc, Bloc!

Bullets entered the BMW killing the driver, King Ike, but the firing continued.

Unable to start the car up because the key had fallen to the floor, King Chulu panicked. He reached for his pistol but was cut short.

"Nigga don't do it," Loco said, with venom in his tone. He aimed a Colt 45 at his head through the open passenger window.

"The money in the back. Take it and go," King Chulu said. He couldn't see the gunmen clearly but he did see the blue flags letting him know they were Crips.

Without replying, Loco shot him in the head and face nine times then grabbed the trash bags from the backseat. As soon as he turned around, a Spanish man burst through the door with a Draco and he realized his big homie, Chulu, was dead.

Before he could even shoot, Big Porky shot the man five times, slumping him, as the impact from the SK forced the man back inside the doorway.

Loco and Big Porky took off and hopped inside the GMC rental. They raced out of the alley and headed back home to Harlem, knowing it was the beginning of a new war.

Bronx, NY

Days later, King Chulu's funeral was held at Wilson Graveyard. The place was filled with Latin Kings and Latin Queens from everywhere. Chicago, Miami, and Boston were all in attendance.

The morgue was unable to provide surgery on his face because there were too many chunks of his flesh missing. So, it was a closed-casket funeral

King Ed was King Chulu's little brother. He would take over his brother's crown since he was murdered. When he heard what happened he went wild. He put money on the killers' head but nobody had a clue who was responsible. However, he was sure to find out soon.

King Ed was a handsome, tall, skinny, Spanish nigga. He only fucked bad model-looking bitches. He was a killer raised in the Bronx.

Looking through his Cavalli shades, he noticed China sitting to his far left. As the ceremony came to a close, he couldn't help but wonder if China had set him up. He knew how New York bitches got down but he also knew China. And she didn't seem like the type, so that idea left his thoughts.

After the funeral King Ed spoke to China. Montonta was with her and the two men mean-mugged each other then went their separate ways, not feeling one another's energy. China was cool people so he just wanted to thank her for coming out, but she looked more broken than him.

Upper Westside

Rugar and PYT both arrived at the nice five-star restaurant. There was a stage for bands who were mostly jazz players. Rugar had Rugardressed in a Dior for men's suit while PYT wore a classy Saint Laurent wrap dress with a diamond necklace and bracelet.

A waiter led them to a nice VIP section where the lights were dim and candles set the mood. They slid in the booth under the gold chandlers.

"This is nice. What are you going to order?" PYT asked, giving him a big plus for the dinner.

"I already ordered for the both of us. That's what I was texting on the way here," he said.

"Oh, I thought you was texting a bitch," she said with a laugh. At least she was being honest.

"I know, but thank you for coming. I would love to get to know the real you because I know there is more than meets the eye," he said, looking into her colorful eyes.

"There is a lot to all of us," she said. For the first time, Rugar finally heard a hint of her foreign accent.

"Can I be real with you?" he asked. "I heard you killed a lot of people." As soon the last statement left his mouth her smile turned to a frown.

"You trying to judge me or take me to fucking court?" she asked. Now she was pissed, grabbing her purse, and ready to bounce.

"No, wait. It's not like that, Jasmine. I just wanted to know why you chose this lifestyle because you're so classy, beautiful, and smart. I just don't see you in this lifestyle," he said. Hearing all the compliments made her loosen up. A few seconds later their food arrived.

"Thank you," she told the waiter as he walked off. "How did you know this was my favorite food?" She gawked at the well-done steak, shrimps, clams, oysters, and wild rice.

"How did you find out when my birthday was?" he replied.

"Next time you ask a crazy question find a correct approach so you don't offend anyone. But I was born and raised in Africa. I was trained to become a hitwoman, an assassin for my family. My father is a King but I moved to Jersey with my sister. And since I was being tortured, abused, and beaten, I was lost.

Rugar couldn't believe what she was saying. She didn't even look like the type to go through struggles.

"Do you know how it feels to be left alone in a wild jungle for three days with nothing but a sword? And all you have to eat are the leftovers from lions and hyaenas?" she asked, looking at him seriously.

"No, I don't," he answered honestly. Now, he was unable to eat because he felt bad he'd even asked her.

"I killed a lot of people. In order to live in America I made a deal to continue taking hits in other countries. I recently stopped six months ago, but this is me. I'm a blood. I killed a lot of people and I'm part of the Empire. That's my life so you can take it for what it's worth or you can leave," she said. She looked down at her untouched food.

"I'm sorry you had to go through that. Just know I accept everything that comes with you. I just wanted to know what I was dealing with so I know how to handle you and understand you, that's all," he said.

"You sure I'm the one you want to really understand?" she asked.

"I ain't stop thinking about you since I meet you, PYT. I know you're a special woman and I like and want you," Rugar said. The two had a thirty second stare down.

"What are you trying to say, Jamel?"

"I want you to be wifey," he said. She laughed.

"I'm sure you heard what happened to my ex?" she said somewhat timidly.

"Yeah, so what? I'll die for your love. I'd rather have you kill me than one of those goofy niggas out there," he said making her laugh.

"I'ma give you a chance, but fuck up and I'm cutting your dick off and feeding it to my pit," she said, holding up a steak knife. I don't care about all that big homie shit either," she said.

"Okay, now let me get a kiss." Rugar leaned in toward her and sucked her lips gently.

"Damn, nigga, bite my lip off," she said.

They laughed and enjoyed the rest of the night.

CHAPTER 13

China laid in her bed trying to let everything register, but it was too much to bare without crying. Losing the love of her life was a hard pill to swallow. Even though she understood it was part of the game, she didn't understand why she had to suffer. Today was her big day. She had recently been accepted to Miami University to major in Criminal Justice and she wanted to become a lawyer. She knew if Chulu or Brazy were still alive, they would be proud of her just like Rugar was.

"Baby girl, you ready? Your flight leaves in an hour," her uncle yelled from outside her door.

"One second," she yelled back.

She hopped out of her bed not realizing she was running behind time. As she began to get dressed Rugar burst in her room shirtless, showing his ripped six-pack and massive chest.

"Nigga learn how to knock," China shouted. He almost scared her while she was fixing her make-up.

"You need to hurry up. I'ma take your big headed ass to the airport and I don't got all day," he said, jumping on her unmade bed.

"You're so fucking annoying. But what's up with that bad bitch I saw you with? She fits you," China said, applying the last bit of make-up under her eyes.

"She wifey, sis," he replied in a cocky tone.

"Damn, already thirsty. But that's what's up. I can't lie, she was making me and Naya look like shit at that block party and you know that's hard to do," China stated as she packed some more clothes in her Coach duffle bags.

"Yeah, I know, but fuck all that. You need to bring your yellow ass on. You know traffic is crazy right now," he told her.

"Okay, I'm done. Grab them bags in the corner, boy. And stop rushing me. I'ma queen. I move to my own beat and your breath stank, nigga," she said walking into the living with bags.

"Damn, about time. Come give me hug and don't be down there partying. Focus on school and keep that pepper spray on you. Also Liea is waiting on you. She lives in North Miami. Your cousin will show you around. We already got your apartment paid in full for a year so just focus on school," Uncle P preached. He was proud of his niece because she deserved it. And she was the first in the family to go to college.

"Oh my God, you told me the same thing five times," she said. She took a deep breath. Then she and Rugar made their way out of the apartment with a hand full of bags.

The whole ride was quiet. Both had thoughts of missing one another on their minds. The two had been close since birth. Plus, they had that twin vibe going on.

"Stop crying, sis. It's going to be okay. When you get on the flight, leave all the negative emotions here," Rugar said, as he pulled up to the airport.

China wiped her eyes. She hated crying, especially in front of people, but lately she was emotionally stressed. "I'm cool, bro, thanks," she said.

"I'ma come to Miami for Montonta birthday but still call me every day. I love you," he told her, as he double parked in the front.

Rugar helped her with her bags and they said their goodbyes to one another.

Queens, NY

Rugar drove through Far Rockaway in Queens to meet with Bullet to discuss business. Queens was a nice area in certain parts but the hood was like being in Chiraq. There was a war zone over turfs and Bullet was the main reason.

When he pulled in front of Bullet's projects, his mans, was already in front of the building. Dressed in a tank top that showed his large muscles, he had his right sweat pant leg pulled up. Bullet was controlling a big dice game surrounded by sixty goons, all ready to move at their big homie's signal.

When niggas saw Rugar hop out with all his jewelry on, they were ready to rob him until they saw Bullet embrace him. Once they found out who he was, the whole hood hopped on his dick because Brazy's name was like GOD in the hood. Since Rugar had taken over, now so was his.

"Welcome to my jungle, blood. I'm King Kong in this bitch," Bullet said. They walked through the projects which was littered with crack baggies, forty-ounce bottles, and fiends running in and out of buildings.

After they talked for about an hour, Bullet had a newfound respect for the young gangsta, not to mention, he had just copped thirty keys and I gave him ten on consignment.

***

Montonta sat in the back of the gentleman's club in the VIP area drinking Ace of Spades while his crew threw money on stage at the dancers. Tonight was a chill night and he just wanted to come out to get some air. He wanted to let his crew enjoy themselves since they had been busy getting big money.

"Yo', Montonta, that blood nigga from the BX on his way over here. Red Hot let him in," one of Montonta's young shooters said from outside the ropes that separated the club from the VIP.

"Let him in, blood," he said. He saw Red Hot coming up the stairs alone and he'd left his crew in the other VIP section.

"What's poppin', bro?" Red Hot asked, walking through the ropes in a Hermes outfit.

"Peace, blood. I'm just mackin', enjoying life. How about you?" Montonota asked, as he watched the strippers twerk on the poles.

"That's a fact. That work got the town litty," Red Hot said, inviting himself to Montonta's Ace and Henny.

Red Hot was twenty-six, light skinned with waves, and he had green eyes. His face sported a small beard and the females loved him. He had five baby mamas. He was from Castel Hill and

Millbrook but he ran the Bronx with an iron fist. PYT was the brains and mastermind.

"That's what's up, bro. But I got a question for ya'. How well do you know PYT? She cool but I don't really know her like that," Montonta asked, trying to downplay his question. He was honestly just being nosey and he was worried about Rugar.

"Listen, I'ma keep it real wit' you. That bitch is coldblooded. A lot of bodies done came up missing fucking with her, bro. She can be deadly if crossed. She killed two of my workers for trying to bag her. But more than anything, she been the muscles and the brains to the empire. She speaks highly of Rugar and that's something I ain't never seen her do," Red Hot said. "I think she really feeling him. All I can say is he wouldn't wanna hurt her because she a different kinda breed," he stated seriously. He let his words linger and let Montonta wonder deep thought.

A bartender bottle girl approached the section.

"Excuse me, papi. I'm trying see what you doing tonight. Take my number and call me. Don't be shy," the woman said. After giving Montonta her number on a napkin, she walked off just as quickly as she'd approached.

"Damn, blood I done fucked every bitch in here expect her. She be curving and shit, so you gonna have to tell me how that shit is," Red Hot said, laughing.

They enjoyed the rest of the night popping bottles and getting dancers.

***

An hour later, Montonta texted the number on the napkin. Her name was on it and it was Salena. They met in a hotel room and he wasted no time fucking her out of her work outfit and heels. She had the best head game and pussy he'd ever had in his life. He was hooked on the beautiful Spanish princess.

Since Chulu's death, Selena had been looking for another baller to replace him. She had studied Montonta and watched him come to the club four times and toss close to sixty racks in one night.

She knew how to work her pussy to make a nigga fall in love. And that's exactly how she was working it tonight—she worked her pussy muscles and her throat muscles.

Montonta fell asleep and woke up the next morning with a hangover. He tried to remember what took place the night before. Then it hit him.

"Fuck, my nigga!" Montonta jumped up and grabbed his Diesel jeans. He checked for the 30K that had been in his pocket along with his pistol. Luckily, he found it as well as his icy Rolex, Cuban chain, and pinky ring. When he saw the letter he smiled.
Dear Montonta,

   From the head to toe, and even the way your cum tasted, I loved every second of you last night. I want more, papi. Call me. My pussy sore but I loved it.

   xoxoxo

Montonta smiled and noticed he had a couple of missed calls, mainly from his goons. But he texted Selena anyway. Shawty was on his mind so he went to her IG. She told him she was the Panamanian Goddess. Her pics were sexy and classy and he knew he'd found a winner.

Rugar called him and told him to meet him at Wilson Projects in two hours. So he got himself together, feeling like a new nigga.

CHAPTER 14
HARLEM

Lil C sat in Jumbo's gym office with his head hanging low. He was deep in thought thinking about how his day of training had went. He wasn't his best during his sparing session and it bothered him.

"Chris, I've known you since you were a baby. I watched you grow into the man you are today. So I'ma be blunt, man. What the fuck is going on?" Jumbo asked. He leaned back in his lazy-boy chair as he waited on an answer.

"Just not feeling it today," he replied, holding back what was really on his mind.

"I respect that. Some of the greatest fighters have bad days, but you got a fight coming up in a couple of days. So get focused before you step foot in the ring again," Jumbo said sternly.

"No problem. What's understood don't have to be said," Lil C said smoothly.

"Save that street talk for them street niggas. By the way, that's a nice BMW I saw you hop out of earlier. I been hearing your name a lot lately. I just hope you're smart enough to keep your personal life and career life separated. The streets will swallow you whole, kid. Listen to me because I know. I just look like this, but you're a good kid, so wise up," Jumbo said, looking at the shocked expression on Lil C's face.

"I feel you, old head. But some paths in life I have to fight alone," Lil C said, as he walked out of the office. Jumbo pounded his fist on his desk. All he could do was hope Lil C wasn't too deep in the game. Because truth be told, he would hate to see another black man lose his life to the streets.

***

"Hey, Mom. What you doing home at nine? I thought you had to work," Lil C stated, as he walked inside and saw his crib and saw his mom sitting on the couch. She had a crazy look on her face, a combination of disappointment and anger.

"Sit down on den sofa," Michelle said in her strong Jamaican accent. Lil C sat down. He sense something was wrong because his mom was never upset.

"What you need this for?" she asked, pulling out a GLOCK 45 pistol. Lil C was at a loss for words. But when she pulled out the Ruger 89, he knew he had to explain himself.

"Mom, what da fuck?" Lil C said. He took the two guns from his mom's possession.

"Get that shit outta my house, Chris! I raised you better than that," Michelle yelled.

"I'm sorry, Mom. I just gotta protect myself," Lil C said, hoping to calm her down. He walked to his room and lock himself in for the night. He could hear his mother crying.

Puerto Rican Day Parade

The parade was like a block party in New York City. For blocks and blocks, people from all over the Tri-State came to enjoy themselves. The Puerto Rican women were barely dressed with their asses, stomachs, and thighs showing. The cops were posted up on every block due to the violence the usually took place.

Drugs and alcohol were everywhere in the 90° degree weather. Crews posted up on each block, some looking for women and others looking for trouble.

"Yo', son, this shit litty, bro" Montonta yelled. He and his twenty-men crew watched beautiful women dance on floaters that moved down the packed street.

"Yeah, that's a fact. I'm glad I pulled up," Rugar said. He watched his homies bag a crew of Spanish bitches who were trying to sell the nutcrackers drinks.

Both Rugar and Montonta were dressed white Gucci outfits with rope chains around their necks and AP watches on their wrists. The crew enjoyed themselves and they tried to bag every bitch they saw.

Block Away

Lil C and Loco sat on the front of an apartment building with a gang of Crips. Everyone was dressed in blue with blue flags. He looked up and saw a bunch of bad ass Puerto Rican bitches walking up and down the block with big asses and camel toes all over the place.

Lil C was dressed in his sky-blue Versace tank top with the shorts to match and his sky-blue Giuseppe shoes. Loco was killing it in a blue Balmain designer outfit with Prada shoes. Letting the world know he was Crippin' heavy, he had a blue flag tied around his neck.

"Yo', ma, come here," Loco yelled down the block. There was a small group of young Spanish women dancing on each other to the loud music that was playing.

"What's up, papi? one of the Spanish women said. She kind of favored Beck G, the Latin artist.

"I'm tryna see if we can be friends, and if my friends can meet your friends, so we can all be friends," Loco stated. The women laughed flirtatiously. He smiled and took a sip of lean from the Styrofoam cup.

"So you Biggie now?" she said, referring to the lyrics he'd quoted from the Rapper Biggie's song. She was with ten of her friends and they told her they wouldn't mind chilling with the guys. So, the women and goons kicked it for a while and a couple of them even boo'd up.

"I'ma go take a piss, cuz," Lil C said. He grabbed his blue Versace backpack with his pistol inside.

"A'ight, nigga" Loco said. He entertained the women while Lil C Lil C was gone. Lil' C passed kids, families, and elderly people, all enjoying themselves on the beautiful day in the city. His mind was on the fight he had later that night. He'd been training hard with Jumbo for the past couple of days.

Once in the back of the pizza alley, he wasted no time pissing on the wall near a trashcan. He jumped when he saw the large rats racing to get the pizza that had been recently thrown out.

"You fucking dumb ass, come here!" a white cop walking by yelled. He had seen Lil C with his dick in his hand pissing in public. To make matters worse, Lil C was pissing on his brother's pizza shop, and his kids also worked there part-time when they weren't in college.

Lil C was stuck after he zipped his pants up. He realized the police had called for backup and another patrol car pulled up with a black officer inside. Then he remembered the gun in his bookbag. He looked behind him and realized there was nowhere to run except past the mean looking officer.

"Don't try it, nigga! Get on the fucking wall you nasty fucker," the white cop said. He threw Lil C up against the wall and began frisking him roughly. The black cop grabbed the bookbag off his shoulders.

Lil C's face was pressed into the wall. Most niggas from his hood had been through police brutally, but this was his first time. He strained to look back and saw Loco coming around the corner with a couple of Crips. When he saw what was going on he reached for his pistol, but Lil C gave him a look that said *chill*.

"Get the fuck outta here," the white cop shouted to the Crips. They didn't move a muscle. When the black cop found the gun, they cuffed him and tossed him in the NYPD van that had just arrived. Lil' C's parade was over.

***

"Damn, daddy. Why you so quiet?" a pretty Spanish woman asked Rugar. He was relaxing as he watched everyone enjoying the parade.

Rugar smelled her breath and it turned him all the way off. He didn't even want to reply it smelled so bad. It smelled like she had just got done sucking ten sweaty dicks.

"Yo', I'ma go get some more Nutcrackers, blood," Rugar said. He left the woman standing there with an attitude.

Across the street, the Latin Kings were selling Nutcrackers by the gallon. Within seconds after he'd purchased two large gallons in a plastic container, the police burst into the lobby eight deep with guns drawn and flashing their badges.

"Don't fucking move!" a Spanish undercover cop, dressed in plain clothes, yelled. Rugar and three of the Latin Kings were thrown on the ground before being cuffed.

Montonta and his goons ran across the street when they saw the jump-out boys rush the building.

"You must be a blood, and a rich blood at that," the DT said, pulling wads of money from his pockets. They placed him in the NYPD van that was already full of niggas. Rugar yelled for Montonta to call Eye Candy which code for his lawyer. Montonta and his crew talked shit to the police until they drove off with their boss in the back.

Romell Tukes

CHAPTER 15

Rikers Island was New York City's county jail for people who committed crimes in the city. The jail was also known for its gang violence. The inmates' signature in war was slashing their victims across the face with homemade knives.

Inmates wore street clothes and jewelry. A nigga had to be official to wear ice without getting his shit snatched. The guards were from the streets so they were just as grimy as the inmates. They brought in drugs, cell phones, and weapons.

Lil C

The holding area bullpen smelled like elephant piss. It was so dirty it looked like it hadn't been cleaned in years. Today, it was packed with robbers, purse snatchers, drunks, rapists, and murderers.

Lil C sat with his back against the wall, thinking about the interrogation he'd had five minutes earlier and about the gun he'd gotten caught with. Of course, he'd kept his mouth shut when they booked him for the weapon and tossed him in the bullpen with the other criminals.

The hardest thing for him wasn't the mandatory three and a half years he was facing, but it was the fight—his big fight he was going to miss at Madison Square Garden that would most likely break him into his career.

He had never been to jail before now. He had only heard about it from niggas in his hood when they would return home from little bids.

After being put in the bullpen, he saw seven young niggas staring at him as if he was a walking lick. He could tell it was about to be a long night. He closed his eyes and leaned back, and let his head rest against the wall.

Rugar

Rugar sat in the bullpen feeling pissed off he'd gotten caught up in that dumb ass raid. They ended up charging him with drinking in public, which was only a small fine. It wasn't his first time on the Island. He had been there a year prior for a school stabbing. He had stabbed another student eighteen times due to a rival gang beef.

With no bail, he knew he was stuck for a couple of days, or at the most, a few weeks; nonetheless, he was still salty about the whole situation. Quietly, he sat in a corner watching the young blood niggas plot on a light skin nigga with dreads. Dude looked like he was Crippin'.

Paying close attention to his surroundings, he noticed the Spanish nigga when he got off the phone. He made his way over to it before someone else could get to it and placed a call to Montonta. He needed to see what was going on with his lawyer and if he could get a bail hearing sometime during the coming week.

***

After minutes of scheming, the bloods made their move. The biggest four made their way to the Crip nigga, while the three shortest bloods played the background.

"Yo', son, you Crip?" the biggest of the bunch asked. The tank top he was wearing showed his muscular frame at six feet, four inches tall.

"Yeah, I'm Crippin'. What's crackin'?" Lil C asked calmly, showing no fear at all.

"We want them shoes, clothes, and that ice. Nigga, come up off that shit, son," he said.

Lil C stood up slowly as if he were about to take off his shoes, but instead, he uppercut the muscle head dude and knocked him clean out. The other three moved in. One tried to hit him with a power punch but he weaved and hit him with a hard two-piece jab, knocking him out too.

"Come on hardback," the next man yelled. He got in fighting position only to get knocked out. The last man ran off to the niggas who were now scared shitless.

Now Lil C was ready to put in work. When he ran up on the four bloods, they backed up against the wall nervously.

"That's enough, homie," a voice yelled out from across the room. Everybody paused.

"Nigga who the fuck is you? Man y'all get that Crip nigga," the big muscle head said. He had stood back up after being knocked out.

"I'm Rugar Brim and if any of y'all move a muscle I'ma have your head on a plate," he said firmly.

"Oh shit! My bad, big homie. We was just—" one of the bloods started to say before Rugar cut him off.

"I wanna know all of your names and where you from. Y'all in violation, homie and this ain't what bloods do, fool," he said.

"We from Brooklyn and we under Bam Bam," one of the men stated.

"Say less," Rugar said. He went to sit down and had to step over blood spills on the floor. Seconds later, Lil C approached him.

"Thank you, fam, but I had that under control," Lil C said. He was a little upset because he could hold his own.

"I know but it's not about that. We move millie and correct. We ain't no clowns," Rugar said, schooling him. Lil C took a seat and nodded his head. He could tell Rugar was somebody in the streets like himself.

"Where you from and what's your handle?" Rugar asked.

"I'm Lil C from Polo, cuz," he stated.

"Oh, so you that boxing nigga I been hearing about?" Rugar questioned him.

"Yeah. That's me, son. Where you from?"

"I'ma Fosta baby, you heard," Rugar said proudly. From that point on, the two talked for hours until they sent to the Beacon building where things were really turned up.

***

The Beacon section of the jail was for the most violent prisoners, or, like the two men, the high profile niggas. The unit was divided by gang affiliation. They had Crip houses, Blood houses, Folk houses, Latin King houses, and MS-13 houses.

When they hit the unit with their bed rolls, it looked like a little Afghanistan. Niggas were yelling, banging, and shouting gang shit.

Listen, we in a blood house and you have to be brave to come in here. You got heart and I respect that. So I'm not about to let no nigga jump you or buck 50 you. But you gonna have to shoot a lot of fair ones," Rugar said, as they walked through the gates.

"Perfect," Lil C said, smiling. They walked down the tier and it looked like death row.

"Where the bloods at? I'm Rugar Brim in the building," he shouted. The whole tier went crazy, happy the big homie was in the building.

The C.O. placed Lil C next door to Rugar which was cool. That night, Rugar had a gang of shit—hygiene items, food, weed, a phone, knives, and magazines. He shared with Lil C so he was straight too.

The bloods asked who Lil C was and when he said he was Crippin', the whole tier got quite. When Rugar said he was good, some were okay with it but some were still salty. Rugar told the niggas if they felt some type of way because a Crip was in the building, they needed to get the one-on-one with Lil C.

As soon as lookout came there was a line of niggas ready to put hands and feet on Lil C, but they had no clue what they had signed up for.

Lil C beat the shit out of eight niggas in the dayroom in less than forty minutes. He sent two of them to the hospital with broken jaws. It was the first day he became respected and feared and he was the only Crip in a blood unit.

Rugar laughed and enjoyed the movie because Lil C was nothing to fuck with. When he told the dorm who Lil C was, they stayed out of his way because they had heard he was a real killer in the streets.

Romell Tukes

CHAPTER 16

Rugar and Lil C had built a bond within days of meeting each other. The two became like batman and robin. Most of the inmates became cool with Lil C because they feared getting knocked out and embarrassed.

Lil C was in the dayroom on the phone talking to Mona. He was trying to tell her to move on and live her life because he had a bid to do, but she refused to walk away.

After the phone clicked off he went and sat next to Rugar in front of the TV where he was surrounded by fifteen goons.

"What's the word, loc? You look stressed, fam. I guess push-ups and jerking off ain't doing it for you," Rugar said laughing.

"Nah, my mom and girl fake stressed out there. I left them a good amount of money and I know my son, Loco, gonna do the right thing. For the time being, I can live off the land in here but I just need a steady connect," Lil C said, thinking about Loco running out of work.

"I feel you, son. But look, I fucks with you and I know you about your chicken so I'ma holla at your man. I get the best work and prices in the city, so I got you," Rugar said in a low pitched voice. "Right after my bail hearing. I got all your info and I'm not gonna forget about you."

"Say no more," Lil C said, hoping he wasn't faking. He had no clue Rugar was the plug and big homie. *Man, you too young even though you move like a boss,* Lil C thought to himself.

Two Weeks Later

Rugar had been waiting a couple of weeks to see the bail judge since they kept pushing his bail hearing back. He sat in the back bullpen for hours. He was hoping Naya had sent a bail bondsman so he could get out if he were given a bond or bail.

The courtroom was huge and bright when Rugar's name was called. The court police cuffed him and brought him in front of

Judge Thomas. The courtroom was packed with families of the inmates and people fighting serious cases who were out on bail.

"I'm Mr. Smith, your bail bondsmen. I'm here to post your bail and give you the do's and don'ts. I already spoke to the judge and we should be okay," the black bailsmen told Rugar just before the judge got started.

The judge talked for ten minutes before giving him a seventy thousand dollar bail which had already been posted, so he was free to go.

Once outside, Rugar felt like a new man, fresh out the joint.

"Naya is like family. I'm SMM but we all fuck with the Queen so take my number, blood, and hit me if you need me," Mr. Smith said walking off.

Rugar knew Naya was connected but to have gang connections in corporations was big. But what he didn't know was Naya owned the bail bondmen company and she was the face and money behind the business.

Beep! Beep!

Rugar saw a white Cadillac Coupe with tints parked in the front of the courthouse. He'd gotten word that Montonta was supposed to pick him up. He walked down the stairs trying to see who was behind the tints. The window slowly rolled down.

"Damn, a bitch couldn't get a jail call or a letter," PYT said shaking her head. She looked beautiful with her hair in a Chinese bun and she rocked a little makeup.

Rugar was shocked to see her. She had been on his mind every night when he would be in his cell staring at the ceiling.

"I ain't want to worry you and I knew you was out there handling business," he said. He got inside and kissed her soft lips. He smiled when he saw her rocking a pair of butter Timb boots.

"Nigga please, we in this together. What type of bitch I look like? I been pressing my sister about ever since you got booked. You got me looking crazy," she said pulling off.

The shorts she was wearing showed off her nice thick thighs and he felt himself getting aroused.

"Maybe. But thank you for caring," he said. "Where we going?" he asked, as she hopped on the express towards the Bronx.

"I'ma take you out then I gotta get back to school," she said. She looked at him and blushed.

"I need to pick up a new fit. I can't walk around like this," he said.

"Chill, I got you, boo. Naya gave me all your sizes. She told me I'm like your first real wifey so I feel honored," she said laughing. She sped down the Bronx Expressway.

"I wonder what else Nay told you."

"Enough, homie. Believe me," she replied.

"I heard the Kings beefing with the homies in Lincoln and Mahattanville," Rugar said.

PYT got off an exit and slowed down. Then she drove through the main streets.

"Yeah, and dude's name is King Ed. He's the one who took over Chulu's position. They beefing with Sause and them APT boys, but they ain't got shit to do with us," she stated.

"A'ight, say less, blood," he replied.

They pulled up to a nice high-rise apartment complex with security guards in the lobby. PYT parked and walked in the classy building with Rugar at her side. She greeted the three large black guards who ice-grilled Rugar. They stared at her perfect round ass as it jiggled with every move, jealous she was above their pay grade.

"Damn, this shit is fly," Rugar said, as he walked into her condo on the 18th floor.

"Yeah, that's a fact. It's low key and you're the only person I brought here besides Naya," she said. She went inside and took her Timbs off, showing off her pretty little feet.

The condo was a large two bedroom, two baths, and living room. There was also a dining room area with a large bar. Chanel carpet and wallpaper was throughout. There were flat screen TVs everywhere, with mirrors on the ceilings. A nice view of the city set it off.

"That's good you know how to move," he told her.

"But I do get lonely," she said. She grabbed his dick and kissed his lips, turning him on. I had to make sure you're the one for me, daddy. But everything is on my bed for you in the room to your far left. I gotta get my test and homework printed out," she said. She walked to her computer and printer which were in the living room where she did all her studying.

Rugar walked in her room amazed at how neat it was and how good it smelled. It was a white room with a fireplace and mink floor.

"Damn," he said, noticing the Louis Vuitton outfit with boxers, socks, and shoes to match. It was all red and white. He also saw hygiene products to use in the bathroom.

He wasted no time undressing and getting in the shower to wash away the jail smell. Luckily, he'd gotten a haircut the day before so his waves were spinning.

Thirty minutes later, the two made their way to City Island to grab some seafood, their favorite food. They enjoyed their lunch together. When it was almost time for school, she dropped him off at Fosta and went to school. She would be happy the rest of the day since her boo was out. Now they were officially stamped.

***

Lil C was a little nervous as he and six other men waited for the judge. He didn't have a paid lawyer so the court would have to give him one.

"Excuse me, gentlemen. Is Mr. Johnson here?" the lawyer asked. He walked into the small room dressed in a fifty thousand dollar suit.

"Yes, that's me," Lil C said, raising his hands in cuffs.

"I've been paid in full. I see you have a gun charge but I'm going to try and get you the best deal possible since you have no record," the man said smiling. Mr. Martinez was Spanish handsome, clean cut, professional, and smart.

"Who paid for you because I ain't got no money," Lil C asked.

"Listen, you're in good hands. That's your last worry. Jumbo is a good man," Mr. Martinez said and noticed the surprise look on his face.

Lil C was ready to cop-out and get it over with. He knew he was facing a couple of years.

"I canceled your court date until I have time to read over your case a little more. Since I just got it, I'll need you to be patient. I'll come see you soon, but in the meantime, take my card and call me," he said. He handed him a business card then turned and walked out.

"Yo', son, that nigga top dollar. He get the big cases so you lucky. Your people must got some paper if he took a gun case," one inmate stated.

Lil C was silent. He wondered why Jumbo would use all his money to help him. He thought heavy on it until he went back to the Island.

CHAPTER 17

Mona sat in the visitation room of Rikers jail for over an hour waiting on Lil C to come out. Before coming inside the jail visiting area, she was searched, patted down, and screened for drugs and weapons.

The visitation room was packed with round tables and visiting booths. It looked like a real prison visitation room, like the ones she saw in movies. Guards were posted in each corner of the room watching the inmates' every move. A couple of young male guards winked and smiled at her hoping for a reaction.

The guards had no respect for a person's family or their spouses. They would try their best to bag a nigga's girlfriend, and sometimes their mother.

Mona felt like her life had been on pause since Lil C had been in jail. Her job and friends helped her pass time but it wasn't the same without her lover around. To make matters worse, she had found out she was pregnant two weeks ago and the baby was Lil C's because she was still loyal to him.

Lil C finally walked out from the back dressed in street clothes. He was wearing a True Religion outfit and Prada shoes. He'd gotten a little bigger since he'd been going hard on his push-ups, pull-ups, and dips.

"Damn, babe, you getting too big. I miss you," Mona said. She hugged him tightly. The other inmates' girl peeked a stare at him as their panties got wet.

"Look at you, summertime fine," he replied. He was referring to her white and tight Fendi dress that hugged her breasts and fat ass. The other niggas stare lustfully.

"Whatever. Gotta look good for you, but how's court going? You never wanna talk about it on the phone or in your letters."

"My lawyer came to see me the other day. He said the best he can get me is a 2–4 years split-bid, boo," he said and explained what a split bid was.

"That's a long time but I'm here for you," she said. She began to cry.

"Don't cry, babe. This shit light weight. Have you spoke to my mom?" he asked, wiping her tears.

"Every day. She's okay, just praying for you really hard. She said you just like your pops. But she really misses you. I had to force her to take that twenty thousand Loco sent me," she said, shaking her head.

"Did you get my BMW and did Loco give you the money?"

"Yes. I told you that. But don't you think we should get a paid lawyer?" she asked. She was tired of him asking about his BMW especially since she was driving it now.

"No, I got a paid lawyer," he informed her.

"But how? They cost a lot of money, don't they?"

"It was a blessing. I'm upset I missed my big fight though. Shit, that was my meal ticket," he said.

"You'll have another chance when you come home. But I have something important to tell you," she said seriously. He became nervous.

"Damn, it's too early in the game for that. I honestly don't wanna hear about your affairs and I don't wanna hear no bad news right now either. I got a lot going on," he told her.

"It's not that, babe. I would never do that to you," she said tearing up again. Lil C had never really seen her cry except when her father was gunned down on duty by a New York gang leader. His murder made headline news for a week.

"I found out I was pregnant two weeks ago. I missed my period and knew something was wrong since I'm always regular," she said. She looked at him and waited for a response.

"Yesss!" He shouted so loud he scared her and the other visitors and inmates. There was no doubt in his mind the baby was his. The timing was on point and he knew she wasn't a hoe. Honestly, she was a good girl.

"Wow, I'm so glad you happy," she said. Her smile grew wide showing her relief.

"I'm sorry I can't be there. That's the shit that hurts the worst, babe." He shook his head from side to side realizing, regardless of his happiness, he was still in jail.

"It's okay, babe. You're always in my heart no matter where you are. But your mom was really turned up when I told her about the pregnancy. She wanted me to move in with her," Mona said laughing.

The two talked for two more hours about court and prison, money and baby names, and boxing and marriage. Then the C.O. approach the table informing them the visit was over. They stood up from the table, sad it was over.

"I love you and take care of my baby," Lil C said. He leaned in and hugged her and squeezed her tightly. Then she watched him walk off and be escorted from the visiting room. She watched him until he was no longer in sight.

***

Once he'd made it back to his dorm he went straight to his cell. He was deep in thought and he needed time to reflect on the beautiful news he'd just received about his unborn seed. Since Rugar had bonded out, a lot of inmates were acting funny towards him, mainly the bloods. A Crip from Brooklyn had been sent to the dorm but he was mainly blood so he was amongst the enemies.

Lil C wasted no time making a big 12-inch homemade knife from his bonk. He could fight but he still wasn't Bruce Lee. Since Rugar was no longer there he would stay to himself. When he wasn't outside he would exercise and watch the news every morning. There was this one female C.O. from Queens who had been trying her best to give him the pussy. He could tell she was the thot in the whole jail. She was ugly with a nice body but she was fucking every C.O. and inmate there. He was good for now though, and he was far from thirsty.

Bronx, NY

The last couple of days had been intense between PYT and Rugar. They had been spending a lot of time together on dates, lunches, movies, clubs, and going to the amusement parks.

Now, they were at PYT's crib on the living room couch. They were cuddled up watching the movie Love & Basketball. Tonight though, she had other plans for Rugar and she was ready.

"Come on. I got a surprise for you," she said. She paused the movie and stood up. When she did, her perky breasts stood out firm showing off her hardened nipples and flat stomach. Not to mention the camel toe bulging through the pink boy-shorts.

Rugar followed her to her bedroom. His eyes stayed focused on her ass as he watched it bounce up and down. He had never realized how fat it was outside of wearing jeans or dresses—it was a perfect fit for her frame.

Take off your clothes," she demanded, as he sat on her California king sized bed on top of the silk sheets.

He did as he was told and watched her again when she walked to her walk-in closet. She reached in and pulled out a one-piece lingerie made by Chanel.

"You like it, boo?" she asked. She stepped out of the closet and twirled around. Then, she took her hair out of the bun and allowed it to drop and hang freely to the mid-section of her back.

"Damn," he said. His dick raised to its full length. Her body was perfect and not a stretch mark or bullet hole was in sight. Her pussy was shaved with perfect lips and her clit was small and fat like a swollen eye.

"All for me?" she said. She grabbed his dick and started stroking it. Sizing his manhood up, her pussy became soaked. She placed her warm lips around the tip of his dick and sucked it slowly.

"Uhmmm, shit baby," he moaned. She took him in and out of her mouth, coating his dick with her spit and his precum juices. She started bopping her head fast, going down deep on his dick. Deep throating it caused tears to form in her eyes. She shook her head like a Pitbull locking his jaws on his victims.

"Fuck ba-by," he cried out. She continued sucking the precum while slurping on his dick as cum dripped from the corners of her mouth and down her chin.

"I'm cumming, baby," he yelled. She deep throated him while sucking faster and doing tongue tricks. Finally, he busted in her mouth but she went to spit it out in the toilet.

She was smiled like a sneaky kid and bent over on all four.

"Fuck me, baby. I want that dick," she moaned. He slowly entered her from behind. At first, he had a rough time entering her because she was so tight. Her pussy was warm, wet, and tight. Once Rugar got into a rhythm, her walls opened and he spread her ass cheeks going even deeper.

"Ohhhh yess, ughh shit!" PYT went crazy, driving her head into her pillow while her body jerked. She tried to run from the dick but Rugar wasn't having that. He grabbed her waist and held it down, and began to punish her with long, deep strokes.

"I'm about cum," she yelled as. Cream started to flow out of her pretty pussy like water. Seconds later, Rugar came also.

'Yo', what the fuck! I never felt this before," she said. Even after she'd released, her body shook in ecstasy. She climbed on top of him and let him slide his semi-hard dick into her wetness while she rode it. Her breast bounced up and down.

'Ride that dick," he said, holding her petite waist. She bounced up and down like a G4 until she felt him cum in her. She was on birth control because she wanted to feel him raw.

Rugar laid her on her back and threw her legs over his shoulders. He made love to her as she dug his back out with her nails, scratching him deeply.

They fucked for two more hours before they both fell asleep. This was the start to a new level in their relationship and they both were ready.

CHAPTER 18
HARLEM

The playground behind Fosta projects was packed as females walked around in booty shorts, and flip flops from Family Dollar. Although cheap, they rocked them as if they were rocking Gucci. Kids were playing on the slides, monkey bars, and swings, enjoying the New York summertime heat.

Rugar posted up on his Benz watching the scene with a smile. He was waiting on Montonta to arrive so he could speak to him before going meet with Naya and PYT.

Five minutes later, he was about to check for the time and he heard a lot motorcycles roaring through the parking lot.

Montonta killed the ignition and hopped off. He had on a big rope chain and a diamond incrusted Bust Down Rolex.

"My bad, son. I was fucking the baddest bitch I ever seen," Montonta said, while shaking his head.

"Yeah, I hear dat, blood. But shit getting serious between me and Jazmine. She wifey now, bro. I just wanted to let you no she apart of me so treat her like a sister," Rugar said. He knew Montonta disliked her for some reason.

"Bro you moving too fast. She not a regular hood chick, bro. She gives me the creeps, and you didn't even do your research, blood. She's dangerous on some next level shit," Montonta yelled.

"Nigga you don't even no her. She's official. I already know she got a body count but who don't," Rugar replied, just as the police rode through the parking lot.

"Fuck all that. What's so important?" he asked.

"Call Ashely and tell her to set up an offshore access account in the Bahamas out of the U.S. Then open a loan account and try to get it done this week so we can transfer more money without the FEDS tailing us, bro," Rugar said. PYT had given him the idea last night.

"Okay, cool. Sounds smart," Montonta replied.

"Then I'ma have Ashely meet with PYT so they can set up new accounts for the Empire. Then our money can expand as well on CD disc accounts in Cabo Verde. I need you to go to Polo Grounds today or whenever you got time. Look for a nigga named Loco Crip, nigga. Tell him we Lil C people and I want to speak to him. So give him my math, son," Rugar said.

"Yo', them niggas is wild over there and you know they don't fuck with us. I heard of that name Lil C before too," Montonta stated.

"Son official, trust me. I just left him on the rock," Rugar said, and hoped in his Benz. Montonta hopped on his Kawasaki Ninja bike.

"A'ight, son. Your call," Montonta said. He popped his clutch and hit the gears and sped out of the lot popping wheelies. Brazy was one of the best in Harlem before he was killed. He was known as the stuntman.

Newark, NJ

The twins stood in the garage area waiting on Naya. They laughed and joked paying no attention to the squeals and cries coming from across the room. They were Naya's main muscle, but they had a large army under them, and the two were ruthless killers.

The brothers had found Ant earlier that morning. He had been trying to creep out of his baby mother's house in East Orange. They pistol whipped him and tossed him in the back of the van.

Now he was tied to a chair by his feet and hands. He was shirtless with a pair of Power Ranger underwear on—the twins thought that was funny.

Ant used to be one of Naya's best workers until he ran off with four bricks that belonged to her. Luckily, he'd been under the radar for six months. A couple of weeks ago, he'd gotten drunk in a strip club in Patterson, NJ. He fucked a stripper and pillow talked about robbing a bitch named Naya from Newark.

The stripper bitch listened and told her older brother who sold guns for Naya. She used to always hear her brother talking about a Queen Pen boss-bitch named Naya. Her brother informed Naya of the news and she had the stripper bitch fuck him again. Her goons got the drop on him and for days, they followed him from Patterson, Newark, to East Orange.

"Never bite the hand that feeds you, word is bond," one of the twins said, while blowing smoke in his face. Ant tried to talk but the socks in his mouth prevented him from talking. His eyes grew wide as if he were seeing ghosts.

Everybody heard heels clicking up the stairs as if someone was walking toward the garage.

When he saw Naya walk in two seconds later, he tried to jump out of the chair. Looking beautiful in a black Christian Dior dress with a slit, it showed off her legs which were perfectly toned.

She took off her Gucci shades and laid her Birkin bag on the table near a scared-shitless Ant.

"Good to see you, Ant. How much of my money you tricked off?" she asked. "Take that shit out of his mouth," she told the twins. "And why the fuck y'all got this nigga in Power Rangers underwear!" Naya shouted seriously. The twins laughed, taking the dirty socks out of his mouth.

"Naya, I swear by Allah, on my kids, on my big toe, I was gonna get your money I-I ju-just—" Ant tried to protest but Naya stopped him.

"Put the sock back in his mouth." She grabbed a pistol from her Birkin bag.

Boom! Boom! Boom! Boom! Boom! She riddled his frail body with bullets and blood leaked all over the floor. His lifeless body was picture perfect.

"Clean this shit up," she ordered. "I'ma go check Rugar. Y'all two stay outta trouble but drop off my shit from the last reup," she said to her most trusted men. She looked at her designer red bottoms stained with Ant's blood.

***

The twins chopped up Ant's body, and within minutes disposed of it in large black garbage bags. This was part of their everyday lifestyle and they got a kick out of it.

Mark and Marcus were ages twenty-nine. Both were brown skinned and tall. The ladies considered them handsome, and their bodies were medium builds. They were what you'd call lady's men. They were both blood under their uncle who used to work for Naya. But two years prior the state had caught him for a murder charge. Since then, they worked as Naya's personal security. They had a large crew in Newark, New York, Brooklyn, Philly, and all over. Together, they had a team of killers.

Hour Later Westchester

Rugar, Naya, and PYT sat in a cheesecake restaurant having a good time.

"I got word them ABC boys are on to me. I don't know how there is a missing link in my Jersey foundation," Naya said.

"I'ma have my people look into it tomorrow. No worries," Rugar said, taking a bite of his delicious Jr. Cheesecake.

"I think you should stay out of Jersey for a while and let the twins handle your affairs," PYT stated.

"I'ma shoot out to Cali for a couple of weeks after our meeting," she replied, taking of a sip of her water.

"That's cool," Rugar said.

"What's poppin' with your jailbird?" Naya asked laughing.

"That shit was wild, but I met a Crip nigga from Polo Grounds. He needed a connect so I think I'ma scream at his people. I like Lil C and I believe he can be a valuable player," Rugar said.

"Oh shit, blood. That's the dude who killed Baby Blu and King Chulu," Naya said in a low pitch voice.

"I heard about him too. You sure he can be trusted," PYT asked. She looked at Rugar as he seemingly zoned out.

Rugar had never found out who killed King Chulu but it did hurt his sister a lot and business was business.

"Damn, I ain't know son was a savage like that," he said. "But I solute him for killing Baby Blu. I was waiting for the right time myself. I guess he had more food than he could chew."

"Yeah, they took over his blocks and all." Naya agreed.

"It's funny how I'm just now hearing about this. Next time let me know what's going on, you heard? I'ma big boy," he said, sounding really upset.

"Okay, sorry. But on another note, the Crips are good for business. I know a couple of Grape Street Crips that get to that bag," Naya said.

"I don't know. It's a dog-eat-dog world, especially on gang time in New York. There is no loyalty in gangland," PYT said.

"There is no such thing as a trustworthy business, but I'm about money not colors," Rugar said to her. Just then, a Spanish waitress approached there table and stared at them— mainly at Rugar. There was no denying she was on him.

"Can I help y'all with anything?" the waitress asked in her Spanish accent. She was beautiful and she looked like a young Jenny from the block, but with a fake ass and fake breasts.

"No we good, ma. You can spin the block," PYT said. She gave the waitress a look that let her know Rugar was off limits, even for conversation.

"Y'all must be serious. This is going to be crazy," Naya said seriously. She was surprised the two had gotten so close so fast.

The three talked for another hour about business plans and about Ashely's meeting with PYT. All in all, the day went well.

CHAPTER 19

The meeting with Jumbo had gone well. Now, he was pushing over one hundred fifty keys of coke and dope within a week. Jumbo had given Rugar a gift earlier in the day and the gift had been a key. When Rugar asked what the key was for, Jumbo told him it was a token of his appreciation. The key belonged to a new yacht which now belonged to Rugar. Jumbo owned a yacht club that networked at a couple of billion.

Jumbo told him he would have an answer for him in a couple of days concerning Naya's situation with the FEDS being on her line.

Now Rugar was in New Rochelle, NY, with a real estate agent and a broker. He was looking at a mini mansion he'd seen online.

***

Ashley sat in the back office of the computer store Rugar had recently opened. He had decided to let her run it since she had a clean record.

Business was slow. She only had two workers, but she was fine with that because she could sit on her ass all day. Life was good. She had a job, her kid was good, she was off Section 8 because Rugar paid her well, and she was now attending college courses.

"Hello," a customer called out, as she entered the store causing the bell ring.

"How may I help you, Miss?" Ashely asked. She walked out front in her khaki's and blue work shirt. She looked at the pretty woman and envy coursed through her.

"I'm Jasmine. I came to show you how to set up the off-shore and loan accounts for this business. I'm sure Rugar informed you I was coming," PYT said, looking at the confused look on Ashely's face.

"You can come to the back," Ashley said coldly. She thought Rugar was going to send Montonta not some boujee diva in a skirt and heels.

PYT walked into the small office, sat at the computer, and began typing fast. She put in a floppy disc to unload the account material in her files.

"You're one of his side chicks or something?" Ashley asked with a chuckle. She knew Jasmine was exotic and his type.

"Listen, I don't have time for small talk or high school gossip. These numbers will give you access to the loan accounts and the pin-numbers," PYT said, pointing at the computer screen.

"How do I know it's correct?" Ashley asked. PYT pulled out a stack of papers from her large YSL purse.

"Listen, here is everything. I know what I'm doing. You just do as you're told," PYT stated.

He should've sent over a professional instead of a wanna-be model. So you can take all this shit with you," Ashely said and threw the stacks of papers at PYT.

PYT couldn't take anymore. That was exactly why she hated bitches. They were the worst haters.

"Okay, I'm out. I'm sure a dumb hoodrat can figure it out," she said, fixing her skirt as she stood up.

"I sure will. Just like one day I'ma be sucking Rugar's dick and swallowing all his nut," Ashley said and laughed. PYT was on her way out but stopped suddenly. *This bitch just lost her mind*, she thought.

"Pop-off bitch! What the fuck you stopping for?" Ashely yelled, taking out her big hoop earrings.

PYT just smiled at her. Then, in one swift move, she pulled out a .357. When Ashely saw the barrel of the gun pointed at her face, she froze.

"I'm sorry. I don't want him. I don't even like him," Ashley said, scared for her life. PYT laughed out loud wondering what happen to all the gangsta shit she had pooped seconds earlier.

"Too late, honey," PYT said. Without a second thought she placed four hollow tips in Ashley's skull and let her body fall on the computer.

"Call the cleanup boys to 117th Lenox," she told Red Hot over the phone before she walked out. Once outside, she placed the *closed sign* over the glass door.

PYT knew she would have to handle all Rugar's business affairs from now on but she was cool with that. She just hoped he was. She hopped in her white Audi A8 and headed to the college to take the exams she'd been studying for.

***

Loco and his crew were parked in front of Fosta projects in a sky-blue Range Rover with rims, waiting on Rugar. Loco had taken over uptown Harlem and all of Baby Blu's blocks as well as King Chulu's blocks on Douglas 105 and Columbia Ave.

Money had been flowing like water since Lil C had got locked up. The only issue was his supplier, Uncle Lo, was over charging him and his work was trash.

Montonta pulled up to Polo Grounds a couple of days before. The Crips were ready to shoot when they saw the red and black ZX -7R motorcycle with the red flags hanging on the handlebars.

Thankfully, Loco happened to see Lil C the same day. He let him know that Montonta was coming to holla at him. The Crips knew about the Fosta blocks getting money.

Rugar pulled up in his Benz and parked right behind the Range. He knew it was Loco because they stuck out like a sore thumb in the sky-blue Range in a blood hood.

"What's good, son? Nice to meet you. I'm Rugar," he said, as he approached the Range. Loco hopped out of the passenger seat.

"Likewise, bro. Lil C told me good things about you and y'all niggas' name is ringing crazy in the city. That's my cuz Big Porky, Lil Jay, Turk, and Rell in the truck security." Loco stated laughing

The two talked off and started networking prices, locations, and drop-offs. Tonight, Rugar planned to drop off their first six keys of coke and six keys of dope in a Wendy's parking lot. After their meeting, the two went their separate ways, feeling like they were about to be on top real soon.

Later that night in Spanish Harlem

The pickup went smooth and the crew busted the keys down and fed the hood. They shut shit down and Polo Grounds was going crazy for the new product.

"I'ma hit up the club later with some locs from the Bronx," Big Porky said. He was posted up on the corner selling grams of coke and dope with his goons, They were in the colony area behind the Polo Grounds building.

"Fuck that, cuz. This shit jumping. I made seven bands in four hours," Lil Jay said, pulling out a wad of blue faces.

"I'm out. Fuck this. Yo' Rell, Bo, C-Roc," Big Pork yelled out to his little homies. He was going to tell them to head to the club in Yonkers. Ten soldiers posted up with Lil Jay slanging drugs until it was time to switch shifts with Turf and his crew. They ran a tight ship with a 24-hours drug ring. They had fiends from all over uptown coming to get high.

Yonkers, NY

Club Hell was litty. There were naked strippers sliding up and down on the poles, while ballers tossed money enjoying the scene.

Big Porky was in the VIP section drunk and ready to leave. His side bitch lived down the block on Elmo Ave.

"We out, Crip. I need you to drop me off at this bitch crib, cuz. Come scoop me in the morning, bro," Big Porky said in a slurred voice as he got up. He left the club with his goons behind him.

The other side of the club in a VIP section was full of exotic dancers. They were twerking and pussy popping for the gangbangers dressed in gold and black.

He was ducked off in the dark side of the strip club watching Big Porky's every move. A couple of days ago, Eddie had found out the Crips from Polo Grounds had killed his brother. He had paid 50K for the info. He'd been given four names, and all of them had something to do with his brother's death—Lil C, Loco, Big Porky, and Turk.

He watched Big Porky toss over 30K in less than two hours. He asked one of the bartenders what was the big man's name. When she said the name *Big Porky,* he kept his eyes on him.

Yonkers was his third home. The Latin Kings ran the small city outside of the Bronx. Luckily, he knew the club owner so he wasn't going to shut it down. He made his way outside with his eight goons.

"Yo', fam, let me holla at you," King Ed said, while running towards the Crips in the parking lot lacking. Before the Crips could even reply, bullets went flying everywhere, Big Porky tried to reach for his burner but it was too late. Several bullets ripped through his stomach and breasts. The Kings killed all the Crips dumping over ten bullets a piece. Afterwards, they ran off and left four lifeless black bodies in the club parking lot.

CHAPTER 20

Two months after going back and forth to court in bullpen therapy, Lil C took a plea deal for two years in upstate prison, and three years parole. He just wanted to go upstate and go home to his girl and seed. But he knew it wasn't going to be an easy trip. He'd heard stories about how the Crips couldn't live up north in prison because it was blood populated.

Most of the Crips had left prison with fresh buck-50s across their faces. Others had hidden in the box on PC but he refused to go out like that. He was going to claim his set even though he knew he was outnumbered zero to a hundred. So, he decided to play it smart.

Jumbo paid for his lawyer and sent him money on the daily. He never knew Jumbo was such an honorable person. Unlike most of his friends who couldn't even write a letter. Loco was holding him down money-wise every week. He'd sent pics, mags, books, and he was looking out for Mona too. Lil C valued his friendship.

"Yo', where yo from, skrap?" a big husky nigga asked. He was chained next to him on the bus headed upstate.

"Harlem Uptown," Lil C responded.

"A'ight, that what's poppin'. You bangin' and what's your name, son?" the muscle head dude asked.

"I'm Lil C, and I bang broke. I'm Crip," he stated.

"Word, son? That's Brazy. You Rugar's people. You was in the three building and the Ole boy building. I heard all about you, fam. I'ma be honest wit' you. It's dangerous behind these walls for you Crips. But my name holds weight off the strength of them two niggas, Rugar and his brother. So I got you," the big dude said, ripping through his shirt.

"Where you from?" Lil C asked.

"Shit, I'm Jamaican, bro. So you know I'm from Flatbush and London," he replied.

"Oh yeah? My Uncle Lo from over there," Lil C said. At the mention of his uncle the muscle head nigga froze.

"Hold the fuck up, Chris," he shouted as if he knew him.

"Yeah, that's me."

"Your fucking uncle was talking about you last night, man. I had niggas looking all over for you in the building. Me and Lo sandbox niggas, bro. You family. I had no clue you was the Lil C nigga. They call me Big Goon," he said excitedly.

The two talked the whole bus ride to Downward prison. It was the transit center for inmates to get shipped to prisons all over the state.

Big Smokey controlled a lot of the drug trafficking in prison and he was a big name. He was sending females to every state prison to drop off drugs daily.

Goon was Big Smokey's capo, so he had pull in every prison with a fifty to life bid to do. He was well connected and respected. Goon gave him the rundown on what to do and what not to do. Of course, he paid full attention.

Once in Downward Jail, Lil C was shocked to see how big it was. It looked like the max prison he'd seen on TV. After being taken off the bus, the thirty inmates were searched, stripped, and placed in a holding cage. Most men stood up, some sat patiently used to the routine.

"Listen up, assholes. Welcome to Downward where we play no games! You fuck up, we fuck you up! You eye fuck us, we fuck you up! You do anything and we'll beat the shit out of you," a big steroid looking C.O. said. There were five other NFL linebacker looking C.O.s behind him ready to beat a nigga up.

"Enjoy your stay, niggers and don't drop the soap. We got a lot of ass bandits around these parts," the large, white, bald headed C.O. stated.

Lil C and Goon ended up in the same building until they separated and went to different jails.

***

Rugar and PYT were sailing on his new yacht near Long Island watching the sunrise fade its purple and orange. The yacht was one hundred thirty-seven feet long. It was fully equipped with lower and upper deck master bedrooms, a kitchen, bar, and two bathrooms with marble flooring and a glass shower in each.

PYT lay on the upper deck in her red Prada bikini catching a light breeze. "Baby, this is so nice. I can't believe you got a fucking yacht," she said laying on his bare chest.

"Something light, ma. But you got a nigga tired, boo," Rugar said, referring to the crazy sex they'd been having all day, all over the yacht.

"I know, nigga. You was moaning louder than me." She laughed playfully.

"Yeah, now you faking. You know what's up," he said. He grabbed her long hair and kissed her glossy soft lips.

"Baby, I know you very independent and self-made, but I think we need to spend more time together. I just bought a mini mansion in New Rochelle close to your college. And since you live in the Bronx—"

"What are you saying, baby? Spit it out," she said.

"I want you to move in with me. I bought it for us," he said. A huge smile spread across PYT's face. She tried hard to contain her excitement but couldn't.

"Okay, cool," she said.

"Good. And oh I forgot to ask you, when you saw Ashley did she say anything out of the ordinary, or act weird when you saw her? She's been MIA for a couple of days now and she knows a lot about my affairs. I can only hope she ain't missing for the wrong reason," he said, shaking his head.

PYT thought about the last time she seen her before she killed her for running her big ratchet-ass mouth. She thought, *only if you knew she is missing, but for the right reasons.*

"Maybe she's swimming with the fish," PYT said with a devious laugh. Rugar read between the lines.

"Jasmine, I asked you to do one job," he said.

"I did as you asked and she got on some crazy shit calling me all types of bitches so I killed her. But no worries. I covered all my tracks. But I had to 'cause she pushed my buttons," PYT said.

"What the fuck you mean she pushed your buttons, Jasmine? She was worker. I could've fired her. You ain't have to kill her. We're more professional than that, and we run a business not a target practice," he said.

"I know, and I'm sorry," she said, giving him the puppy dog eyes. If he was any other nigga, PYT would've killed him just for raising his voice, but Rugar was different. He was special.

He lowered his voice but he was strong on not mixing business with violence.

"I'll make it all up to you," she said. She pulled down his Gucci boxers and released his penis before sucking his dick slowly. She played with the head of it with her tongue ring then she deep throat every inch.

"Damn, baby," he said. Hearing him moan made her faster and faster until she tasted his precum. Then she stopped because she wanted to feel him inside her.

For hours, they fucked on the upper deck in every position they could think of. You could PYT's screams throughout the sea as her voice seemed to echo off the water.

Harlem

Loco was pissed when he'd heard about Big Porky and the Crips' murder. It was big since the murders made World Cast news. There was only one Crip who had survived, but he was in a coma. But word on the streets was the Latin Kings had done it and claimed it proudly.

"After I get the drop on these niggas it's litty, cuz. We ripping on all them niggas, Crip," Loco told Venny, who sat posted on the block on his Impala. Loco had a truck full of security guards and young shooters parked in front of the corner store.

He parked down the block from the store so he wouldn't be noticed. He walked down the dark street and passed by a beautiful Latina woman with her boyfriend. She passed him and smiled while giving him a quick wink.

Loco paid them no mind. He continued walking to his car. Then he saw a shadow creeping up on him from behind the van. He wasted no time pulling out his GLOCK with the 30-round clip attached to it. Bullets weaved past his head as he ducked, shooting at the van. Unaware where the bullets were coming from, he took cover behind a truck and saw the couple he'd just seen. He walked past both firing but missing.

"Come out to play, Crip-ass-nigga," the voice of the shadow yelled.

Boom! Boom! Boom! Boom!

Loco fired towards the van and shot out the window and light pole.

Out of nowhere, shots came from the middle of the street. The bullets took out the couple with four shots to each of their faces.

The last shooter took off running down Madison. By now he knew he was outnumbered, and the police were speeding down the block.

Everybody took off running in separate directions. The police only caught one of the Crips and he had a gun, but there was also two dead bodies on the scene.

Romell Tukes

CHAPTER 21
BROOKLYN, NY

Rugar drove his motorcycle through the Red Hook section of Brooklyn. He had just come from a small get-together and he'd been discussing business with Bam Bam.

Lately, things had been successful for the Empire, even Bloody was getting on board, because with Rugar's prices, it was hard *not* to get aboard. PYT had their mansion looking like a home now, and it was beautiful.

Within days from now, Rugar had plans to open a small restaurant. It was a small Caribbean restaurant near uptown and he couldn't wait for the grand opening.

He needed air in his rear tire so he pulled over into a BP gas station up the block. Once he parked at the air pump, he hopped off, digging in his pockets for change.

A Spanish nigga with long hair, wearing all black, walked past him heading to the restroom. Rugar gave the man a light head nod while he placed four quarters into the machine.

After filling his tire, he felt a hard pressure to his helmet.

"Stand the fuck up, nigga. Any funny moves, I'll blow your shit off," a man wearing all black with a yellow flag tied around his mouth said.

"A'ight, be easy, son. I got five grand in my pocket," Rugar said, raising his hands in the air.

"Turn around and shut up. I like that chain,' the gunman stated and snatched the chain off his neck.

Rugar played it cool. It was a good thing his helmet was bullet proof. "You can take it, B. Just let me make it home," Rugar cried. The robber admired the heavy rope chain and he was happy he'd came up off a good lick. He was so caught up in admiring the chain, he didn't even see Rugar when he pulled out a pistol from his back side.

BLOC! BLOC! BLOC!

The robber fell to the ground. Rugar snatched his chain back then pulled the yellow flag off the robber's face as he inhaled and exhaled, taking his breath.

"HK for life," the robber moaned before everything went black. When more cars started to pull up at the gas station, Rugar hopped on the bike and burnt rubber out of the gas station. He left the gunman lying dead in a darkened area—there were no cameras and since it had taken place on the side where the restrooms were located, Rugar was safe on any possible indictments.

He was pissed he'd let a Latin King almost get one up on him. But it could've been a hit, so the dead man had just started a new war in the city. The Kings had just signed their death certificate.

Meanwhile in Harlem

Montonta was posted in the heart of Wagner projects talking to his workers.

"Okay, blood. We got you this time. That's my word, B," Lil Dee said. He had been sitting on the benches waiting for Montonta to put his re-up in the bookbag.

"Come up short this time we got a issue. All that Blood shit gonna go out the window, five. Have mines or be mines," Montonta said. He passed him the bookbag he'd filled with ten keys. Then he turned and walked off to his car.

Selena was posted up on the outside of Montonta's Lexus Coupe talking on the phone to her mom in Spanish.

She hung up the phone when she saw Montonta coming out of the projects. She really liked his company and he was spending bands on her daily. She already had a closet full of designer shit since dealing with him. She had even gave up bartending at his request.

When Selena saw a familiar face walking her way she froze with fear. King Ed approached her smiling.

"Well look who we have here. It's been a while, but I see you get around fast," he stated. The look on her face let him know she was at a loss for words.

"What's popping, fam? You lost?" Montonta asked as he approached his car. The butt of his pistol was poking out in plain view.

"I'm far from lost. I'm just saying hi to an old friend, but I come to speak to you in peace. I'm King Ed."

"Let's walk," Montonta said and started walking down the block." I don't know or care who you are, bro. But you got balls coming to look for me solo," Montonta stated. Selena hopped in the car and put the child safety locks on.

"No disrespect, bro. I'm here to talk business. I'm tryna regain some of my brother Chulu's turfs around the city and you got a couple of his spots," King Ed said.

"I'm not giving up shit. nigga. Chulu gone, homie. By any means if you want my blocks you know how to get 'em," Montonta said pissed off.

"Okay. I thought you would say that my friend. I'll see you soon, and watch your company. Her looks can fool you," King Ed said. He smiled at Selena and she quickly looked away.

"The only reason you still alive is because I don't want your blood on my white Givenchy shoes," Montonta said.

"Sometimes you gotta get dirty," King Ed said, as twenty bloods came out the building towards them.

"You got five seconds to get off my block," he said. And four large vans, filled with Latin Kings ready to kill, came speeding down the block towards them.

"Oh yeah, and I'm never solo. Take care," King Ed said. He hopped in the first van that had drove up and left him standing there. Montonta was pissed as he hopped in his Lexus.

"You got one second to tell me what that was about," Montonta asked Selena who sat silently looking out of space. "OK. Speak," he said. He pulled out a pistol and placed it to her head. She started to cry like a baby but managed to tell him the whole Chulu story and how she knew Eddie.

Brooklyn

Uncle Lo had just come from his gambling spot on Utica St. near Flatbush to collect some money. It was a nice, warm summer night as he rode through the dirty streets in his navy blue and white Hellcat Camaro.

Once he'd made it to his pawn shop in Brownsville, he rushed inside feeling something was off.

"Mike, what's up, white boy? How we looking?" he asked, not really caring, just trying to make small talk.

"Busy with a lot of jewelry. I know a lot of good people got robbed this weekend," Mike said. He was watching First 48 on the TV behind the counter.

"Welcome to Brooklyn. I'ma check you before I come out," Uncle Lo said before turning to walk to the back. The place was full of boxes and junk and a bunch of used shit stuck to the ceilings. This was one of Lo's stash places. He'd opened up the pawn shop two years ago with the help of white boy Mike who was a known hacker.

Lo stashed the money that was in the garbage into the sofa. His phone started to ring non-stop. He saw Meka's name and thought against answering it. Meka was a boujee chick from his hood he'd fuck daily, but she was a sack chaser.

"Hello," he answered, wondering what the fuck she wanted.

"Lo, the FEDS just busted into your gambling spot and clothing store. They got everybody in cuffs," she yelled until she heard the dial tone.

"Yo', Mike, hide everything illegal! The FEDS ran up in my spot, son," Lo screamed. He locked the sofa full of money. He ran to the front and found Mike held at gunpoint by four Federal Marshalls dressed in combat clothes and vests. Six rushed him to the floor as if it was the NFL football pre-season, and cuffed him up without reading him his rights.

Manhattan

Twenty-five minutes later, Lo was in a secret federal building somewhere downtown. He was given his indictment paper and he was the ringleader, the head of his indictment. He was being charged with racketeering, the R.I.C.O, money laundering weapon charges, and conspiracy to murders.

"Mr. Lo, what's cracking Crip? Big homie, we got your black ass now. I can't wait to see my bonus. You and your crew are gonna be on the front page of the New York Times," Agent Jones said dapping with his partner.

"It took us eight years. You can't even imagine how much shit we got on you. Not to mention all the rats that are begging to take the stand like this." Agent Richardson raised his right hand and stood at attention laughing. Both of the federal agents were black and both were assholes.

"What the fuck you dickheads want? Just give me my call so I can go to MCD," Lo said, leaning back in his chair smirking.

"We want that Jamaican drug lord you re-up from. Shotta. Help us bring him in, you walk. You don't we'll get him anyway and you'll get eight life sentences, and you know the appeal rate is 0 to 10," Mr. Jones said, fixing his tie tighter around his neck.

"I go free? Damn that's sweet," Lo said. Seeing that he was thinking hard made them smile. "Can I get Newport?" Lo asked. One of the agents pulled out a box and lit one for him. Lo blew smoke in their faces. Then he grinned a wide grin causing both agents to excited.

"How about this? You two bumbaclot fuck niggas get on your knees and one of y'all suck my big blood clot dick, and the other one suck mi balls while mi suck your blood clot mother," Lo shouted in his Jamaican accent. Now he was laughing hard and the agents were pissed.

Agent Richardson jumped across the table and slapped the cigarette from his mouth. His partner had to get him off him before he got suspended again.

When they left, Lo was pissed he'd gotten jammed up. As he sat there thinking with a swollen lip, he hoped his girl had heard what happened and called his paid Jewish lawyer by now.

Lo refused to snitch on any nigga. That was against his code. He was a street nigga and Shotta was like a brother to him.

Shotta was one of the richest men out of Kingston, Jamaica. He'd been banned from the U.S. years ago when he ran a large drug ring all over Miami, NY, Texas, and Arizona. They could never charge him or find him, he was a ghost. He was close to Michelle and Lo and he considered them family. He was an elder but he had seen them grow up. He had watched over them since they barely knew their parents.

Lo closed his eyes and prepared to face the music of reality from living a real-nigga life...

CHAPTER 22
HARLEM

"Ayo, fam. John John told me y'all niggas went out to the BX and robbed them Parkside niggas at a high school party," Lil Hype shouted in front of his building in Fosta projects.

"Yeah, son. They tried to front on us. We trying to go back out there but we need a burner. Go get one from your brother. We'll bring it back," John John said, as Lil Hype looked at him like he was crazy.

"Hell no, blood. You know how Montonta is, "Lil Hype said, hopping off the bench, brushing the ash off his clothes from the weed smoke.

Lil Hype was Montonta's little brother and one of the best basketball players in Harlem. He'd already been offered eight D-1 college scholarships. At fourteen, he was six-four in height, handsome, smart, and gang affiliated by choice, though Montonta was against it.

"Let's go to Turf projects across the street to holla at Mookie. I know he got a strap, blood. Come on, we out," John John said, walking across the street. John John was a known troublemaker. Not only in Harlem but all over the city.

"Damn, what's up with this nigga?" John John said, as a black GMC truck pulled up on him, almost hitting him. It was 90° out at two in the afternoon. There was no way the driver behind the dark tint didn't see him.

"Where the Demo's at, homie?" a Spanish man said, while rolling his window down halfway.

"We all blood. What's poppin'?" John John asked. He walked a little closer to the truck.

"Good," King Ed said. He rolled the window all the way down and came up with the barrel of a AK-47 assault rifle so long it looked like a pole.

Boom! Boom! Boom! Boom!

John John caught two shots to the chest while Lil Hype froze. Getting cold feet, he took off like a track star. Seconds later, four bullets pierced the mid-section of his lower back. He fell on his knees right in front of Rugar's building where he always hung out.

"This is the takeover," King Ed shouted from his window. He threw up his Latin King set and sped off.

The police came ten minutes later. Two fourteen year old's had been left in critical condition in the projects. People everywhere were crying, especially for Lil Hype. He was the hood superstar.

***

Montonta was doing 90 mph down the highway, rushing to the hospital for his little brother hoping he was okay. When his sister texted him informing him his brother had been shot, he left Selena's crib on the lower Eastside and rushed to the hospital.

Montonta left the hospital and found two cops placing a gang of tickets on his car windshield.

"Officer Parks, there's no need for the tickets. We got him covered. We'll take care of this asshole," Detective Howard stated, smiling when he saw Montonta.

"I'm just doing my job," Office parks, the ticket man, replied.

"I said get the fuck out of here," Detective Howard shouted, running him off. Detective Howard was a grimy detective known throughout Harlem for robbing, killing, and stealing from the poor to get rich.

"How can I help you?" Montonta asked.

"Good question. Two dead fourteen year old boys, or should I call what it is, murders? Do you at least have any info for your brother?. The murders have been rising in Harlem ever since the new leader took over Brazy's empire. Who took it over, Montonta? I know you know, blood," The detective asked.

"I'm sorry officer. I don't speak English," Montonta said as he got in his car and pulled off. The only thing he was thinking about was revenge for his little brother.

***

The next couple of weeks were like World War III in Harlem. Rugar and his large crew were crushing Latin Kings on sight, and they were up by four bodies.

Niggas were getting killed on corners in broad day light, at funerals, in clubs, and subway stations. One nigga was even killed in front of a daycare center because he was wearing a yellow flag. The Kings were shooting back but they were losing a lot more than gaining, which made King Ed skip town. He had no clue Rugar could be so reckless and ruthless.

King Ed hid out in San Juan, Puerto Rico, with one of his baby's mothers and his family. He felt like he was trapped. He still had issues with the Crips but the main problem was the Bloods. They were coming too strong for him. At times like this he wished his brother was still alive.

There was only one thing he could do, and that was throw the ball in and call a truce. He was losing men and money.

Month Later

Rugar sat in the back of his Caribbean restaurant in deep though, smoking a Cuban cigar. He was contemplating life and where he wanted to go with his.

A week prior, the Kings called for a truce and Rugarhe agreed. However, he had other plans for King Ed but it was all about timing.

Naya was in Jamaica laying low. PYT was about to graduate from college with a Master's in Business and Accounting (MBA) any day now. Their love life was great, and everything was smooth besides the King Ed situation which was heavy on his mind.

***

Loco and Poo Bear were in Polo Grounds reminiscing on back in the day.

"Why them King niggas called me for a gang truce a couple of days ago, cuz?" Loco asked, smoking a blunt watching a basketball tournament.

"What you tell them, Loc?" Poo Bear questioned, wanting to know.

"Nigga, I told King Ed to suck my dick! He know what it is, Crip. They killed Big Porky so it's *never* over. We gonna get a line on, son. I think them Blood niggas ran him outta town but them niggas been turning the city up," Loco said. He looked up at the gray skies knowing rain was near.

"What's crackin' with the big homie?" Poo asked.

"He in Attica right now. He good. . . working out and reading on some Malcom X shit," Loco said laughing.

"The Damus letting him live?" Poo asked. He knew up north could get real for a Crip since he'd been there before.

"He said Rugar sent word and he was good. He whooped a couple of niggas out but he good," Loco said, looking at the eight Crips who had just walked into the packed park.

"Did you tell him about Lo and Porky?" Poo Bear asked. "I heard his BM throwing a big baby shower," he added.

"Facts. Mona's baby shower going to be litty. I ain't tell cuz about Lo or Porky. I need to do shit like that face-to-face. I'ma go see him soon. Money been flowing all the way in Westchester with Turk and his crew of goons." Loco said, feeling rain drops. Anyway, he was ready to go because he needed to pick Selena up.

CHAPTER 23
HARLEM

Loco drove through the dark Harlem streets looking for niggas as if he were their fathers.

He pushed his Range down St. Nicholas Ave and saw Lil Jay's baby's mother, Yvonne. He wanted to see if Lil Jay was there since he owed him and he hadn't heard from him in days.

Yvonne lived in the hood. Loco told him to get his family out the hood the first chance he got because that was a nigga's downfall.

He walked in Lil Jay's building and saw a crew of young niggas in the lobby with blue flags hanging from their left side, shooting dice.

"What's crackin', cuz? Who you? I hope you got a visa pass," the little Crip said, with snort in his noise that made Loco laugh.

"Yeah, lil homie. I got a pass, cuz. I'm Loco. What your Crippin' like, cuz? Know who you pulling up on before you pull up, cuz," Loco told all ten of the goons.

"Oh shit, my bad. We ain't know it was you, Loco. Yo' name heavy out here."

"Lil C like GOD to the hood," one of them stated.

"Y'all seen Lil Jay around?" Loco asked.

"Nah, we ain't seen the big homie in some days. Normally, he would pull up every other day. But his BM live in apartment 4D."

"A'ight, good looks, son," Loco said, taking the pissy stairs to the fourth floor.

After knocking four times, he was about to leave until he heard someone unlocking chains.

"Damn, papi, you knocking like you the police," Yvonne shouted. When she opened the door and saw Loco, she paused. He was handsome and dripped out in ice and designer clothes from head to toe. She walked back in the apartment and he followed. She sat down and crossed her legs.

Yvonne was an ex-stripper. Lil Jay had cuffed her and put a seed in her early in the game. She was one hundred percent Dominican with bronze skin and long blonde hair. Her breasts were big and she had pretty hazel eyes. She had thick lips, a flat stomach from getting liposuction and a fake big ass that was too big for her skinny legs.

"Is Lil Jay here? I need to holla at him," he asked, trying not to stare at the large camel toe that poked out through her tight leggings.

"No, I ain't seen him. But he might be on Grant fucking that dirty Puerto Rican bitch. But who are you?" she asked in a sexy voice. She uncrossed her legs so he could get a better shot at her fat pussy.

"I'm Loco," he said, noticing her hard pierced nipples.

"I heard a lot about you, big money. You can sit down and sit a while," she said licking her thick dick-sucking lips.

"I'm good. Just tell him I stopped by," he said, watching her play with her tongue ring. He could tell Lil' Jay wasn't there because the apartment was too quiet and Yvonne was practically begging him to take the pussy. So, he walked back to the door and left.

Yvonne slammed the door when he walked off. She was pissed she'd missed her shot. She wished he would've stayed longer. She would've dropped to her knees and engulfed his whole dick in her warm mouth.

She had heard so much about Loco—how he had millions. Unlike Lil Jay, an average block nigga. She was a sack chaser and needed a baller. She went in the bedroom, undressed, and played in her wet pussy while her son slept next door.

***

Loco drove towards 134th and Lincoln where Lil Jay sold most of his keys and where he was raised. When he pulled up to Lincoln he saw Big Duce talking on his phone

"Yo', Big Duce, what's poppin', bro? You seen Lil Jay around here?" Loco asked with his window partially down.

"I ain't seen him in a couple of days but I think he might be at that little stripper bitch's crib on Grant—the bad Puerto Rican," Big Duce yelled.

"A'ight," he said and pulled off. Loco knew Grant was a Latin King block. He had told Lil Jay several times to stay away from there until shit cooled down.

Once he was on Grant, he drove slow. Fortunately, nobody was out. He saw a familiar car parked at the end of the block. It was a navy blue Lexus SC 430 with tickets all over the front windshield.

Loco parked on the side of the car and looked in the clear windows and saw that everything was intact. He wondered if he was just upstairs laid up in some pussy. He pulled on the handle of the car door, and to his surprise, it was unlocked. He opened Lil Jay's glove compartment and his pistol fell out, which was odd because Lil Jay stayed strapped. Then, a strong odor hit his nose and made him want to vomit.

"What the fuck is that smell?" he said aloud. He walked around to check the trunk for drugs or money.

When he popped the trunk he jumped back when he saw Lil Jay's head cut off and detached from his body. A yellow flag had been tied around his forehead.

Loco slammed the trunk, wiped down his prints, and hopped in his Range filled with anger.

Queens

Everybody was present at the Empire meeting except Naya. She was still in Jamaica, low-key, until the FEDS eased up on her New Jersey affairs.

"I'm losing a lot of sleep and money warring with the Latin Kings, homie. They got numbers in the Bronx, so me and PYT losing a lot of good men. I don't even know what the fuck we beefing about but I'm tryna get money, not sell homemade

147

cheesecakes in the FEDS," Red said. Bloody nodded his head in agreement. Then again, he was with anything that went against Rugar.

"Y'all niggas scared of a little war? We got money, guns, soldiers, and strategy," PYT stated to everyone.

"More money, more problems, blood. Some things we can't run from," Big Smokey stated strongly.

"This is all part of the game, gentlemen. Hate, envy, murder, robberies, jail, success, prayers, and the trials. I can assure everyone in this room this war will be over with before the end of this week," Rugar said sternly. His capo, Montonta, was right by his side, smiling and holding an AR-15 rifle.

"Regardless, blood, I'm with you. We ran all them niggas out of BK, son. Believe that," Bam Bam stated sharply.

"Well, y'all niggas beef all you want down here. We focused on this bag upstate, son. We don't need all y'all niggas' heat. Brazy ain't never move like this, son. You should rethink your position," Bloody said with a smirk. PYT gave him an evil eye.

"Nigga, when we had to send a crew to Rochester to save you and your soft ass crew from them MS-13's you ain't say shit! And we lost a helluva lot of good men and you still here, alive and breathing, so you need to be the last nigga talking," PYT said.

"Who are you? His spokesperson? I thought he ran the Empire," Bloody said rebelling.

"I'm not a spokesperson. Do you know who I really am love?" she said shutting him up.

"Sorry for your losses. I'ma handle it ASAP. All the shipments and drop-offs will remain the same until further notice. Thank you," Rugar said. He got up and left the old warehouse with Montonta.

PYT wanted to stop him to speak to him. She hadn't seen him in three days but she decided to give him space until shit died down.

New York City

Mona's baby shower was held next door to the famous Apollo in a large ballroom that did big events. Michelle, Mona's mom, Loco, and her friends all helped turn the baby shower into the event of the year. There were at least eight hundred people who had come out.

Gifts were stacked to the ceiling. There were balloons, cartoon mascots for the kids.

"Damn, this shit is lit," Mona said to her friend, Amanda. She was seated in a chair made for a Queen and Amanda was standing next to her. She wore a Nicole Miller white gown and her stomach looked as if it was about to pop any second because she was due any day now.

Loco approached the two making small talk.

"I wish bratty was here, sis," Loco said. He looked at a beautiful light skinned thick chick wearing a yellow and green dress. The dress hugged her curves and went well with her blond hair. Her breasts were round and plump like ripe melons.

"Yeah, facts. That's why after I go into labor and take some time to heal, I'ma go see him. You should come with me," Mona said, just as Michelle was walking toward them.

"Say no more, we out then," he said. Then he and the light skinned beauty made eye contact.

"What y'all kids up to?" Michelle said in her Jamaican accent.

"I'm trying to see what's up with her over there," Loco said smirking and pointing to the lady in the yellow and green dress. "Who that?" he asked out loud to anyone.

"That woman is old enough to be your mother. That's Lil C's cousin. She's been in the state two years from Kingston," Michelle said. Amanda sucked her teeth because she had been trying to get with Loco for years. But she wasn't exotic like he liked his females, she was just a regular plain Jane.

Before he could get ten feet away from his new mistress, his phone rang. It was Yvonne again. Since Lil Jay's death, she had been blowing his phone up. She told him she wanted him in her life but he curved her. He told her he was an official real nigga and he would never fuck his dead man's girl.

He gave her and Lil Jay's mom some loot. He had also paid for the funeral expenses, but that wasn't enough for Yvonne, she wanted some dick.

"Hello, Yvonne, why you blowing my shit up?" he snapped, stepping out of the ballroom where it was quite. "I don't know what type of games you playing, Yvonne, but we can't do this," Loco told her. He was beyond sick of her shit.

"Can you just make sure my child is good, Loco? I'm nothing no more. I guess I'll see you the next lifetime. Maybe then we can be a couple. Bye, handsome papi," she said, before the phone hit a dial tone. Loco rushed to his car to get over to Yvonne's as quickly as he possibly could. He knew several women who battled with mental health issues. He'd even witnessed one of them kill herself. Since then, he'd been on alert for shit like that. He only hoped she didn't do it too.

CHAPTER 24
BRONXVILLE

Rugar was dressed in all black sitting behind the wheel of an old Buick with Montonta in the passenger seat.

"Yo', blood, we been stalking this nigga for three days and it's now or never. We gotta make a move while he upstairs before he leave again," Montonta said. He kept his eyes on the white two-story house with the neatly manicured grass, located in the suburban area of Bronxville.

Rugar looked around the dark quite neighborhood thinking the same shit. He had to agree with Montonta, the two been following King Ed around since he'd gotten back in town. Thanks to Selena, they had everything they needed to know about Eddie. They even knew where both of his babies' mothers were born at.

"Come on. Fuck it, let's get it," Rugar said, placing a silencer on the tip of his P85 Ruger Pistol. He could've sent a crew to kill King Ed but this was personal, and he knew to never send a boy on a grown man's mission.

***

King Ed was in his master bedroom fucking his baby's mother like a porn star.

"Uhm, ugh, yes, papi, fuck me, baby," Lori yelled. She was throwing her ass back, making it clap knowing he was about to cum.

"Damn, you missed a nigga," King Ed gritted. He slapped her ass while giving her deep strokes and she went crazy.

"Ohhh, fuckk, ughh!" Lori screamed at the top of her lungs while grabbing the edge of the bed for dear life, ripping the cotton out.

After he nutted on her fat ass, she cleaned her cum off of his dick by sucking it and making loud slurping sounds while doing it.

"Damn, you tryna wake my son up," he said as he slid his dick in and out of her mouth, all ten and one half inches. "I gotta go baby. Let me hop in the shower," he said, pulling his dick from her mouth, before cumming down her throat.

Lori was Bolivian. She was born in La Paz, Bolivia, but raised in the Bronx. She was a NYPD officer. At twenty-four years old she had her life together. She was a college graduate with a home she owned, and she had several luxury cars. The two were high school and middle school sweethearts with a three-year-old son. She had a perfect body because she exercised. Her hair was long and brought out her blue eyes and high cheekbones. The tattoo on her ass was an added bonus to look at. She was bad with 34-28-40 measurements.

She threw on her Valentino silk robe and walked in the bathroom where Ed was soaking his body. She knew he had been under a great deal of stress lately from the way he'd been moving and acting.

She also knew it wasn't the right time to tell him she was two months pregnant. So, she walked down the hall to check on her son, Eddie Jr. He looked so cute lying in his pajamas cuddled up with his teddy bear.

Lori made her way downstairs to eat some more of the peaches she had left from earlier. Since being pregnant, she had been craving fruit lately. As she dug in her refrigerator, she was unaware of the terror lurking in her rearview.

"Oh my God," was all Lori could say when she saw the two masked men with guns pointed at her. "Please, I have a child. I'm begging you," she pleaded with tears.

"Where he at?" Rugar asked just as he heard the water from the shower stop running.

"Go upstairs, bitch," Montonta demanded when he heard the water turn off upstairs. Lori walked upstairs with two guns trained on her. This was why she wanted Ed to leave the streets alone because it could harm their family.

Once in the bedroom, Montonta posted up by the bathroom wall while Rugar held her at gunpoint. "You a beautiful woman but the choices you make within these next couple of minutes will determine your future, so don't be a superhero," Rugar stated. Lori's police instincts kicked in and she thought about her work gun under the mattress, but it was too risky.

"Just don't hurt my son," she said. Then she heard King Ed drying himself off.

"Lori, what should we do for Lil Eddie party and why you so quiet? I know you're not sleep, love," Kind Ed said, as he walked out of the bathroom. He had a towel wrapped around his chiseled waist, showing his tatts and six-pack.

"Y'all disrespected my home?" King Ed said, as he took one step out of the bathroom coming face-to-face with Montonta's pistol. Both gunmen took off their masks.

"Take a seat, and there's no such thing as a truce in the street," Rugar said. King followed orders.

"I'm sorry, baby," King Ed stated when he realized Lori was crying.

"Listen, let my family live. I promise she won't say a word," King Ed said, knowing Rugar was a dangerous man.

"Bitch-nigga shut yo' ass up! You ain't let my fourteen-year-old brother live," Montonta shouted in tears.

Lori looked at Ed as if he was crazy. She had heard of the horrible death of the two teenagers in Harlem. It was a big deal all over the city but she had no clue Ed was responsible.

"Your time is done here," Rugar said.

Psst! psst! Pssts! psst! pss!

Rugar shot his pistol first and the bullets cut through the silencer and entered Lori's skull. Then, Montonta emptied the clip into King Ed's face leaving their white bed sheets crimson red.

Rugar looked back and Montonta was gone. A few seconds later he heard three muffled shots and knew Montonta had also killed their three-year-old infant. On the way out of the house Rugar paused when he saw the photos of Lori dressed in a police uniform. There were even a couple of pictures she'd taken shaking hands with the mayor of New York.

He had no clue the bitch was a cop. If he did he would've played the scene because he didn't need the heat of killing a cop on his hands.

The two drove off in silence, both in their own thoughts. Although they had gotten rid of one problem, now they had an even bigger problem.

Rochester, NY

Upstate niggas were very different from city niggas and most upstate niggas hated city niggas.

Bloody controlled the whole upstate area from Albany, Buffalo, Rochester, and anything in between. He had an army of soldiers in each town. Brazy had met Bloody years ago in an adolescent prison upstate known as Green. Green was a gladiator school and the two stuck together until Brazy left to go home first. He held Bloody down with food packages, pics, and money orders, but when he touched down he invited him into his family.

Months prior to Brazy's death, Bloody met a Jamaican connect and he was making side deals without informing the empire which was rude. When Brazy died, Bloody started overcharging the gang for his bricks. Since there was a drought and Bloody was the only one with product, the gang had to pay whatever price he charged until Rugar came in the picture. As long as nobody found out about it he was good.

Bloody never traveled with security because he was feared by many, but he always had a crew when he went to the city.

Every Friday Bloody would go out clubbing, but tonight he was at a lounge he owned in his hood. He had just dropped off nine bricks to Elbow, one of his homies from Central Projects across town.

"Damn, Bloody, how much you gonna drink tonight?" the bartender, a childhood friend, asked him, "the bar closed at 1 o'clock."

"As much as I want to," Bloody said slowly. Then he downed a shot of Incredible Hulk. "I'ma take a piss, but go 'head and pour me another one. Then I gotta go, Mark. I got some pussy waiting on me," Bloody said, as he stumbled towards the bathroom. A few minutes later he stumbled back to the empty lounge.

"Excuse me, sir. How do I get to interstate 8? I'm not from around here," a beautiful young lady asked. She was dressed in a nice dress and heels. When Mark saw her he almost knocked over Bloody's drink of Henny as he admired her perfect size round breasts.

"Ummm, make a left down until you see Exit 2, then make two rights and it should be right there near a gas station," Mark said, looking into her pretty eyes.

"Thank you," she said, pulling something out of her purse then throwing it inside Bloody's drink.

"Here, let me write it down," Mark said. He turned around to look for a pen and paper but when he found it she was long gone.

"Where the fuck is my drink?" Bloody yelled, coming from the bathroom. When he saw his drink on the counter he drank it in one shot before he made his way to the door.

"Drive safe, Arnold. I know how you get. Do you want me to call someone?" Mark asked as Bloody walked out laughing.

Once he was outside he hoped in his red BMW truck heading to Chelly's crib. She was an ex-model snow bunny. She was bad but she was a cokehead.

Minutes later, he pulled into her parking lot and almost hit two parked cars. Bloody was feeling dizzy and weak.

"Fuck!" he yelled as he coughed up blood.

"Damn, daddy. You really on one," a female said from nearby. Her heels could be hard clicking on the pavement with every step.

"Chelly, is that you? Come help me, boo," Bloody said with a slur. He was unable to see who was standing in front of him in the dress and high heels.

"It's me, Bloody. I'm the spokesperson and that evil pretty bitch. Remember me, Bloody? I'm the grim reaper," she said.

Suddenly, Bloody recalled the voice and knew exactly who it was. He tried to crawl away from his BMW as quickly as he could. If he wanted to live, he knew getting away from PYT was the only way he would see another day. To his dismay his body wouldn't cooperate. The liquor mixed with what she'd dropped in his drink had him feeling as if he were moving in slow motion.

"You made side deals so you broke a rule of the family, bratty. Then you upped the price on my family," PYT yelled. She kicked him viciously in his ribs and he rolled over helplessly. Bloody couldn't get up or move his legs because it was poison she'd put in his drink at the bar.

"I'm sorry," he mumbled because he was unable to talk. Blood spilled from his mouth like a baby drooling.

"You disrespected my man and I've been waiting for this day you bitch-nigga." PYT smiled deviously and pulled out a .38 caliber Derringer that held two hollow tips.

Boom! Boom! She placed both bullets in his forehead before walking off singing a Lil Kim song.

CHAPTER 25
HARLEM HOSPITAL

Mona delivered a baby boy the same day as the 9/11 terrorist attacks hit New York City's twin towers. She name him Garbiel Karah and he weighed in at a healthy 7 ½ pounds with green eyes like his father.

Attica Prison

That was three months ago, today was Christmas. Mona, Loco, and little Garbiel were on the visitation floor waiting on Lil C to come out.

The visiting room was huge and packed with friends, families, and children. There were over thirty round tables and plastic seats, and there was also a few snack machines. The big white guards stood off to the side watching everyone's hand movements to see who the dummy would be trying to pass off drugs or phones.

"This shit looks scary. I don't know how y'all niggas can do this shit," Mona said, watching Garbiel sleep in his baby chair. She looked around and saw plenty of large buff niggas who looked like they were on steroids.

"Yeah, it's part of the game," Loco said. "I'ma go get some snacks and drinks," he told her. Then he stood up and followed the red line to the snack machine. When he came back five minutes later, he had over forty dollars' worth of snacks, foods, and drinks.

"Damn, nigga. You tryna get me fatter? You know I'm tryna lose this baby weight?" Mona laughed. She grabbed a pack of Twix candy bars but Loco snatched it out of her hand.

"Nigga this not for you. I know my bro hungry," he said as he sat down laughing.

The past couple of months the two had become closer, especially when he chose to be Garbiel's godfather. Loco had his own responsibility taking care of Lil Jay. He had become an orphan child because Yvonne actually ended up committing suicide the day of Mona's baby shower.

By the time Loco had made it to her crib, her wrists were cut open and she had swallowed a bottle of pain killers that killed her. Loco had a nice condo downtown and a new girlfriend named Hasely. She was black and white and worked for the city court clerk's office.

"There goes my baby," Mona said. She was so excited seeing him walked towards them in his Fendi top, Fendi loafers, and green state pants. Lil C's dreads were neatly done and hung down his back. Every bitch in the room eyed him. Not to mention, he had thick muscles and his body was ripped to perfection.

"Damn, bro. You done got big as hell, cuz," Loco said. The two leaned in and embraced one another then dapped it up.

Lil' C turned his gaze toward Mona. "Come here, baby." She walked up to him slowly and when he hugged her she cried. They held on to each other for as long as they could without the C.O. saying anything. When he let her go, he quickly grabbed her ass in the tight Seven For Mankind jeans. Everybody else in the room looked because they couldn't help but notice how fat her ass was. She was the baddest bitch in the building.

"You got thick, baby," Lil C said, smiling. After all the pleasantries, he sat down and laid eyes on his son. It was his first time seeing his baby boy aside from his pictures. Staring at him sleeping so peacefully, he became overwhelmed with emotions.

"Merry Christmas. He's so cute and handsome," he said, trying to hold back his tears.

"Who got all this shit?" Lil C asked, opening a bag of chips. He had to be strong for Mona and his son.

"So, what's going on in there? You good?" Loco asked.

"Yeah, just exercising, studying, and staying on point. It be a whole heap of cutting, gay shit, and tension up in here." Lil C started looking around the visitation room, but made sure not to lock eyes with Loco.

"Yeah. Big Porky was killed, Lil Jay gone, and Lo locked up, bro. It's crazy out there but the Kings not an issue no more. They found King Ed dead a few months ago," Loco said sadly, hating to break the news to him.

"How's Rugar and the business affairs going?" Lil C asked. He needed to change the subject because losing his niggas hurt the worst.

"Son official. He looking out, bro. He kept his word," Loco said. He didn't want to go into details right at that moment, especially since Mona was there.

"How's work and mama, love?" Lil C asked Mona.

"Everything is great. Your mom and my mom are helping big time. I'm tryna get my own spot before you touch, but everybody miss you," she stated.

"Come to daddy," Lil C said when he saw Garbiel's eyes slowly open. He looked just like him—light skinned with green eyes. "He's so small," he said rocking his son in his arms for the first time.

"Of course he's small, nigga," Mona said laughing, "he's a baby." She said and laughed some more. Watched the scene of her two favorite guys she had to hold back her tears.

"When he get older, he gonna have so many thots. I'ma have twenty grandkids from all over," Lil C said. Mona shook her head in disapproval.

"When you get out cuz?" Loco asked.

"With my merit board, in a couple of months," Lil C replied.

"We gonna throw a big party in a club, cuz," Loco said. Mona looked at him oddly.

"Yep, and I'll be right there," Mona cosigned.

"Cool. But how y'all get up here?" he asked, playing with his son.

"In Mona new E-Class." Loco had let it slip out without even meaning to blow her spot up. Mona cut her eyes at him.

"Where my Benz? And when was you gonna tell me you had a new car?" Lil C asked

"I traded it but you gonna love it, babe. It's sky blue and it's new. I'm about to open a clothing store in Queens," she said, changing the subject.

"That's what's up, but we gonna finish that conversation later on the phone," Lil C stated. They talked for another two hours before their visit was over.

Washington Heights, NY

Rugar left his goons parked outside in the Cadillac Escalade truck as he walked into Jumbo's Cuban restaurant. He walked to the back area. The place was small and empty but it was a decent lowkey establishment.

"Good afternoon, my friend. Looks like your gaining weight," Jumbo said. He was dressed in a three-piece suit. He stood up to shake Rugar's hand firmly.

"I'm eating good and networking all over the tri-state, N.C., ATL, and Nashville, TN," Rugar stated. Jumbo could tell he was proud to have keys all over the Tri-State and south now.

"Good, good. You're a smart businessman. But my people reached out to me about your friend Naya again. And I must say, they got a hard-on for her in Jersey. They got a big case with a lot of murders," Jumbo said.

"I'll be sure to tell her, thank you," Rugar said, wishing he could help her. But it seemed to be over his head.

"Also, something has been brought to my attention," he said seriously, "a gang war within the city streets with your people and the Kings. If I got wind, I know them people gonna be cleaning up gangs with federal indictments soon. And since I have to look out for my own safety, if any of this stupidity shit gets to me I will cut myself loose from you," Jumbo said.

"I understand," Rugar replied.

"No. You have no clue, Rugar. I control a very big empire as well. My empire deals with the cartels and they highly disapprove of gang activity and gang wars. Your brother never had this issue because he was about business. The gang life was only his foundation," he said.

"I'm sorry for the trouble. I can assure you, it won't happen again. But with all due respect, the gang life is my temple and money is my foundation," Rugar said. Jumbo shook his head in the affirmative because he understood his logic.

"Listen, I'ma cover for you the best I can, son. As of now, they don't have a clue who runs your empire. They think it's Naya but a woman over an empire is rare. In twenty-four hours, I'll have an eighteen wheeler drop some shit off to you. But besides that, I want you to come to a fight in Vegas with me next weekend, front row," Jumbo offered. Rugar agreed, and after conversing business a little while longer, he bounced.

Romell Tukes

162

CHAPTER 26
MIAMI, FL

Fall in Miami was summertime. Women walked around the beaches half naked and clubs were packed. The strips were lined with nothing but luxury cars, driving up and down the Miami streets.

China loved it, and her college was a regular party central. Miami was better than New York in so many ways because she lived carefree. She was a cheerleader for her school and the campus was huge. Most of the students were Haitians, Cubans, Whites, and Africans, but there weren't many Blacks. Most kids thought China was one hundred percent Korean. Most of the dudes in her school, or in Miami period, were stocky with muscles and tans, She had a thing for dark niggas with muscles but she was still single.

Uncle P had paid her lease up for two years. She had pink rugs, photos of Biggie and Brazy, surround-sound, pink curtains, and two fifty-two-inch flat-screen TVs—one in her living room and one in her bedroom.

"Damn, China. Why you always in here by yourself, girl? You need a roommate 'cause I know this shit expensive," her friend, Fatima, said in her country voice.

Fatima was Haitian and white. She had a small waist and wide thighs. She was light skinned and sexy. She was from Opa Locka, which was across the bridge. The two went to school together and they had built a strong friendship over the past couple of months. Fatima lived on campus. She didn't have a job but her niggas tricked their bag on her as if she were a trophy.

China would always take her shopping with her and Fatima would take her out to the hottest clubs. China had a new white Benz S Coupe with a body kit, and a new FI CRONO. Rugar and Uncle P would Western Union her five thousand dollars every other week for her car note, bills, and living expenses.

"You coming to Nicole's pool party this weekend?" Fatima yelled from the restroom.

"Fuck no, I got exams on Monday and I hate that bitch," China stated with passion. Nicole was a rich white bitch on her cheerleader squad, and she was popular. "Don't you gotta study too," China asked. Fatima laughed loudly. China never understood how Fatima was an honor student yet she never studied. Every time she asked her about studying all she'd say is it's a gift and a curse with a little trick.

"I'ma slide to Dre's spot. I'll be back later just call my line," Fatima said. She grabbed her Coach purse and Honda car keys.

"Hello," China said, answering a call with a blocked number.

"Hey, girl. This Naya, what you doing?"

"Oh shit, hey! Long time no speak. How is your vacation going?" China asked, getting comfortable in her sofa chair. She folded her legs then crisscrossed them and sat Indian style, allowing her fat pussy print to show through her boy shorts.

"I'm on South Beach at the end section. Come chill if you're not busy," Naya suggested.

"Really? Okay. I live around the corner so give me five minutes and I'll be there." She jumped up to put on her Chanel bikini ensuring she'd show off her flat stomach, round ass, perky breasts, and pierced nipples. Her manicured nails and toes always looked good.

***

Naya had fun in Jamaica but she got tired of it quick. She met some very important people. One nigga was a powerful man and she promised to keep in touch.

Rugar informed her the FEDS had a warrant for her arrest, and coming home anytime soon would be a bad idea. She let the twins take over and she heard they were running shit smoothly. She was proud since she'd raised them from teens.

She thought Miami would be the best place to lay low and still enjoy her daily life. She had a fake name, a fake ID, fake visa, and she had her security accounts hacked so she was able to change her social security number thanks to PYT.

With a new identity she was able to get a new hook-up on a fancy condo in the skyrise, and a new all white Lamborghini Aventador worth four hundred thousand dollars.

Naya was sitting on the beach in a folding chair tanning her golden skin. Her long hair hung past her shoulders and she was wearing a two-piece Gucci bikini with her shades on looking like a model not a killer. When she saw China looking all over the place for her, she waved for her attention until she saw her.

"Damn, you look different, girl, word," China said. She couldn't help staring at Naya's perfectly toned body. She had never seen her without clothes on and she was a little jealous. Naya saw the way she was staring and gave her a compliment, admiring her bikini.

"Nice two piece. So how's school?" she asked. China sat in the empty folding chair laid out for her and watched the jet skiers tear the clear water up.

"It's okay and I'm making the best of it," she replied.

"That's what's up. Just stay with it. I know the boys are in line for you," Naya said laughing.

"I wish. Most of them niggas gay," she said laughing, "but what brings you down here?" China asked curiously.

"To be honest, I'm on the run so I'm down here laying low. I got a condo so I'ma chill for a minute," Naya said not wanting to lie to China.

"Damn. So what's your plan now?" China asked. Now she was worried.

"Shit, gangstas don't die. They get money and move to Miami," Naya said being honest.

The two spent the rest of the day together on the beach. They laughed, drank, and let corny Miami niggas play pull up on them with their lame game.

Atlanta, GA

Glizzy sat in his Maserati Ghibli S Q4 listening to Fat Mac talk for ten minutes.

"Aye shawty, that brick came back like magic. I never seen no shit double up," Fat Mac said with excitement in his tone.

"That's what's poppin', five," Glizzy said. Montonta sat in the passenger seat smiling, loving the ATL.

"I'ma need four of them joints tonight. Meet me in Zone three. Them niggas ran me out of Zone six, shawty. But get at me," Fat Mac said, showing his gold mouth.

"A'ight, fam." Glizzy pulled off from the block and turned up the Lil Durk's mixtape.

"I been down here four years, blood. And ATL is where it's at. You and Rugar need to get a crib down here," Glizzy said, driving around the city.

Glizzy was born and raised in Harlem. He had moved to Atlanta four years ago to finish high school but he never did. Instead, he got into the street life.

"What's poppin' with bro? I don't even hear from Rugar no more," Glizzy said.

"He cooling, blood. Tryna check a bag," Montonta said. He let some of the smoke escape his mouth as he smoked on a blunt of OG Kush they picked up from Stone Mountain.

"We going out to Magic tonight?" Glizzy asked. He already knew Montonta was a club nigga. He had just blew 20K in Mr. Lueis' the night before.

"Hell yeah, nigga, I'm in the A! You know I gotta put on for up-top."

"Too late. I already did that," Glizzy replied. He strolled down the block in the East Atlanta hood he controlled. He was the plug out there and Brazy used to be his plug. But now it Montonta and he was Rugar's capo. The work was the best he'd ever had. He only hoped his blood homies would continue blessing him. He had an army he had to feed and he was a general in Rugar's blood set in Atlanta.

"I got seventeen bricks left at the hotel. I'ma leave it to you tonight. Then I'm out. Just wire the money to the account. I gotta get back home. I'ma leave the bitches down here to trap with you," Montonta said. He was referring to the two blood bitches who had transported twenty-five keys of coke and fifteen keys of dope in a rental car.

"A'ight. Just so you know, I'ma try to fuck somethin' too." Glizzy laughed even though he was dead ass.

"Shit, go 'head. I already did and them bitches ain't got no walls or tissue left in their pussies," Montonta said honestly. They both burst out laughing.

Romell Tukes

CHAPTER 27
BRONX

Red Hot was in his stash house in the Sandview projects listening to the money machines work. Naked women stood in a room bagging up crack, while security posted up around the house with assault rifles.

"Shit been going smooth since them King niggas disappeared, blood," Murder said. His eyes were trained on the women bagging up drugs and counting money—it was a beautiful sight. It was nine o'clock in the morning and Red Hot looked out of his window. The kids were playing on the playground enjoying the last of the nice weather.

"I forgot to tell Moola Hand and you what happened when we went to Albany, bro. Some niggas popped up on us with twenty or more niggas with pistols and Dracos. They thought we was Jackboys," Murder said, recalling the events of the previous night. He had gone to drop off some work to Moola Hand's people in Downtown Albany.

"Move a little different, kid. I like Moola," Red Hot stated.

"What's up with the boss though? I ain't seen her in a while," Murder asked. He was Red Hot's capo and he was referring to PYT. He had a major crush on her. In his opinion she was hands-down the baddest bitch he'd ever seen. Murder was the only person besides Red Hot to see the PYT and that was a mistake.

Red Hot had got shot in the head in Brooklyn after being set up by a bitch he'd met. Since then, Murder had an emergency number to call if anything serious like that ever happened again. The number belonged to PYT.

So Murdered called her and met up with her and she was one of the baddest bitches who ever crossed his path. He tried his hand but PYT curved him. She told him if he ever tried his hand again she would cut it off along with his head. He left it alone and explained what happened. Within hours, the bitch who set Red Hot up was found dead along with the two shooters who almost killed

Red Hot. Luckily, Red had survived the hit. Murder never said a word but he knew PYT had put the hit out. But only if Red knew she was the hitter.

"Nigga she good. Stop asking about her 'cause you barking near the wrong tree. I feel sad for Rugar though. I hope he a heartless nigga," Red Hot said then walked out of the apartment.

East Orange, NJ

"You still owe me ten thousand from the last key, nigga. you think I'm dumb? Listen, just because you got cash on deck, I'ma give you two bricks, playboy. But I'ma tax you so now you owe me twenty thousand and you can get the fuck out," Mark said from the driver seat of his Infiniti Q 70L 3.7X. Muhammad stuffed the two keys in his small bookbag.

"Brother, Naya never taxed me. She knew my money was always good. What part of the game is this?" Muhammad stated.

"It's my game, nigga. Pay like you weigh. What the fuck you gonna do about it besides pay me?" Mark looked the Muslim nigga straight in his eyes.

"A'ight, you got it. I'll have your shit by the weekend." Muhammad handed him forty-six thousand in cash. When he got out of the car he was pissed, so he slammed the car door.

Muhammad and his crew of Muslims controlled the whole East Orange and West Orange. The extorted drug dealers sold weight and killed. Muhammed hopped in his Yukon truck and pulled off. He kept replaying how Mark had disrespected him. He knew Mark was a hotheaded trigger-happy gangsta from Brick City, but Muhammad didn't care about a rep he was about respect.

Newark, NJ

Marcus was in the projects with some of his goons trapping, smoking, and drinking. He had a war going on around the corner with Papi and Flaco, some Dominicans who sold weight. The beef started because Marcus wouldn't sell them bricks of dope at a reasonable price. That led to shoot-outs every day and the hood had been on fire for the past two weeks.

"Yo', twin, you remember that nigga, J Mack, who ran off with that G-pack three months ago?" Live asked as he approached the gang in front of the first building out of eight.

"Yeah, what's poppin' with him?" Marcus asked, blowing out PCP smoke, something he did daily—most niggas in Brick City smoked wet.

"The homies got him held hostage in build seventy-five at Kat's crib," Live said. Then seven niggas pulled out their straps and walked toward the back of the projects.

Once they had made it in the apartment, they saw J Mack sitting on a child's size seat, naked and crying trying to cover up his little dick.

"Give me one reason why I shouldn't kill you and have the homie run a train on Ms. Kat? I always thought your grandma had a fat ass anyway," Marcus shouted.

"I'm sorry. I had to use the money to bail out, so I been fucked up," J Mack said. While he was explaining his case, he heard the sounds of sexual moans and groans coming from his grandmother's room. The goon had his grandmother suck five nigga's dicks back to back, with a gun to her head.

"Look, blood, this nigga got eight hundred dollars in his pocket," one of Marcus' soldiers said, emptying J Mack's sweatpants.

"I was going let you live," Marcus said. Then he shot him three times in the chest before walking to the back room. When he opened Ms. Kat's door, she was screaming one nigga fucked her in the ass, another in her pussy, and one fucked her face. Her sixty-year-old sagging breasts flopped like water balloons as the men ran a train on her. Before they could finish, Marcus shot her in the head and took her out of her misery.

"Come on, nasty niggas. Just remember, that's y'all DNA in her. Now let's hit up some clubs," he said. He walked out of the room smiling and laughing at how wild his goons were.

New Roc, NY

Rugar sat in his office thinking about a new plan to invest in so he could clean as much money as possible.

"Baby you bossy," PYT said. She had strutted in wearing a silk robe with lingerie underneath.

"Come in, love," he stated. Seeing her bright smile always made his day.

"What you doing, babe?" she asked.

"Nothing much. But how was your meeting with the investors?" he asked. He'd planned on asking her earlier but he was so busy it slipped his mind.

"Everything went good. He gave me a lot of new ideas but I like what you did with the place." She sat in his lap and gazed over the large library shelves realizing they took up two walls. There were security cameras, file cabinets, paintings of MLK, Ghadi, Malcolm X, and Fred Hammonds.

"Maybe we can have sex in here on your desk," she said as she kissed his lips softly.

"Not this second, baby. But I have a question I been meaning to ask you... Do you know what happened to Bloody?" he asked her straight up.

"Yeah, I killed him. I found out he had a new connect and he was taxing the empire. I hate snakes," she said as if it were nothing.

"Listen, Jasmine... next time let me handle it. I need you to fall back. You're the brains to the empire and my backbone," he said shaking his head.

"Okay, I'm sorry. Now can we get down to business?"

"Go. But I'm not playing. Fall back," he said again more sternly this time.

"Look, we set up a quarter million dollar' worth of offshore accounts overseas in China, Asia, Japan, and India. Then, we buy out stocks over there and sell them to the US and Canada for triple the amount. That's how we crash the stock market," PYT stated.

"How much is that?"

"If everyone in the empire comes together we'll need three million," she said.

"Three? What? I don't know where to find half of that," he said.

"Sleep on it, boo. It takes money to make money," PYT said. Then she stood up to leave. Switching her round, soft ass, turned Rugar on and he needed some sex. "Hold up a minute," he told her." She smiled knowing she had him..

She dropped her robe putting her perfect body on full display. Within seconds, his dick was brick-hard. He led her to his desk and kicked everything off. Then, he slid inside her slowly and deeply.

CHAPTER 28
ATTICA, NY

Lil C sat at the bus stop across the street from the Attica prison. Looking at its big walls, now he was dressed in street clothes instead of state greens.

He rocked a Louis Vuitton sweater, jeans, and boots with spikes. The credit card the jail released to him had over 60K on it, so he was good to go, unlike most niggas who were fucked up, homeless, and broke after being released.

The bus was forty minutes late. Him and three other inmates were waiting on their wheels to freedom. The bus ride was a seven-hour ride with a couple of stops. The main stop was at Montcelo, NY. From there, he would transfer and take another bus to 42nd St.

Lucky for him, it was Friday. So he had the whole weekend to himself until Monday. Then he would have to go report to his parole officer. He had plans to spend the night with Mona but Loco said he'd made arrangements to hang in Miami which he knew would be exciting.

Lil C was so happy to make it out the same way he went in because Cripping in a New York jail wasn't easy. But he'd done it, and now he was focused on a bag.

Hours Later, Grand Central

Mona stood outside the big train station waiting on her Benz. Her arms were crossed and she kept checking her watch.

"Where is this boy at?" she mumbled aloud. Every now and then she'd brush her long hair behind her ears. She watched thousands of people walk up and down the busy 42nd street and still no Lil' C.

Finally, she saw him bopping as he walked. His dreads hung to his stomach.

"Oh my God! You home, baby!" She ran through the crowd and jumped in his muscular arms. The two kissed passionately, something they had been unable to do for years.

"Let's go, sexy," Lil C said. He grabbed her hand and escorted her out of the train station. When she walked up to the Benz, Lil C was amazed. The shit was exotic.

"Damn," he said. He climbed into the deep white leather seats. He reached his hand out and felt on the wood grain dashboard. Avant played in the loud surround sound system.

"I told you this shit was litty," she said, pulling off into the busy New York City traffic.

"Where is my son?" Lil C asked, hoping to see him.

"He's spending the night with your mom because I want you all to myself tonight. Then, I guess Loco got that Miami party planned for you too. I'll be working so you lucky," she said.

"Where we going?" he asked.

"I'ma about to get what I been missing, daddy. And it's something no nigga out here could've gave me," she said. He nodded his head and thought about what she truly meant by that.

The Season Hotel

Mona paid two thousand seven hundred dollars for a one night stay in the penthouse suite. It was at one of the fanciest hotels in the city.

The place was decorated from top to bottom, upstairs and downstairs. There was wall-to-wall carpet, a bar, three bedrooms, two marble-floor bathrooms, marble sinks, and gold toilets. There were also glass showers, and indoor, a jacuzzi, and a view of Times Square.

"You out did yourself," Lil C said, walking around in his socks. He had a big smile on his face.

"I'ma order us something to eat, babe. I know you sick of jail food, nigga." Mona sat in the living room and placed her feet on the white leather leg rest.

"I'ma take a shower first," he said. He couldn't wait to get the smell of jail smell off him.

"Okay, daddy," she said, "I bought you some clothes. Everything is in the bedroom," she yelled to the bathroom.

She called room service and ordered plenty of seafood, wine, and whip cream, as well as ice.

Lil C took a hot shower, allowing the shower to rinse away the stress. He thought about Mona and how blessed he was to have a rider like her. Unlike most niggas whose girlfriends or baby mother's would leave them for dead and fuck their man while they were on lock.

He never questioned her loyalty or whereabouts during his bid. The way he saw it, if she was doing anything behind his back he'd rather not know; besides, he understood, just like a man, a woman had needs too.

Mona heard the doorbell ring and rushed to open it, snapping her from her train of thought. She tipped the Spanish nigga thirty dollars. He smiled as he stared at her thickness. She rolled her eyes, took the food, and slammed the door.

Lil C was out of the shower. He felt like his old self dressed in a pair of Polo boxers, Rag & Bone jeans, and Timbs. Seeing him shirtless, Mona admired his toned chest and stomach. His body was riddled with tattoos and the more she stared at him, the wetter she got. She loved his artwork of MLK, his mom, and animals. The colors really stood out since he was light skinned.

"Uhm, damn light skinned... That six pack looks good on you," she said.

"You lighter than me," he said. He sat down next to her and she stood up. "I'ma go wash up," she said. She rushed, wanting to hurry up and get her panty's off since they were soaked from her pussy juices.

As Lil C waited for her to return, he thought about his boxing career. He was twenty years old with a son. He knew he needed to make money, now more than ever. The streets were like second nature to him, but he had to make the right choice and think about his son. He planned to go see Jumbo after he saw his P.O. on Monday. By then, hopefully, his mind would be made up.

Mona entered the room naked, except for red high-heels. As she went to her knees and slowly crawled over to him, Lil C's manhood stood to attention. Smiling, she maneuvered between his legs, pulled his dick out, and went to work.

"Uhhmmm, you taste good," she moaned. She sucked on the head of his manhood doing tongue tricks. His toes curled as he went in and out of her warm mouth. She made loud slurping noises as she got his dick wet. She began deep-throating him, taking him with ease, causing her eyes to fill with tears. She bopped her head up and down so fast, she didn't even feel it when his cum shot down her throat. She swallowed every drop.

"I'm not gonna let you tap me out," he said. He placed her on the bed and moved her thong to the side. He slid inside her tight, wet walls making her bite down on her bottom lip. She moaned softly. He slowly stroked her until he felt her warm pussy open up wider.

"Ugghh, ohhh, fuck me," she screamed out. This made Lil C go crazy. He started tearing her pussy up and within minutes they both released an explosion that made their bodies tremble. After being in the missionary, he bent her over and dogged her from behind. He gripped her waist so she couldn't run and then eased his thumb inside her butthole.

"Fuckk, babbyyy, yesssss," she yelled. She took the dick deeply and her eyes rolled from ecstasy of it all. By now, she'd had three orgasms in seconds and the room had a strong sexual order.

He placed her on her side and lifted one of her legs over his shoulders. Then, he went crazy. The sounds of her gushy wetness was like a waterfall. His balls clapped on her fat ass with every long stroke. When he started hitting her G-spot, she placed a pillow over her mouth to muffle her screams. Again, they exploded and continued making love until sunlight covered the room.

CHAPTER 29

The bright light shined through the bedroom curtains and woke Lil C from his sleep. He stretched his long boxing arms out and felt around the bed for Mona, she was out of sight.   His   body was sore and weak from the crazy sex they'd had the night before. Their first night back together had been amazing on some triple X porn-movie shit. She had even let him hit it anally until she tapped out.

The strong aroma of breakfast filled the air prompting him to get up from the bed. He opened the double doors that led to the living room and kitchen.

Mona was standing over the stove in a pink G-string that was being swallowed up by her big ass. Her hips and curves poked out as she stood bowlegged.

"Good morning, baby," she said, looking over her shoulder at him.

"What you cooking?" he asked, as he grabbed her waist from behind.

"Pancakes, eggs, jerk chicken, and hash browns," she said. She sprinkled a little curry powder on the chicken.

"Who taught you how to cook? You used to be a fast food girl," Lil C said in his Jamaican accent.

"Michelle did. She taught me everything she learned from the yard. And I don't mean no harm but your breath stank, nigga, you need to hit them hygiene," she stated, covering his mouth.

"Whatever," he said laughing. He went to the bathroom to get himself together. Afterwards, they ate breakfast and talked for hours. After they got dressed, they left the hotel and she dropped him off at Polo Grounds to visit his mom and son.

Polo Grounds

Lil C sneaked into the back of his building because niggas were out in the front deep. He knew they'd want to talk and welcome him home but he was on a time schedule. Once upstairs, it was all love. He played with his son on the living room floor while Michelle fixed a warm bottle for the baby.

"Me t'ank you a lot but t'ings mi do'nt wa'n put you through," Lil C said.

"It's okay. Mi your mother," Michelle replied feeding Garbiel. "That Loco kid been here all day and yesterday checking on me," she said, watching Garbiel down the warm milk and getting sleepy.

"Okay, but how's work and life?" he asked.

"Good. Ever thing crisp," she replied. The two hung out for another hour until Loco came by again. He wanted to make sure they wouldn't miss their flight.

***

"Nigga you smoked out," Lil C said, throwing up the Crip set.

"Shawty in window four is the plug. Pull up on her with your ticket and ID. I know you got a jail ID but you good," Loco said, walking through the thick crowd.

Lil C pulled up to window four where a pretty brown skinned chick was typing fast on a keyboard.

"Excuse me, here is my ticket and ID. Loco sent me," Lil C said, looking in her brown eyes.

"You don't remember me, Chris?" the pretty woman asked. She looked as if she were shocked to see him.

"Am I supposed to?" he asked rudely. He had no idea who she was.

"Wow. I sat behind you in the 7th and 8th grade. They used to call me brace-face," she said sadly. She was disappointed he didn't know who she was. Especially since they were cool back then. She felt like he should've remembered her because he was the only one who defended her against bullies and she had a crush on him.

"Oh yeah, what happened to your braces? You look different," he said. He was shocked she was so beautiful.

"Thanks, I guess. I heard you a boxer now."

"Nah. Not yet," he said. She stamped his ticket and handed it back to him. He walked off and left her confused. She wanted to talk more until he rudely walked off.

After clearing the metal detectors, they hopped on a flight to Miami. They were ready to enjoy the weekend. Loco, Turk, and Lil C had never been to Miami so this was big.

Miami, FL

As soon as they touched the pavement, the Miami heat hit them and it felt like a desert in the middle east.

"This shit is crazy," Lil C said, observing all the exotic bitches rushing past, him in and out of the airport.

"I think this is us right here," Loco said when an Audi limo pulled up. The limo was like a small club. The inside was fully equipped with dancing lights, a bar, flat screen TVs, laptops, and it seated fifteen people.

They drove through Miami admiring the clear water, white sand, beaches, and palm trees. The scenery was beautiful as they drove down the Miami streets making their way to the Luxury Express in North Miami.

Once at the rental dealership, they all went crazy like kids in a candy store.

"Yo', son, I gotta bring one of these to New York. A nigga might try to rob me and kill me for this," Turk said, admiring an all-white Rolls Royce Wraith Coupe 6.6 Twin Turbo.

"Gentlemen, your three luxury cars are already parked out front. Thanks to Mr. Rugar, the insurance and registration are in the driver's seat. Enjoy your stay in Miami," an older white gentleman dressed in a business suit said. He handed them each a set of keys.

Turk had the key to the new Audi R8 Daytona with the clear doors. "Damn," he said, as the doors lifted in the air.

Lil C climbed in the sky-blue McLaren 570s GT, and Loco had a Bentley Continental GT, all white.

All three raced down the Miami streets with the Audi and McLaren doors in the air, heading to a designer outlet to run it up shopping.

Club Express

Night life in Miami was like no other, everyone stepped out in their best gear, best ice, and best cars. Niggas brought them racks out.

Lil C, Loco, and Turk pulled up to the front of the club in the foreign whips, looking like rappers or basketball players. The line to the club was wrapped around the block. People were waiting to get in the hottest club in Miami. Rugar had brought the club out for the night. They had big name rappers coming to perform in honor of Lil C's welcome home party and there was also a birthday party taking place.

Two large bouncers who stood six feet, seven inches tall, weighing three hundred pounds each, stood at the entrance.

"I'm Lil C and this my welcome home party," Lil C told the guards. They looked like they were trying to suck in their guts.

"OK, welcome home. Y'all got anyone else with you?" the light skinned, bald head bouncer asked. Lil C looked back at the ten bitches in line. They were trying to get his attention hoping to get in for free instead of paying.

"That whole crew," Lil C said, pointing behind him. The women rushed inside and hugged while laughing at the bouncers.

"Good looks, son," Loco said. He handed him a stack of fifties which amounted to eight hundred dollars.

The inside was the length of a football field. There were two bars, one in the front and one in the back, two stages, four VIP sections, an upstairs and downstairs, and several big disco ball lights.

As soon as Lil C walked, in the DJ gave him a shout-out. The crowd went crazy as he made his way to the VIP where Rugar stood waiting.

Lil C felt like a boss. He didn't know how the DJ knew it was him but he loved the atmosphere. He wasn't even from down there.

"My man, Lil C, what's the word?" Rugar said, embracing him. Welcome home. Have a seat Loco and Turk. I'm glad everybody made it. Them bottles for y'all," he shouted over the loud music. A local rapper was on stage performing and he had the crowd going crazy as he waved Haitian flags in the audience.

"Thanks for the love and for holding it down, bro. That's some real nigga shit, fam," Lil C said, looking at the only three females in the VIP section, They were quite, but hands down, they were some of the baddest bitches he'd ever seen.

"No problem, son. I told you I don't see color. But let me introduce you to my fam. This Montonta to my right, this my sister, China, this wifey PYT, and this is Naya," Rugar said, introducing everybody.

China nor Naya could stop staring at him because he looked fine as hell in his all white Gucci outfit.

"Your name heavy in the city, loc," Naya said to Lil C. More bottles were brought to the table because Loco and Turk were running through the Ace of Spade.

"Thanks, but I heard a lot about you too, Jersey girl," he replied catching her off guard. She smiled, letting him know he was on point. Naya couldn't lie—the boy was fine as hell. Her pussy was wet but she wouldn't dare cross the line since her heart was with Brazy.

"Naya, come with me to the ladies room," China said. She stood up and pulled her Fendi dress down. Loco noticed how fat her ass was and had to turn his head to keep from getting a hard-on.

"Yo', we about to hit up the dance floor," Loco said as Turk, China, and Naya followed them.

'Make sure they all good, blood," Rugar told Montonta. Montonta had snuck in the club with a pistol. He left the VIP area and had a hard time tracking them because the club was so big.

PYT shook her head because she knew what Naya and China was on. She was a woman also and couldn't deny the fact that Lil C had a nice body. The nigga was handsome and a rep, but he wasn't her type. PYT hated light skinned pretty boy niggas, and Lil C was at the top of the food chain.

"What's your plan now that you're out?" PYT asked. Her legs were crossed and she sat militant.

"Open some businesses and invest some money. I got a seed and a city of Crips to feed," Lil C said.

"Sounds like a plan," she told him. "PYT will plug you into agency brokers, investors, and we also got you a new ID, and a business license. So you'll have everything you need with a business account in your name and A-1 credit thanks to PYT," Rugar said, handing him a folder with the important documents.

"Thank you. Ima be ready next week. I already got a business plan. And you can continue dropping off keys to Loco, but I need you to double up now," Lil C said. Rugar nodded.

***

"Girl, that nigga sexy," China said, "I'll fuck the shit outta him." The drinks she'd consumed had her felling tipsy. She looked in the mirror as she stood in the bathroom applying a new coat of gloss to her lips.

"You gotta respect your brother's business. It's a thin line between business and family," Naya said washing her hands. She exited the bathroom and Montonta was at the entrance talking to a thick pretty Cuban chick.

"Damn, you stalking?" Naya said in front of the Cuban chick. Montonta looked at her sideways before walking off.

"Why you cockblock like that? I no y'all don't take shits in clubs 'cause y'all too classy," he said, following them back to the VIP section.

China sat next to Lil C while Rugar and PYT went to dance.

"I heard you box?" China asked over the loud music.

"Yeah, but I'm more focused on another chapter in my life," he said.

"I feel you and I know your girl glad you home," she said, fishing for info.

"Yeah, she is. She held it down my whole bid and she gave birth to my seed," he said proudly. The two talked the rest of the night and became friends. She and Naya both now considered Lil C a cool dude.

Turk and Loco had two Spanish bitches each to bring back to the hotel for the night. They planned on turning up among other things. Their flight back to NY wouldn't leave until the next morning.

Romell Tukes

CHAPTER 30
PAROLE OFFICE

Monday morning the parole office was packed like a welfare line. Lil C sat in the back of the waiting room with other convicts on parole, waiting to see the P.O. to find out if he was going to get violated. He'd spent the previous Sunday afternoon with his son and Mona. He was still tired from the trip and Miami had did a number on him. There was no question he was ready to get back in the game and take over.

"Mr. Johnson! Do we have a Mr. Johnson?" a fat older lady yelled. She stood at an open door that led to the offices in the back.

"Yes, right here," Lil C shouted. He got up from his seat and walked towards the fat bitch. Once in the office, she sat down behind the desk with a computer and a stack of folders, and one of the folders belonged to him.

"Why welcome home. I'm sure that little bid did you justice," the parole officer said.

"Yeah, it did. Gave me time to think about getting my life together," he replied looking at her family photos.

"Well good for you said. I'm Ms. Wilson, your parole officer. I've already read over your caseload and I see you're a member of the gang known as the Crips," she said, while looking through his thick folder.

"I'ma Crip and that's just who I am. This ain't Compton where we do drive-by shooting or all that extra unnecessary violent gangbanging shit. I'm just affiliated. I'm older, more mature, and wiser now. I came home to a newborn son. So now that I got a seed, my insight on life is different," Lil C stated. She looked him in his eyes to see if he was sincere.

"When I did a home check I saw you had a beautiful son and girlfriend. You have a nice family. I just hope you do right by them. I'll be doing my rounds daily. You have a 6 a.m. – 8 p.m. curfew until you get a legal job or get enrolled in school. No drugs because you'll have random drug screens," she said. She knew the rules by heart because she was strictly by the book.

"What about driving? I have a license, and I've got a job lined up already," he inquired. Loco had just brought his 600 Benz to him the day before and he had already been driving.

"Well, get the job and bring your first pay stub and we'll take it from there," she said. She smiled and had took a liking to him already.

"Okay. Anything else?" he asked.

"No, I think that's all for now. Have a good day and stay out of trouble," she said as he stood to leave.

***

Lil C drove his Benz through the snowy streets of Harlem watching the light snowfall hit the windshield. He was on his way to meet Jumbo at a restaurant on Lenox and 6th Ave.

He had told himself due to New York's snowy conditions and being like the North Pole, he was ready to cop a Range because of its four-wheel drive and snow tires.

Once at the Spanish hole-in-the-wall restaurant, he parked on the curb to gather his thoughts. He had made up his mind and he was prepared to tell Jumbo he was ready to give up his boxing career. It was going to be rough because he had been training under Jumbo for ten years. He took a deep breath and exited his vehicle.

He entered the restaurant and he was greeted by a couple of waiters. Walking inside, he looked around, surprised at how nice the place was. The floors were all marble and there was a stage. There booths all around and bar fully loaded bar. Round tables with white cloths had been placed throughout, and there were a ton of Spanish guests enjoying meals.

"Hey, Chris. Back here." Jumbo stood and waved him over from a private booth. He was dressed casual in a business suit. Seeing him dressed that way was new to Lil C but he hadn't seen him in two years.

"You must've just come from a funeral," Lil C said as he embraced him with a big hug. "Thank you for the lawyer, Jumbo. You didn't have to waste your money like that. I know how bad it is out here for you," Lil C stated as he sat down.

"First off, welcome home, kid. A cell is no place for a sane man, so stay out," Jumbo said seriously.

"You right, but I've been doing a lot of thinking lately. I'm going to put my boxing career to the side because I have a family I have to provide for now," Lil C said, getting right to the point. Jumbo was silent as he thought about how to respond.

"So everything you put into it goes to waste? I respect your choice because you're an adult now. But what's your plan?" Jumbo asked.

"To be honest, I don't really know, but I do know I gotta find a way to provide for my family," Lil C said.

Without asking questions, Jumbo read between the lines. "Follow me," he said. He stood up from the booth and turned around headed toward the kitchen located in the back. Lil C looked at him as if he were crazy for walking through somebody else's restaurant. What he found even stranger was how everybody, including the workers, nodded at Jumbo as if they knew him personally.

"You must know the owner?" Lil C asked. "Either that or you come here a lot," he added.

"Something like that," Jumbo said. He led Lil' C into a small office near the bakery area.

Lil C looked around the office and noticed all the pictures of Jumbo lined on the walls. Some of the pictures showed him shaking hands with the police chief, the governor, or other men who looked powerful and important.

"You in a lot of these photos," he said. Jumbo laughed.

"Let's have a face-to-face. See, Chris, I been knowing you since you were a little kid and I know everything you do in them streets. I'ma give you a chance to make some real money. But I want you to promise me you'll turn it into something successful like a business. Because what I'm into isn't a lifestyle one should commit to," Jumbo said with a strange look on his face.

"I told you, I'm done boxing," Lil' C reiterated.

Jumbo put his hands in the air gesturing him to listen. "Look, kid, you not slow," Jumbo continued, "how you think Rugar and all of your neighborhood role models became so wealthy?" he asked.

Lil' C pondered the question. And then, as if a light bulb had gone off over his head, he said, "Ain't no way. So you telling me the lawyer you sent wasn't by luck or sacrifice?"

"That was for free, but you let the old car, bummy cloths, and assuming I was having a rough time, fool you," Jumbo said laughing.

"So what the fuck do you do?" Lil C wondered aloud. He had an idea but he needed to hear Jumbo say it.

"I supply the east coast and I'm part of a large cartel family—one you'll never see or hear of. But that information can't never leave this room," Jumbo said seriously and in a stern tone.

"Of course not," Lil C said. His tone reflected the shock he was feeling.

"I like the way you move and I've had my eyes on you for a long time. I think you ready now," Jumbo told him.

"I'm definitely ready," Lil C said. His mind began to contemplate just how big Jumbo was in the game. Even though he, himself was making money, he still knew there were levels to this street life shit.

"Money can turn one into a monster," Jumbo told him, as he changed gears on the convo and began schooling his new young protégé. See, that little Benz you pushing, and the two hundred racks you got saved? That's what I pay my maid, " Jumbo said honestly.

"I feel you," Lil C replied.

"You remember Big Meech?"

"Hell yeah."

"He was seeing plenty, but his ego was his downfall. I was riding in a fucked up Honda and dressed bummy for a reason," Jumbo said.

"I'm always on point and I move smart," Lil' C said.

"I know. So here, take this address. There's gonna be a shipment waiting for you under the door panel of the van. On Fridays there will be pick-ups. Don't ever call me just come here if there's ever an issue. Understood?"

"Copy. Question though... How do you know Rugar?" Lil C asked, as Jumbo handed him a piece of paper with an address written on it.

"He's my Godson. But from now on, you'll only deal with me, and you can deal with your own crew too. But you don't know me and I don't know you," Jumbo said.

And with that, the meeting was adjourned.

CHAPTER 31
MIAMI, FL

It was around four in the morning. China and Naya had just come back to China's condo. They had hit up a couple of male strip clubs and gentlemen clubs. It was Naya's birthday so the women enjoyed themselves. It was the only time of year Naya could come out of her shell, and tonight she did.

Rugar had hit her up on facetime earlier that day to wish her a Happy B Day. Fatima had taken them to every hotspot in the city, and by the time they returned they were good and drunk.

"I ain't had that much fun in a long time," Naya said, sitting on the couch.

"I never seen dicks that big in my life. Them shits look scary," China said from the kitchen. She opened a bottle of wine as she tried to control her balance. "Do you want a glass?" she asked once back in the living room.

Naya was reading all the birthday wishes she'd gotten from people on her iPhone.

"Nah, I'm good. I can't believe how your friend grabbed that big muscle-head nigga's dick and kissed it," Naya said.

I think she used to fuck with him," China said. She sat down and took her high heels off. She had worn a see-through Versace dress with a Versace bikini underneath. You could see her whole body in plain view.

Naya wore a tight, short Prada dress that hugged her thighs and you could see her panties and ass cheeks when she sat down.

"That dark skin brother with the dreads, tatts, and muscles almost made me kidnap him. He from New York and his name was Remell. I was ready to bust it open for him," Naya said laughing, and feeling tipsy.

"You crazy girl but you look nice in that skirt," China said, She stared at Naya's thick upper thighs.

"Shit, you killing that Versace too. I should've rocked that," Naya replied. She stared at China's perfect breasts.

The two eyed each other lustfully and the room got silent for a minute. The wine had them feeling horny and vulnerable. The two women were now face-to-face and they leaned forward and locked lips, catching each other off guard.

"Ummm, I'm so sorry, Naya," China said. Coming to her senses, she backed away.

Naya was at a loss for words. She had never kissed another woman but China was so beautiful. so she was also at fault since she returned the kiss. There was something sexual between them but both women knew it could never be.

"It's cool. It's on me too, so don't sweat it. Let's just act like the shit never happened," Naya said and stood up.

China opened her mouth to speak. "I just never—"

"It's cool," Naya said. "I gotta go. I have to open my salon tomorrow. Make sure you be there," Naya said and began to walk out.

"You sure you cool enough to drive? I can take you," China asked.

"Nah, Remell just texted me and I got a date. He might be the one to knock the dust off this good ass pussy," Naya said, laughing and walked out the door.

***

Naya was parking her car in the underground garage. She texted Remell her address so he could meet her. Tonight was her night and she planned to live it up by any means. Her pussy hadn't been touched by a man in a long time, but she planned to change that tonight. Within seconds he texted back confirming her address. Earlier, they had two talked for two hours and it seemed they had a strong vibe.

Naya rushed to her apartment to shower and get ready.

Fifteen minutes later, her doorbell rang. She rushed from the back wearing high heels and a lingerie set that exposed her nipples, and fat, shaved, juicy pussy. She opened the door to and he was holding a big teddy bear and some chocolate candy in his hands.

"Happy B day, beautiful," he said, giving her a hug. He could smell the scent of her strong Dolce & Gabbana perfume.

"Thank you," she said. She walked off making her ass clap and jiggle with every step.

"My room is back here," she stated sexually. He looked around admiring her pad which was expensive and classy.

When they got in the room it was on and popping. They undressed each other until they were naked. When Naya saw his massive twelve-inch pipe she got chills, but he promised to go easy.

He slid his dick in her tight pussy making her go crazy. He stroked her slowly and gently.

"Uhm, ohh, fuck," Naya gritted. She felt the pain. After they both came, she was ready to ride. "Aweee, ugghh, yess babyyy," she yelled, as her C-cup breasts bounced up and down. She rode his dick while he glided her hips into his. "I'm cumming," she yelled. Her cream exploded from her pussy.

Remell laid her on her back and opened her legs. He dived in head-first and began eating her pussy and sucking her clit until she climaxed again.

"Ohhh, damn," she moaned. She pushed her fat pussy into his face and continued squirting her juices. Remell laid her on her stomach and licked her asshole clean, shocking her as he licked her brown, small booty hole.

He wasn't done yet and he bent her over and pounded her back out roughly.

"Damn, you feel so good," he moaned, as he long stroked her tight pussy. He tried hard not to lose control, but her shit was so good they nutted again.

Naya started licking his balls then made her way up to his dick. She wrapped her perfect lips around the head and went to work. She spit on his dick and took as much as she could down her throat.

"God damn," Remell said as his toe began to curl like noodles. Then he came in her mouth. When she felt his thick cum, she kept sucking until he was empty. Then she went to spit it out in the bathroom.

They made love under the sheets and all that could be heard was ass clapping on dick and they fucked like wild animals for the rest of the night.

***

The next morning, Naya woke up sore. She could hardly move and all she wanted to do was soak in a hot tub. She saw a letter on the pillow next to her from Remell that read:

You're the best thing I ever came across. I want you right now, but we've got a 6 p.m. date. Be ready. There's something about you I've never felt before. – Remell

Naya smiled after reading his neat handwriting. She looked at the time and she had an hour to get ready for her salon opening.

She decided she didn't have time for the tub and hopped in the shower. She could feel the pain of their sexual escapade all through her body. She had never had a dick that big and she loved it. However, her sore pussy said different.

Remell was heavily on her mind as she got dressed. She decided to wear a business suit and high heels and looked like a real businesswoman.

She got in the elevator and rushed down the stairs so she wouldn't be late. As soon as she pulled off in her Mclaurea, a black truck cut her off. Then, six other trucks ambushed her from all directions.

"Freeze, bitch! Don't move and put your hands on the fucking steering wheel." Naya froze with tears in her eyes as she did as she was told. There was a gun under her seat but that was easy to beat.

The FEDS slammed her to the ground and cuffed her while talking shit.

Romell Tukes

CHAPTER 32
MOUNT VERNON, NY

Loco had just gotten back from dropping Turk off to re-up so he could disburse product to all the workers. He had recently bought his mom a house in Mt. Vernon, in a quiet neighborhood away from Polo Grounds, his stepping grounds.

Nobody would ever suspect a gangbanger of living in that house which was perfect.

"Hey, Mom, what you doing?" Loco asked walking into the house. She was sitting on the couch flicking through old photos.

"Hey, baby. Just thinking about when you was baby and looking through some pics," Ashati stated as she took off her reading glasses. She was beautiful—half Native American with perfect skin and long silky hair—she looked like a young Lisa Lisa.

"Damn, that was so long ago," Loco shouted when he saw a picture of him in a clown suit for his fourth grade Halloween party.

Ashati was raised on the Harlem streets and she'd grown up around gangstas and hustlers. That was how she'd met Loco's father—he was a known robber and killer.

"You remember this picture at Disneyland?" she asked, as he placed his gun on the dresser. She was used to it and she had always told him to protect himself.

"I pissed on myself that day," he said laughing.

"How about this one? Your first grade picture. You and Chris. I remember the both of you was so scared," she said. She passed him the photo with him and Lil C dressed up in there little suit.

"Yeah, that's bro," Loco said smiling.

Ashati turned a photo page and a small photo slipped out and Loco picked it up. "Who's this?" he asked. There were two niggas in fur mink coats and big icy rope chains, and they were sitting on the hood of an old school Cadillac. Ashati's facial expression changed. She hadn't seen the picture in years. By the look on her face Loco knew something was wrong.

"I don't know if you're ready for the truth. Just go wash up and get ready for dinner," Ashati said.

"Mom, don't do this. I been ready. Please just let me close this chapter in my life," he stated.

She took a deep breath. "That man was your father's connect. He grew up with us he was like family to us. He let greed take over his honor in the worst way. Your father ran a dope house in Queens. One day your father called me out to Queens and told me to pack up everything. At the time I knew something was seriously wrong," she said and paused, as she tried to hold back her tears.

"He left and told me he would be back in a couple of hours and then we would be leaving town. I was pregnant and young so I didn't question him. Long story short, two hours later he was gunned down in the streets by the man in the picture," she stated.

Loco looked at the man in the picture and noticed there was something familiar about him, but he couldn't put his finger on it.

"The next day I was ready to leave town. Your father's death demolished me in every way, Pete showed up at my house smiling. He had the nerve to tell me he killed his own friend because he'd stolen four bricks and one hundred fifty thousand dollars in cash from him. He told me I was safe. See, me and Pete went to school together. We even dated before your father but I hate him now. He's still alive, running around doing good, owning businesses, and raising a family in Fosta projects," Ashati said. Just as the name left her lips, Pete's face started to come to light in Loco's head.

"I believe his son or nephew was recently killed by police. It was all over the news but karma a bitch. The name finally clicked and Pete was P. The old head that used to be with Rugar in the projects when he used to go check Rugar.

Loco had also heard about Rugar's brother shooting it out with the police. Everything started to connect and he had a feeling it was about to be a hot winter.

Days Later

Loco had been parked in the rear parking lot of Fosta, in a black minivan, waiting on P for three days. With no choice, he had taken all his shits and piss in bags not wanting to blow his cover. He had also been snorting cocaine for three days straight which helped him stay up and alert. An all-white Jaguar F-type R pulled up and parked near him, but it looked out of place.

Uncle P parked a couple of spots near Loco. He had a pretty Spanish bitch named Omari with him. She was from the Heights.

"We had so much fun, papi. I can't wait until we fuck upstairs. The car was okay but I love to fuck wildly," she said as he got out of the car.

"Yeah, we gonna have a long time," he said, realizing it was close to 11 p.m. The hood was empty and cold as they walked through the parking lot.

"Don't fucking move, and turn the fuck around," Loco yelled, creeping up behind them. Catching them both off guard, he'd scared them nearly to death. His pistol was pointed directly at their backs, and they were confused and afraid to move or turn around.

"I said turn the fuck around," Loco yelled. He was geeked and coke dripped down his nose.

"Don't I know you? Look man, you can have the money but you making a big mistake," Uncle P said. Omari had started crying.

"Please, kill him and not me," she pleaded, throwing P to the wolves, "I got six kids," she continued. P looked at her oddly. The bitch had told him she didn't have any kids.

"You killed my pops, JR. Remember him?" Loco asked.

"Listen kid, your pops was a thief. It's a cold game," Uncle P said honestly. A couple of fiends were walking by and saw the interaction. They turned around and went the other way forgetting all about the late night hit they were searching for.

"Okay, gangsta. You right, it is a cold game.
Boom! Boom! Boom! Boom! Boom! Boom!

Loco killed them both and took off running in the dark parking lot. He didn't stop running until he'd made it to his van. Then, he jumped inside and pulled off without looking back.

Peekskill, NY

Lil C had Michelle's eyes covered as she stood in front of the mini mansion upstate.

"Okay, you can open them now," he said and uncovered her eyes.

"Oh my God, baby! It's so nice," she yelled. She looked at the nice size mini mansion with the large grand driveway. The yard was huge and there was a waterfall in the middle of the driveway, glass doors, and a perfectly manicured lawn.

"You like it? Come on, it's yours," he said. He led the way inside and allowed his mother to admire the shiny marble floors, high ceilings, and the expensive wallpaper.

Lil C was up in the game. Jumbo had been blessing him with tons of keys—so much so, he had to rent an eighteen wheeler to move work. Jumbo still hadn't had time to tell Rugar he was supplying him but he'd called a meeting later that week to sit down with them both.

Turk was making major moves in the Midwest while Poo Bear had connections in Philly and Delaware. Loco was nowhere to be found, of course. But Lil C had money to get and he knew Loco was good. He figured he was probably in some pussy somewhere uptown.

CHAPTER 33
BROOKLYN, NY

Naya sat on her bunk in a federal holding cell staring out of her cell window. Her eyes were fixated on the Empire State building. She remembered her first time she'd paid a visit to the Empire State building when she was fourteen years old. She was with Brazy.

That was the same day they started the empire. And a year later, the empire was the talk of the town. Brazy and Hound had robbed and killed a Dominican connect for two hundred keys and they never looked back. At the age of sixteen they were the richest niggas in the city.

The FBI in Miami had flown Naya to New York because her charges were in New Jersey and New York. She was being charged with twelve murders at Queen pen status. She was also charged with the RICO Act, weapon charge 924(c)(j)(i), and running an organizational criminal enterprise on a 56mcn indictment. She was the leader and only female.

She had seen saw her paid lawyer two days prior. Mr. Calhoun, her lawyer, had almost made her vomit when he have her the news that she could possibly be sentenced to death penalty.

Her judge, Mr. Lopez, was the worst judge in the Southern and Northern district. Her lawyer had already informed her a cop-out with 70–100 years on the table. And that was *if* they chose to lift the sentence of the death penalty.

Mr. Calhon told her they really wanted her boss, Brazy, but since he was dead, she would have to do. The case was so strong someone would have to take the fall. The FEDS didn't have much on Naya but they had enough to indict her.

For 24 hrs., they tried their best to break her, playing good cop/bad cop. They tried to persuade her to give up her crew, her new boss, and her connect, but she remained silent and militant.

They showed her pictures of her and Brazy five years prior in the DR, Cali, Miami, and in Cuba. She was surprised because she had no clue they'd been watching her that long. They told her when, and why they had started investigating Brazy six years prior

***

Over six years ago, Agent Carver, a twenty-two-year-old rookie had gone on an undercover bust alone. He wanted to gain a name in the Bureau. The FEDS wanted Brazy and his name was ringing bells in the streets but they could never get enough to build a case on him.

Agent Carver was a young black male acting as if he was a street nigga trying to find a new connect. After months of hanging with Brazy, he was still unable to get him to sell him work or bring him in his organization.

One day, Agent Carver's body was found floating in the Hudson River. All the evidence Carver had on Brazy had disappeared from his apartment. There were no links to the murder but the FEDS had an idea it was Brazy. With that thought in mind, they began to dig deeper into him and his empire.

***

Luckily, the FEDS had no photos of the empire's members. Most importantly, they didn't have any photos of PYT or Rugar, so that made her feel somewhat easier.

"Miss Naya, you've got a visit girl. Cheer up, I've known you forever. Just stay prayed up," Ms. Clay said, walking inside her cell. Ms. Clay knew Naya from Newark and the two had been friends from the streets. Ms. Clay's husband was an ex-worker for Naya until he opened a car dealership.

"Thanks, girl. I'm about to get ready," Naya said, fixing her hair. Naya was beautiful even at her worst. Her Indian and Arabian features were amazing, plus her body was toned thick and perfect.

Naya looked at the letter she'd received from Remell and she was shocked he'd told her he'd seen her on CNN news. He had no clue she was a Queen Pen but in his letter, he let her know he was going to ride the bid no matter what. He was recently in the FEDS so he knew the ins and outs. He sent her an email address so she could request him on Corrlink and he also put twenty-five hundred dollars on her account.

Now wasn't the time for romance for her. She was fighting a death penalty sentence but she did have a lot of respect for him now.

PYT and Rugar sat in the small visitation room watching lawyers run in and out of small private booths with their clients. Most of them had sad, stressful facial expressions.

When Naya got booked, China called them and informed them of what happened. They got in touch with Naya's personal lawyer. PYT knew her sister was very militant and strong minded but she also knew Naya was stressed out sitting in a cage all day, waiting on her fate.

PYT graduated college days prior and received a Master of Arts Degree in Accounting and Business Management. She wished Naya could've been there to see her walk across the stage.

"You okay, baby? She'll be out soon," Rugar asked, seeing the discomfort in her face.

"I'm cool, love. Thanks. I'm just worried about her," PYT said. When she looked up, Naya was walking from the back in a brown jump suit, smiling when she saw her visitors.

"What's up? Why the long faces?" she asked, hugging them both tightly, before sitting down. She looked around the packed room.

"We miss you already," PYT stated.

"Yeah, me too. But I'm so proud you finally got your degree. Now you can open that account agency," Naya said as PYT shook her head.

"How is it looking Nay?" Rugar asked softly, asking the big question.

"My cop-out is one hundred years but I got the death penalty on me now. And if I go to trial they can hit me with a couple of life sentences," she said with a deep breath.

PYT shed a tear, something she never did. Not even in front of Naya. She stood up and rushed to the restroom.

"She'll be okay. Just please take care of her. She got love for you and that's rare, bro," Naya stated.

"This is some fucked up shit. You don't deserve this," he said pissed.

"I know, blood. But when me and Brazy started this shit I knew the outcome. So I can't cry now. They wanted Brazy but I'm the next best thing. They had no photos, wiretaps, videos, or nothing on the empire. Or on you two. Just me, Brazy, and a couple of Jersey and city niggas. I don't think it was smart for you two to come up here at this time," Naya said as PYT walked out the bathroom.

"Chill, it's covered. We used fake official ID's and license's but what can we do to help?" he asked as PYT sat next to him holding his hand.

"Kill all eighteen witnesses," Naya said seriously.

"I'm on it PYT," said without hesitation.

"Nah, I'm just joking. They'll put me in the chair," she said, laughing trying to have a sense of humor. But PYT was serious.

"What did they take from you?" PYT asked.

"Just my condo and three hundred thousand," Naya said as if it was nothing.

"Everything else is in yours and Aunt Pat's name in Atlanta. That's all safe down there. Just hold it down. But one important thing for you both," Naya said with a pause.

"What?" Rugar asked, wondering why she taking so long.

"I never told either one of you about this, but me and Brazy had a child when we were younger. We were in Jersey that's one reason I was always in Jersey. Me and Brazy thought it wouldn't be smart to tell nobody unless it was an emergency. As of now, I'm sorry," Naya said. PYT and Rugar looked at each other then, Naya.

"Hold on, so you telling me I have a nephew and I'm fucking his Aunty?" Rugar said confused. But me and PYT are stepsisters—same mother different fathers," Naya replied.

"This is crazy," PYT stated. She wondered why she would keep a secret like this.

"Where is he and how old is he?" Rugar asked.

"Seven years old and he lives in Elizabeth, NJ with his nanny, Monica. I spoke to her last night and she's waiting to hear from y'all. Please take care of Brandon. He's a good kid and he's my heart," Naya stated.

"We will," Rugar said.

"Don't worry too much about me. I lived my young life," Naya said being honest.

"Stop talking like it's over," PYT said.

"You two got a nephew to raise and an empire to run. I'm focused on this case and I'm thankful to have y'all," Naya said. They talked for the rest of the visit. She was the baddest Queen Pen in the media.

Romell Tukes

CHAPTER 34

It was night and Montonta was sitting sat in front of the projects with a couple of hoodrats and goons smoking and drinking. He was ready to hit some clubs.

"Damn, Montonta. When you going to let me taste that dick? I heard that shit on point, daddy. But I don't even see you no more," Alica said softly in his ear. Montonta looked her up and down with a chuckle.

Alica was a bad boujee bitch from uptown. She had curved Montonta three years ago at a basketball game and played him in front of everybody. She was short at five feet, one inch. She was light skinned with hazel eyes, tattoos, and she built like a brickhouse at 36-26-40. She had ass for days. However, if your bag wasn't up she wouldn't even let you lick her ass.

"Alica, I wouldn't let your thirsty lazy eye, big boob, small boob, dirty same-clothes-wearing-ass suck my dick with yo' mouth. I heard your pussy smell like the Bronx zoo," Montonta said loudly, making everybody in front of the building laugh including the residence walking by.

"Montonta, hold on big time. Let me holla at you," old school said. He approached him with a bag of stolen raw meat he was trying to sell to get high.

"Old school, you know I don't sell drugs. You see all these hustlers out here?" he said pointing to the twenty niggas shooting dice. There were plenty of them in the back on the basketball court.

"Nah, slim. I come to holla at you about some real shit. Take a walk with me," old school said, showing his gums and five bottom gold teeth. Old school was from New Orleans and he'd been in Harlem over thirty years. He used to be a big time drug dealer until he met a white bitch who got him hooked on dope after he came home from the Navy.

"What's up?" Montonta asked, walking off to the side.

"I saw some shit weeks ago that won't let me sleep, young blood. Listen, Pete was a good man. I've seen him come up from nothing so when I saw the little nigga who used to come out here with you in the blue Range kill him, I was hurt," old school said. Montonta was at a loss for words.

"Old school are you sure it was him?" Montonta asked. He knew he wasn't a liar and he was a stand-up nigga and well respected.

"I may smoke crack but I'm no liar. I saw his face as clear as day. And he saw me before I ran," he said. Montonta thanked him and left. He thought about Loco and why he would have done it.

Jersey City, NJ

Mark was sitting in his black Honda Accord waiting for Muhammad to show up. He was going to sell him the twenty keys he'd put in an order for the night before when he was in Philly.

After these twenty keys, Mark planned to go lay low down south in North Carolina with his cousin BJ and Lil B. Mark was on the run and the FEDS had got his twin brother two days prior after he'd made a big boy sell to his main client in Newark. The FEDS had waited for the deal to go down and then they had cornered him in. They charged Marcus with four murders, and that was enough to convince Mark to get low.

Parked on the side of a dark block, he finally saw Muhammad pull up in a Yukon with tints, and someone else was in the driver's seat.

"Peace, brother. Why you wanna meet way out here?" Muhammad asked, as he hopped inside the Sedan with all black garment on and a kafi, as always.

"Nigga, come on so we can get this over with. Where the money?" Mark asked noticing he was empty handed.

"Everything good ock. I saw you on the news on that big blood indictment. But where the work?" Muhammad asked. He hoped Mark wasn't a FED because he'd just been on the news.

"Right here. Now go get my shit, I gotta go!" Mark shouted. As soon as he did, he heard a soft knock on his window distracting him. "Who the fuck is this?" Mark said when he saw a light skinned Muslim nigga with a big beard. The dude was looking at him. He started to reach under his seat until he felt the cold steel press against his head.

Muhammad wasted no time since he already had the duffle bag in his lap with the twenty keys in. He blew his brains out onto his headrest and driver-side window.

"Allah Akbar, bitch nigga," Muhammad said. He climbed back into the truck with his Muslim brother twenty keys richer.

Muhammad looked like an average nigga but he was far from that. He had come home from a ten year bid two years ago and he'd taken over East and West. He was a plug and he ran a large group of Muslims trained to kill and rob.

He rode back to his hood with a smile on his face. He was ready to make salat and bust down the bricks with his team. He hated gang members with a passion and it was a lot in Jersey. And they were all was on his hit list.

Crown Heights, Brooklyn

"Aye cuz, you should've been on the block. I moved a whole key yesterday. It was like the first of the month," Big Two told Loco, as they posted up around a gang of Crips. Everybody was chilling and this was Loco's second hood. He had this section of BK on lock thanks to his homie Big Two.

Loco was laying low after killing Pete. He had a condo in Downtown Brooklyn and he had a bad Ethiopian bitch from D.C. Northeast living with him. Lately, he'd developed a bad coke habit but he felt like it was his meds.

"I'ma slide to Yonkers to holla at Benger, Kip, and YB. Then I gotta pull up on Lingo Loc. They got shit moving out there," Loco said sniffing.

Tell them I send my love, cuz. I fuck with my Y.O. niggas," Big two said with his deep voice. He was six-six and three hundred five pounds fat. He had a large buck fifty across his face from prison bids and gang wars

" I'm out, son," Loco said. He hopped in his blue Range and took off his Valentino Pee coat. It was getting cold in the city and this was hoodie season for hood niggas.

Loco drove down the Brooklyn streets and saw niggas hustling in hoodies and timbos on the blocks. He loved BK. He pulled up to a red light banging Jadakiss, his favorite rapper singing his song:

> *All the rumors and I ain't get robbed yet/ bitch ass niggas ain't stop actin' like broads yet*

Boom! Boom! Boom! Boom! Boom! Boom!

Bullets shattered his front window as he pulled off. He saw two gunmen running down on his truck with red flags around their faces.

By the time he bent the corner, twenty-six shots had hit the truck and he'd been hit seven times in the legs and chest. Loco pulled over when he was blocks away and pulled off the vest he kept on, which had just saved his life. He felt pain in his lower foot where he was shot twice but he was able to drive home with his good foot.

Draya, the Ethiopian bitch, was a nurse. So when he got to the condo she took care of his wounds. But he was pissed he'd got caught slipping and somebody knew something.

Loco texted Lil C and told him to bring his ass to Polo in the following morning. Importantly enough, Loco knew it was a blood and he knew why. The question was who was ready for another war.

Polo Ground

"So you telling me it was the Bloods just because they had red on, cuz?" Lil C asked as Loco walked back and forth with a cane, limping.

212

"Yeah, nigga. I was on their block, son. Bam Bam, run that shit."

"But why would they cross the line and violate?" Lil C asked.

"I don't know, cuz. You know how it be," Loco said, as he looked at him oddly.

"I just saw Rugar last month at his Uncle P's funeral and everything was cool. Why flip now? I'ma call him. Maybe it was a mistake," Lil C said. He pulled out his phone and saw a crazy look appear on Loco's face.

"Damn, cuz. I fucked up but I didn't fuck up. He had it coming," Loco stated.

"What the fuck you saying?" Lil C asked.

"That nigga P killed my pops. I just found out so I killed him. I'm sorry I had to, bro," Loco said. He looked at Lil C who was silent for at least four minutes.

"Tell all the Crips in the city to strap up 'cause it's about to be a war with the red nation," Lil C said, walking off saying no more.

Loco hopped in his Lexus truck to hit a white line of raw coke. Then he pulled off with a hundred grand drum Draco in his passenger seat.

Romell Tukes

CHAPTER 35
HARLEM

"Yo', blood. You heard what happened to Scram, Trap, and Blicky last nigga in the hood?" lil Jen asked his road dawg, Mundry.

"Nah, but I know it's beef with them hardbacks," he said. He was watching his mom cop some crack in front of their building. Then she rushed upstairs. He hated when she copped from niggas he knew.

"They found all them niggas dead in the hallway stairs in building 67. That's why it's still yellow tape in there," Lil Jon said, as four bloods walked towards them yelling and laughing.

"Munchy and Lil Jon were poppin' bratty," Beanz said. He passed him a box of Dutch Masters after making a run from the store.

"Shit crazy over here, skrap. Word-to-mother, the homies' deaths all over the news. I swear if I catch any Crip 'it's on-sight," Homo said. He opened up a Dutch.

"What's goody for tonight, son?" J Rocc asked, blowing Kush smoke in the air. They passed blunts around.

The sound of gun shots made the crew duck low, catching them off guard. J Roc was the first to catch two to the stomach from the MP assault rifle. Beanz pulled out a plastic GLOCK and Muncy pulled out a .380 special and both of them got busy.

Bullets were flying everywhere while everybody ran for cover in the buildings. Muncy was hit in the leg and Lil John shot two of them before he ran out of bullets.

Beanz got hit ten times in the chest. The bullets killed him right next to a little girl who had caught a stray bullet and died instantly. The little girl was coming out of the building to go to the store to buy candy with the dollar her mommy had given her.

The four Crips ran toward the building when five other niggas ran in trying to get low. But once in the lobby, none of them had the key to get into the building because they all lived in the back buildings.

An older lady was coming out of the elevator when she saw the teens and grown men pounding on the glass door trying to get inside. She was scared and she had gone outside to check on her daughter, Lieu, who she'd allowed to go to the store for candy. Sorrowfully, her little girl was dead. She was deaf so she was unaware of any gunshots being fired. Even so, she was scared to let the hoodlums in. She'd seen them around the projects and knew they were always up to no good.

Rata-Tat-Tat, Rata-Tat-Tat, Tat, Tat, Tat

An AK-47 ripped in the lobby nonstop, even shattering the glass. It hit the fifty-year-old lady and left everybody in its path dead.

The Crips ran out of the building with their masks on. They ran across the street and climbed inside two minivans burning rubber as they pulled off from the crazy gun battle they had just been in.

"Fuck!" Turk yelled. He was upset he'd just lost his little cousin, and Poo, little brother. Now, they were headed back to Polo Grounds.

Meanwhile in Brooklyn

"I just ran up a check. Maybe 40 bandz. Now I'm about to go to Miami and run it up even more," B.T. told Big two. Big Two was standing outside his Benz AMG truck looking at the bad Jamaican redbone with the long dreads. She was sitting in his passenger seat playing with her tongue ring, letting him know she was ready to eat his dick.

Big Two loved the strippers. He only dealt with them because there was no strings attached and they were freaks in the bed.

"I'ma trapper not a scammer. That's y'all Flatbush niggas. I'm the king of this," Big Two said, extending his big muscular arm. As he was shooting the shit, he saw two fiends he'd never seen before walking down his block. "You see them? What I need to scam for and I got them crackheads?" Big two said with a smile. He didn't have no shame in selling drugs. He ran crown Heights. Thanks to Loco he was able to feed Brooklyn.

"Them niggas don't look like fiends," B.T. said. He wasn't a street nigga but a college kid and scammer.

One of the fiends was dressed in an old FUBU sweat suit. The other was wearing a pair of ripped jeans, old sneakers, and a Goose coat. Both men had clean cuts.

When Big Two got a better look at the niggas, one of their faces looked familiar and he realized the dude had been in a spot up north with him and he was blood.

Bloc! Bloc! Bloc! Boom! Boom! Bloc! Bloc!

The fiend shot towards Big Two causing Big Two to take cover and shoot back. He tried to get back at them while ducking down but they were coming too hard. The bitch in the passenger seat was already dead and so was B.T. Then, out of nowhere, ten Crips came running down the block shooting all types of guns.

B Real and Double O took off running. Big Two ended up shooting B Real in his left ass cheek as they ran up the block, through a park, where they had parked an old Toyota.

"This nigga shot me in the ass, blood. Ughh, shit! We gotta get rid of this," B Real said, swerving down a main road. Two cop cars pulled up behind them as they drove through Flatbush driving wildly.

"Damn," B Real said pushing 80–909 mph. He was trying hard to lose the cops, but more had joined the pursuit. Double O rolled down his window and did the unthinkable: he started letting off shots into one of the police cars and hit an officer in the neck.

"This shit slowing down, blood. Keep shooting! I'm not going back. Last time I dropped the soap in a sixty-man shower! Do you know how that feel? No, so shoot, nigga," B Real yelled, bending a sharp corner.

Out of nowhere, a NYPD van crushed into them making the car spin. When B Real gained control, the engine wouldn't work. They were in the middle of the street next to a project building.

"Freeze you ass hole," one cop yelled with his gun pointed four feet away from B Real. B Real was still dazed and banged up.

"Put the gun down now! Now!

Bloc! Bloc! Bloc! Bloc!

The police ended up killing B Real and Double O and both men's' guns were already on the floor emptied.

***

Officer Wilson and Thomas arrived at the scene. They had been on the gang war case and it was so messy, a cop was also dead. "This shit is sad. I got better shit to do. Let these dick suckers clean this shit up. The two niggers dead anyway. They're useless now," Officer Wilson said. He turned and walked away from the crime scene. By now, there were several EMS workers on the scene, and cops were crying over the death of Officer Jones.

CHAPTER 36
WESTCHESTER, NEW ROC

Rugar and PYT stood in the kitchen of their mansion watching lil Brazy. He was in the living room watching the Angry Birds movie on the large flat screen TV. Brazy and Naya's son looked just like them. His golden complexion, long braids, and Indian hair was the spitting image of Naya's. His black and Arabian features and grayish eyes stood out the most. Most of his facial features would put one in the mind of Brazy.

"He's so cute and quiet," PYT said, smiling as she fixed her nephew lunch.

"He's smart too. He knows how to work the TV, computer, and phone. He's so polite to be so young too—he always says please and thank you. I'm upset they kept me from him. I wonder if Uncle P, God bless the dead, knew about him?" Rugar asked, wondering aloud.

"I don't know. I'm just glad he's here," PYT said.

"It's going to take time for him to get used to this lifestyle. I'm glad his nanny, Monica, is here to help," Rugar said.

"She's nice too. I even offered her three thousand dollars a week to be full-time but she said no, she was willing to do it for free. They got a good nanny."

Monica had the guest room. She was a pretty lady in her late forties. She had been looking over lil Brazy ever since he was born. Her own son had been murdered years ago at the age of sixteen.

PYT took her nephew his lunch tray with a PB sandwich, cookies, chips, and a juice box.

"Here go your lunch, Brandon," she said, placing his tray on the Maplewood table. PYT saw tears form in the corner of his eyes while he watched TV. He didn't even bother to look behind him.

"Thank you," he said in a soft child's voice. The strong emotions could still be heard in his tone and his voice cracked as if he wanted to cry.

"You okay?" PYT asked and sat next to him Indian style.

"Mommy Naya not coming back, is she?" he asked as his eyes changed to greenish color. Naya and PYT's eyes did the same them whenever they were sad or crying.

"Ummm, mommy will be home in a little while Brandon. But you have me, nanny, and your uncle. We're family and we're all you need. Mommy will always love you so there's no need to cry, baby. We'll always have each other, she said. Rugar shook his head making the kid smile

"You have the same color eyes as me and mommy," lil Brazy said. He grabbed his sandwich and bit into it.

"That's because we're blood," she said. Rugar stared at her oddly. RugarHe thought about what it would be like to have a child with PYT because she was so good with kids.

RugarHis phone was ringing so he stepped out back to answer it near his pool area. "Yo', talk," he said. Seeing it was Montonta, he closed the door behind him for privacy.

"Watch the news later. We losing a lot of goons. We lost eight this morning, bro. We losing money and it's so much beef, niggas can't even hustle on the blocks.

"Nigga, I been laying low for some weeks. I gave you the greenlight to kill these niggas once you found out what happened to P. You sending hustlers on a shooter's-mission. I told you to take out the main sources but you only drawing unwanted attention. You playing checkers in a chess game. I'ma be in the hood tomorrow. If it's too hot in the kitchen get out the oven," Rugar said, banging his phone into the cement wall until it broke into pieces. He was unaware of the eyes that were watching him from the window.

Somewhere in Harlem

Montonta rode in the backseat of a red GMC truck, through the ghetto streets of Harlem, a place he loved and would never leave. The news was calling Harlem the bloodiest winter in New York since the 60's riots.

Lil C and Loco were nowhere to be found in Harlem. It was as if they had fallen off the face of the earth. But he wasn't letting up. He and Rugar had a meeting the upcoming day and he knew his friend was pissed the Crips were getting their shit off on the Bloods. But Montonta was in the field hunting while he played house.

"Pull over, Blood. I need some wraps and K-2," Mighty Blood said from the passenger's seat, as they rode down Carver 105.

"Damn, nigga, you still smoking deuces? You not in jail," Levi said as he pulled up to a corner store.

"Man, come on, I got shit to do, blood. Go with that nigga Coke," Montonta told his homie sitting next to him. He was busy texting some Mexican bitch from the Bronx he'd met in the club.

Within seconds, two masked men snatched Montonta's door open and grabbed him out of the truck. A third masked man shot the driver in his head and Levi's brains were painted on the steering wheel.

Mighty and Coke came out when they heard the shots ring out. To their surprise, they saw two big men dragging Montonta inside of a small U-Haul truck with four goons already inside it.

Coke wasted no time and started shooting in the kidnappers' direction. He got caught slipping when three Crips came from a side block behind them. They aired him and Coke out and left them dead on the sidewalk.

Queens

Montonta woke up in a cold warehouse cuffed to a table. He was surrounded by twenty-four niggas in blue flags all staring at him. He slowly opened his swollen eyes and started to laugh.

"Am I supposed to be scared, blood? I do this gangsta shit, nigga," Montonta yelled as nobody said a word.

A light skinned pretty-boy nigga walked in and Montonta knew he was wild because he'd seen him on the Miami trip.

"You got heart. You just fucked with the wrong Crip, cuz," Lil C said. He pulled up a chair and sat directly in front of him.

"I told Rugar not to trust y'all niggas," Montonta said. Then, he spit in Lil C's dreads causing a couple of the Crips to rush the table.

"Chill. Stand down," Lil C said. They followed his orders respectfully.

"We was cool, cuz. We don't see color but P killed Loco's pops so he had to honor his pop's. Business is never personal," Lil C said, while pulling out a Ruger pistol.

"You a bitch, nigga. All y'all niggas bitches. My wolves gonna eat you alive," Montonta yelled with venom in his voice.

"Maybe you right. The East bloods got us in numbers but we got y'all in heart," Lil C said then emptied the whole seventeen-shot clip in his face.

"Boo, clean this shit up and cut off his left hand and put a blue flag on it before you wrap it up nicely and leave it at his door for an early Christmas gift," Lil C said walking out of the warehouse with his goons in tow.

Days Later

"What, wait? Hold on, slow down. Say that again," Rugar yelled in his phone. He had just woken up in the middle of the night to the phone call.

PYT woke up a hundred percent when she heard him yelling since he never yells. She immediately became startled.

"Okay, I'm so sorry. I'll be there in the morning, better yet, in a couple of hours," Rugar said. He hung up the phone shocked from the news he'd just heard. Although he was a true G, he had to try hard to hold back his tears, because like the Author Ca$h said, 'Thugs cry too'.

"What's wrong, baby?" she asked, covering up her nipples and breasts.

"They found Montonta's body parts all over Harlem. His hand was found on his mom's doorstep with a blue flag tied around it. I'ma go check on my nephew," he said and quickly left the room.

PYT laid back down after he stormed out of the room. She knew Montonta was his best friend, everybody knew he was Rugar's right hand man and capo. She hated to see him stressed so she lay in bed thinking of a master plan. She'd been watching the news lately so she knew about the gang war and killings. Rugar kept her and the empire out of his street affairs. PYT refused to sit back and watch him get killed or hurt so she planned to interfere after the holidays.

Christmas was the next day and Brandon had so many gifts it would take hours for him to open them all. She couldn't wait, to see the smiles on his little face. She went back to sleep with one thing on her mind... revenge on the Crips.

FBI

"Well, it looked like there was somebody pressing some service buttons from the backseat," Agent Patterson said sitting in his office.

"Yeah, that chopped up disposed body was a blood kid they called Montonta. He was from Harlem. We got a couple of pictures of him," Agent Knowles said, passing him some pictures.

"Who's this young kid on the Benz with the Yankee hat low?" Agent Patterson asked. The kid looked familiar to him.

"I don't know but I bet that watch wasn't made in China. What's that anyway? One of them Bust Down shitty Rolex's?" Agent Knowles asked.

"How the fuck would I know, Billie Jean? God damn, find out who the fucker is. I gotta go. Happy wife, happy life," Agent Patterson said, grabbing his coat to leave. Knowles shook his head because Agent Patterson's wife was fucking the Captain, a black personal trainer. Oh, and she was also fucking him, Agent Patterson.

CHAPTER 37
SOHO, NY

The upscale and classy restaurant was full of powerful businessmen and women. Everybody was dressed in their best suits and ordered the most expensive meals in the city.

Jumbo and Mayor Nelson had been close friends since being teens. The mayor knew Jumbo's lifestyle, and even though he disagreed with it, he still went the extra mile to protect him.

John Nelson was a hip white boy, almost sixty years in age. He was full blooded Slovenia-Eastside and had wealthy parents.

"Jumbo my friend, I've known you for over twenty-five or thirty years, throughout both middle school and high school. There is no difference between us," the mayor said, eating steak with a fork and knife.

"John, cut the bullshit. What are you getting at? I've known you long enough to know when you're cutting corners. Plus, you've never invited me to lunch, you're cheap and you're a fucking Jew," Jumbo said, as he smoked on a Cuban cigar, making his friend laugh.

"Them Crips and Bloods are making a bloody mess in my city, and now the FBI and D.C. got their heads up my ass," John Nelson stated as he brushed his slick hair back. Jumbo listened in deep thought.

"I can hold back the DEA and NYPD, but me and this new chief of police not seeing eye-to-eye. So please control your people and dealings," the mayor said. "The city never saw a body count so crazy—it's like Chicago out there. I heard nothing of your name besides you being a legit powerful man. I can't deal with nobody under the radar, or my job and career will be in a casket. They're about to start cracking down on theses gang bangers and these young kingpins, but I can only cover you for so long," the mayor said. He stood to leave and gave his four-man security team a nod, letting them know it was time to go.

"Thanks," Jumbo said. He tossed his napkin on the table.

"No. Thank *you*," the mayor said nonchalantly, "the bill's all yours. And for the record, I'm not a Jew, asshole. I'm Jehovah Witness," he said and walked off.

"Same shit," Jumbo said, putting his cigar out. He had to come up with a plan quick before he got jammed up, and before the cartel heard about this.

The cartel was against dealing with gang bangers because they were too deadly and too costly for their investments and empire.

Bronx, NY

"Oh shit, baby girl, Uhmmm, take this dick, nasty bitch," Turk said fucking Tammy from the back. He talked dirty to her while gripping her soft ass which had another nigga's name tattooed on it.

"Ugghhh, papi. Fuck me harder, papi," Tammy screamed. She breathed heavily as she threw her ass back on his dick.

Turk slammed his dick in and out of her soaking-wet pussy. He went deeper into her ocean making his balls slap against her pussy lips, which hung like roast beef.

He felt himself about to cum so he pulled out. The condom he had on was gone. *Damn, the bitch pussy must'a swallowed it*, he thought to himself. Tammy turned around and began sucking the life from his dick.

"Uhmmmm," she moaned. She opened her mouth wide and wrapped her lips around his dick, taking it in inch-by-inch. Deep throating him, she slurped and slobbered sloppily, eating up his pre-cum as if it was the last meal on Earth. He bucked and fucked her mouth until he finally busted down her throat, hitting her tonsils as if it were the bullseye. He held her head on his dick and wouldn't let her come up for air until she swallowed every drop.

"Thanks, papi. I needed my protein, and you hurt my pussy too," she said. She stuck her tongue out and slithered it around her lips, licking the nut off the corner of her mouth. Afterwards, she got up and got dressed in her Fendi dress.

Tammy was a beautiful Brazilian. She looked mulatto, mixed with black and white. She spoke Portuguese, her land language. She was a part time student and model. She had blue eyes, pretty dirty-blonde curly hair, and thick curves but a slim waist from hitting the gym three times a week. She had met Turk downtown the week before when she was shopping. She loved big black dicks and dark-skin niggas.

"I'ma hop in the shower," he said, still naked with his manhood swinging .

"Can I come?" she asked. She got undressed again letting her B-cup small breasts pop out freely.

"As long as I can fuck you in the ass," he said.

"Sure, papi, but go slow this time. You fucked me too hard last time and I had to go to the hospital. My husband found out because it was too loose. So please," she said following him into his apartment bathroom.

Tammy was married to a black NYPD cop. He was older than she was and she was twenty-five. He was a nerd at thirty-five years old and ten years her senior.

An hour or so later, they came out of the shower smiling. Tammy was walking funny because he fucked her tiny asshole so hard, if she farted she'd probably shit on herself.

"I won't be able to sit for weeks again," she said sitting down in the dark room slowly, as if she was seriously injured.

"Smells like must in here. It stinks," a female voice said, softly. She was sitting in the corner chair in a black dress with high heels on. She scared them both as she turned on the bedroom lights.

"Who the fuck are you?" Turk said. He wondered how she had got in his apartment but her beauty had him with a hard on. He look at her legs crossed and noticed her smooth skin, tanned thighs, and nice firm breasts.

"While y'all was fucking, I came through the living room window. Since you live on the first floor, you made it to easy for me. But it looks like somebody is happy to see me," she said, looking at his hard dick. He was still naked and obviously still horny.

"Jasmine, is that you? Oh my God, what are you doing here, and with a gun?" Tammy said. She was still naked too but she covered herself with the silk sheets.

"Tammy, how do you know her?" Turk asked. He was trying to figure out why Jasmine looked so familiar.

"I go to college with her and we do study-hour together," Tammy said as tears filled her eyes as she began to fear her death.

"Hold on, you PYT. Fuck!" he yelled. He remembered her from the club in Miami. She was quiet but she was the baddest bitch in the club. It was hard not to remember her. Turk thought about his gun under his mattress. But PYT was right next to it so there was a zero chance he could pull it off.

"Yeah, guilty as charged," she said, aiming her 9mm Beretta with the thirty-round clip on the handle.

"Jasmine, please. I don't have nothing to do with this. We're friends and I don't even know this guy's name," Tammy begged.

"Too late. You should of thought about that before you sucked his dick," PYT said. She realized Turk was trying to ease his way to his bed so she blast the stereo up louder.

Bloc! Bloc! Bloc! Bloc!

She shot Turk in his forehead right between his eyes four times, a professional shot each time.

"Oh my God, Jas. Please don't," Tammy said, when she saw Turk's body fall on the bed.

"Please don't beg," PYT said. Then she shot her twice in her upper-torso hitting main arteries.

PYT left the same way she came in. She hoped the loud music had muffled the gunshots.

Once in her BMW, she called a clean-up crew and turned up a Mary J Blige album before pulling off.

Finding Turk was easy. It just so happened Tammy always talked about him and showed her his picture on social media every study-hour. Tammy told her she was going to get some dick today from her side boo. PYT followed her to Turk's apartment. It was snowy and foggy outside so she knew Tammy wouldn't see her tailing her.

Harlem

Poo Bear sat in the far back in a cage of an black Dodge police van with tinted windows.

"You been working for us now for close to a month and you still ain't got shit?" Agent Thomas yelled.

"I've been trying but everybody low key and hiding. What you want me to do?" Poo said, sweating bullets. He was hoping nobody saw him meeting with the police.

"Oh yeah, so why are there bodies still popping up every night and we have no arrests?" Agent Wilson asked.

"I don't know. It might not be Lil C. It's beef all over," Poo said.

"Listen, dick head, we gonna give you one more week to come up with something big. If not, we're going to charge you with the murder wrap we got you for. You know Crips can't live up north most turn Lion, Muslim, or somebody's bitch. They end up sucking the whole tier's dick like a hooker when a big black muscle head tells you to," Agent Thomas said, as Poo Bear hopped out.

"You think he's reliable?" Agent Wilson asked, pulling off

"Hell no. Can't never trust a nigger. Shit, they don't trust themselves. But call Paterson and see what he got for us," Thomas said. He heard his walkie talkie responding to a double murder in Manhatanville area.

The police had Poo tied up to a murder but they had nothing on him. They knew he would be dumb enough to turn rat on his friends with a little bit of pressure. They had him right where they wanted him. But they needed Lil C and Loco and needed Poo in order to bring them down.

CHAPTER 38
MANHATTAN

Jumbo sat in his restaurant even though it was closed. He was waiting for Rugar and Lil C to arrive for the meeting he'd called. This gang war-shit was getting out of hand, and to make shit worse, the war wasn't even over money.

Someone entered the place and it was Rugar wearing a fur coat. He was smiling, and happy to see Jumbo. He hadn't seen him in a while because life had been busy.

"What's good, OG? What's up with this emergency meeting? Everything okay?" Rugar asked. Sitting down next to him, he noticed the serious expression on his face.

"I called this for a reason just be patient," he said lighting a Cuban cigar.

"I thought everything was in order," Rugar said, instantly thinking there was something wrong with the re-up.

Before Jumbo could reply, Lil C walked in alone with a blue Mink on and shirtless, and dreads hanging low like a true Jamaican.

As soon as Rugar saw Lil C, he stood up and pulled out a pistol. Lil C reacted the same way.

"I should kill you right here," Rugar shouted angrily. His mind went back to how Lil C had burned Montonta weeks ago.

"Try it bloodclot, mi gwan blow your bumbaclot brains all over tis table," Lil C said with fire in his eyes. His mind went back to having to bury Turk the other day.

"Men, there will be no killing in here. This ain't the streets. It's my establishment so please respect me and lower your weapons," Jumbo said softly. Both men put their guns away.

"This crazy," Lil C said. Now he was mad he'd come. He and Rugar continued to ice-grill one another.

I called both of you here because you two are fucking up my business as well as your own success due to the bullshit. I'ma businessman and a successful one at that. So I will not let stupidity ruin the legacy I fucking built. I heard what happened to Pete, and

I'm sorry for your loss. He was my family as well," Jumbo said. Lil C smirked.

"A hunter needs to understand and remember that in a jungle, a hunter sometimes becomes the hunted," Lil C said.

"I ain't come here for this. He know what's popping," Rugar yelled as he stood up to leave.

"Both of you are going to fucking listen. Sit down. I got the FEDS breathing down my neck, I don't need that shit. I told the both of your never mix money and violence," Jumbo shouted.

"But Jumbo, you know the rules to the streets. If somebody comes for you then you come back ten times harder," Lil C proclaimed.

"You a dead man walking, so I advise you to come a little harder," Rugar said grinning.

"Listen, I called you two here so we can end this beef and get money. Both of you have very strong potential to become very successful," Jumbo stated.

"I understand that, and I respect you, Jumbo. But once blood is drawn and the line is crossed, there is no coming back," Lil C said strongly.

"Well, if the blood can't stop here today then I'ma have to cut all ties with both of you," Jumbo said sternly. Both men looked at Jumbo with confusion etched across their faces.

"What? That's bullshit," Rugar stated angrily.

"I'ma give both of you an option. Take it or leave it, men. I been in the game a long time and I'm entrusted with a lot of powerful people. I can't and *won't* let y'all bring me or *them* down.

"This bitch nigga brought harm to my people," Lil C shouted loudly.

"Watch your mouth, Crip-ass nigga," Rugar said, clutching his pistol.

"Enough gentlemen. Since we can't come to an agreement or conclusion then we will have to depart from here. Pride is a good man's downfall," Jumbo said.

"All due respect, Jumbo, I respect your wishes but I'ma man of honor and respect too. Therefore, this shit can never be over," Rugar said as he stood to leave.

"I'm sorry, Jumbo. It is what it is," Lil C stood up.

"Chris, both of you are smarter than this. But I wish y'all the best of luck. I have too much to risk. But on another note, Antianer Wards aka Poo Bear is working for the people. The government is building a case against you, Chris. Be smart, kid," Jumbo said, before he walked out of his restaurant. Lil C couldn't believe the information he'd just heard about his childhood friend, and along with the news of Jumbo cutting him off, it was all too much.

Long Island, NY

"This is one of the few houses we have on the block that has an inside and outside pool, a full courtyard, a garden, basketball court, and a ten acre backyard,' Maria, the real estate agent said. Her, Mona, and Lil C were walking through the beautiful mansion in South Hampton.

"This some MTV cribs shit," Mona said, looking at the fireplace and marble floors in the living room. It led to the dining room area where there was a big glass table and a large China cabinet worth twenty-two thousand dollars.

"Everything in this house has a lifetime warranty," Maria said, running her hands across the stainless steel oven and stove.

Maria was from the hood in L.I. but she recently became a real estate agent after she graduated college. She was twenty-six and brown skinned. She had a nice smile and she was classy. Her ass was fat and her thighs were thick. She had short hair and looked a lot like LaLa from the *TRL* show and *Power*.

"We should throw a party here," Mona said stepping in the movie room.

"Damn, love. We ain't even bought the place yet," Lil C said. Maria's heels clicked as she walked down the hall.

"This place is too huge for the two of us and son. What the hell are we going to do with four other rooms?" Mona wondered as they toured the mansion for another half an hour.

Lil C and Mona were both impressed. They wanted it. They told Maria they were ready to sign but Maria told them she had to print out the contracts and deeds for them to sign. Then they could close the 1.2 million dollars' deal. But with Mona's A-1 credit and Lil C's 750,000 cash, everything worked out perfectly. Now, all they were waiting on were the deeds.

***

Lil C was parked in his Benz truck at the waterfront near the train station. He was looking out the tinted windows thinking about all the crazy shit going on within his life.

"You good, son?" Loco asked. He was in the passenger seat rolling a blunt, waiting on Tone from School Street projects to drop off the 250,000 he owed.

"I'm good. But this Poo situation gotta get handled soon before it's too late," Lil' C told Loco seriously.

"Facts. He called me a few days ago telling me he was in Vermont trapping. But I know he got a lowkey spot in Ossining like twenty-five minutes away from here," Loco said.

"We gonna get him but I'm focused on a connect right now. Shit, we running outta work. I hope Tone did his homework," Lil C said just as he saw Tone hop out of a Range in the snow. He climbed in Lil' C's truck with two bags.

"Here go the money, cuz. This nigga always wearing a conehead hoodie," Loco said when Tone hopped in the back. He informed them of a Mexican connect who wanted to have a sit down in two days, and Lil C happily agreed.

Ossining, NY

Simone Dominguez was on her knees giving Poo Bear a mean head-job as she bopped up and down slurping and spitting on his dick.

"Uhhhgg, shit, damn, ma," Poo said as his fat hands grabbed the armrest of the chair for dear life. She picked up the speed sucking his dick like Christy Mack the porn star.

Simone was Black and Dominican. She was pretty short, light skinned with blonde hair and thick at 36-27-38. She could pass for twenty-five because of her crazy insane body but she was only seventeen years old, still in high school.

Poo Bear was hiding out in Westchester County outside of the Bronx. He had given the cops enough information to bring Lil C down but they wanted more and he couldn't push himself to do it. He still had mad love for Lil C.

Loco had him nervous. Every time he'd call he'd question his locations but Lil' C always answered, Vermont or Philly.

Ossining was a lowkey town. Poo's cousins lived up there but only Turk knew about the area. He had brought him up there years ago but he was dead so he didn't have to worry about him.

Since being in the small town, Poo had taken over the drug track in less than two months, thanks to the FEDS supplying him.

Poo Bear had a clue Simone was young because her pussy was tight, small, wet, and her walls were too intact.

"Ohh shit, ma... I'm 'bout to cum," Poo yelled, as he tightened his ass cheeks.

Simone deep-throated him like a wild bull and swallowed his kids down her young throat. She continued to wrap her thick warm, young lips around his dick, bopping up and down until his five-inch dick got soft in her mouth.

"Daddy, I love your dick. I wanna be yours," she said, standing up naked. Her big breasts flopped in his face.

"Of course, you wifey," he said, getting his dick harder looking at her thickness.

"Okay," she said. She climbed on his dick ready to ride so he could come in her young pussy like she liked. His small dick was perfect for her tight, small pussy, and he tricked racks on her.

That's what she loved about him. She had another two hours to fuck until her mom's night shift at Wal-Mart was over, then he would have to go.

Simone used to go to school in H&M clothes and JC Penny gear no-name brand. Now, she had designer everything from head to toe. He would let her push his Camaro SS to school and around town while he drove his Porsche 911 in and out of town.

She had a young girl mentally and she only saw material shit. She even let him fuck her raw and she would swallow his seeds. She did anything to keep him under her spell. What Simone didn't know was Poo had given her herpes and genital warts. She didn't do check-ups because she thought it could never happen to her.

CHAPTER 39

Rugar had PYT's smooth toned legs in the air making passionate sex to her. They had been getting it on in their California king sized bed for over two hours.

"Yesss, daddy, uhmmm, go deeper," she moaned biting her bottom lip. She was feeling pain and pleasure as he slowly long-stroked her tight walls that gripped his dick like a glove.

"Damn, baby," Rugar grit as her pussy farted like a hand clap. PYT's pussy was so wet, cum was dripping down her thighs.

"Ugghh, shit, fuck me, I'mm cumming," she yelled. She rubbed her breast while he pounded her pussy out. She busted two nuts back to back and he also nutted in her before pulling out of her warm gushy pussy.

"Mmn, that pussy getting gooder and gooder," he said as they lay in the bed out of breath.

"I feel like we don't even make time for us with so much going on with lil Brandon, the empire, a new connect, the beef... You know I'm sorry," he said playing in her long wild silk hair. Her head laid on his chiseled chest.

"I understand, babe. Don't stress yourself. Trust me, it'll be all over with soon," she said.

"Hope so," he replied.

"I'ma go see Naya tomorrow, you wanna come?" she asked.

"I can't. I gotta meet with Big Smoke," he said. "He got some important shit he gotta tell me face to face," Rugar told her. She nodded her understanding.

"Don't forget. Wherever you go, have a team member with. I know you can handle yourself but it's a direct order. I don't trust Jumbo, and I know Lil C ain't playing by the rules," he told her.

"I told you okay before," she said with an attitude. She was well trained and he was worried about a wannabe thug who only had a couple of bodies. She turned around on him and went to sleep.

***

PYT had been throwing up all over the place all morning. She went to the bathroom and vomited all over the floor. She was feeling like shit and she thought she had a food virus. Naya had just called her to see if she was still coming to visit her. She told her she would after she went to see her doctor.

"Aunty, are we going to Chucky Cheese again today?" lil Brazy asked, standing in her room in his Batman pajamas, with a toy in his hand. She gave him a hug and she sat on the bed while he jumped in her lap.

Before she could even answer him, the nanny came down the hall.

"Brandon, didn't I tell you to always flush the damn toilet after you use it?" the nanny yelled walking into the room.

"Dang, sorry," he said climbing off the bed, then running off as PYT and Monica laughed.

"Chile, that boy is a handful I swear," she said with her strong Alabama accent.

"I know," PYT said with a weak voice. She was trying to get herself together for her doctor's visit.

"You okay, love? For the last couple of days you haven't been looking too well. I'm not nosy but you look pale and you don't look like your usual self," she said honestly.

"I know but I think it's just stress," she claimed.

"Stress? Girl you too young and beautiful for stress. You might be pregnant," Monica said, walking off when she heard what sounded like Brandon breaking something downstairs

PYT laughed it off. She knew she wasn't pregnant. It was impossible. Then she thought about the last time she'd had her period.

"Can't be," she said grabbing her car keys, purse, and pistol. She threw on her North Face coat.

When she made it outside she saw a gang of bloods waiting on her to move. So, she went back inside and snuck out the back. Then, she went in the garage and hopped in the black Range.

When she drove past the security team, they didn't even see her because they were all too so caught up in war stories and shooting dice on the side of the mansion.

PYT thought about how you could never take the hood out of a nigga no matter what.

Forty-five minutes later

PYT was in the doctor's office in the waiting area biting her nails. That was something she hadn't done since she was a kid. She looked around and saw five pregnant women with long sad faces wishing they could get abortions. Since it was too late in their cycles they couldn't.

A couple of teenagers were there for STD checkups. They looked at PYT admiring her beauty, but most of them envied her. PYT played on her phone as quiet as a mouse, waiting on Dr. Karp's results from the blood test she'd just taken 10 minutes prior.

"Miss Jasmine, good to see you. Are you ready?" a handsome white male in his thirties, wearing a white lab coat, asked.

"'Bout time," she said walking to the back to the third room. She sat down and her leg bounced up and down nervously.

"Well Jasmine, the tests came back," he said.

"That was fast. I just did it," she said.

"We work fast here. But, you don't have any viruses or STDs. However, you are five weeks pregnant," he informed her. She sat still, frozen in place.

"It's okay, dear. You'll be okay. I can be your permanent doctor. I also do emergency home visits if needed," Dr. Karp said, reading over the clip board.

PYT's mind was running wild. She refused to get an abortion so she had to come up with the balls to call Rugar.

"Here goes some information on pregnancy. Try not to stress or do too much, and I'll see you next week," he said, leaving her to her thoughts.

Long Island, NY

Big Smoke looked at the two large trucks parked behind Rugar's BMW M5. It was full of shooters.

"Damn, blood, you pulled up to my hood like Obama, nigga," Big Smoke said. He was posted on his block at a corner store he owned.

"Shit a little crazy right now but we need to call a new meeting soon because we need a new connect. I only got about a hundred keys left and Glizzy on his way up from Atlanta to get fifty of them," Rugar said, as the snow suddenly started coming down.

"I feel you, but we been warring with the Crips, out here going toe to toe. All them niggas be in Hempstead and we next door, so bodies be dropping er'day. I already got the blue print, bro," Big Smoke said. Rugar shook his head. He didn't want his beef to extend into the Empire like it had done with the Latin Kings.

"Don't worry, blood. Your beef is my beef. We family. But I called you out here for a reason. so let's take a walk," Big Smoke said, walking down the block.

"My girlfriend, Maria, is a real estate agent out here and she told me about all of her business affairs because I own property and I re-sale it. I let her do the book work and so forth. Anyway, she told me about a chick named Mona and her boyfriend whose name is Chris. She overheard her call him Lil C, a Harlem nigga with a bag. She said son dropped 700K or some shit in cash then it hit me, that's our guy," Big Smoke said, smiling.

"Are you sure?" Rugar asked.

"Bro, he had a Jamaican accent and swag. My girl from the Island, bro. That's son," Big Smoke said. Rugar wrote the address down.

***

PYT drove through the snow thinking about the seed growing inside of her. She wondered if Rugar was going to be happy or mad.

Once she made it to a red light she picked up her phone and texted Rugar, letting him know she was pregnant and they needed to talk ASAP. She was too scared to talk right now but she knew she would have to see him anyway at home tonight.

When she put her phone down, she was caught off guard by bullets from an AR-7 assault rifle. The powerful bullets were tearing up her driver side and window.

PYT put the truck in drive while ducking from the bullets that bypassed her head as they flew from a van outside her door. Once she got her pistol out, she started shooting back into the van. She killed two of the men but the van door slid open. When she busted a left, the van turned right. She was pissed she'd got caught slipping. She tossed her gun out the window.

She saw blood leaking down her side from her stomach. Police saw her swerve down the block and they pulled her over thinking she was drunk. Unable to drive anymore, she parked in the middle of the street and passed out due to the heavy loss of blood.

When the police saw bullet holes in her truck, they became alert. But when they saw her hunched over the steering wheel shot two times, and passed out, they called the EMS, hoping she was alive.

CHAPTER 40
HOSPITAL

Rugar sat in PYT's hospital room listening to the machines beep, looking at all the IV's hooked up to her body. She was in a deep sleep in critical condition. Still, he was happy she was alive but upset he'd lost his unborn seed.

When Rugar got the text saying she was pregnant he started blowing her phone up, excited to hear the news. He called over twenty times then a cop answered informing him she was shot twice and that she was the victim of a hit and run shooting. The cop also let him know she'd been hospitalized.

Sitting there thinking made him regret taking over Brazy's position because it was all falling downhill.

The police considered PYT a victim of a shooting. Since that was all the information they had, they left her alone. They could care less if she was shot dead. She' just be considered another black life killed due to violence.

Rugar had plans to send PYT to Atlanta with her Aunt Pam under the protection of Glizzy and his army until shit died down.

When he saw her eyes open he saw tears. She heard the doctors say she'd lost the baby when was conscious earlier and they were working on her. They said she was lucky the bullets only pierced her transversus abdominis, a muscular sheet found on the lateral sides of the abdominal wall, and her thoracolumbar fascia, which they explained as a deep investing membrane, instead of hitting her organs.

"Good morning, babe," she said softly, waking up from her nap.

"It's not morning now," he said, still a little mad she'd gone out alone when he'd specifically told her to have security with her at all times.

"I see you still mad, huh? I told you I was sorry," she said. She tried to move around but the pain was too severe and she was groggy from the pain killers she was on.

"I told you to do as I say for your safety. Now we lost our seed," he said pissed.

"Please, I don't want to talk about it," she said. She watched members of the blood pace around the door.

"Listen, I'm sending you to Atlanta until shit dies down, love. I can't afford to lose you or let you get harmed. I love you too much. You all I got," he said sincerely.

"How long?" she asked like a little kid with an attitude.

"Until it's over. Then, if you let me, I wanna marry you," he told her. "I mean, I want you to marry me," he said half smiling.

"What? Are you sure? Marry me, baby? I'ma gangsta," she said being honest. Even laying in a gown she still looked beautiful.

"I know who you are and what you are. I love you," he said again.

"I'll be glad to marry you," she said and began crying.

"Good. The doctors said you should be ready to leave tonight. And you got a flight tonight so be ready when I come back. I gotta go prepare for my event. I'ma leave a crew outside and they do know to check on you every two minutes so no sneaking out," Rugar said. He leaned down and kissed her before leaving.

PYT wondered who the nigga or gunmen were who shot at her. Then, it hit her. She saw a nigga with long dreads shooting at her, but she remembered hitting two of them. Hopefully, she killed them.

The nurse knocked on the door and brought her in some JELL-O and toasted bread with a chicken breast in gravy.

Days Later Atlanta, GA

"Damn, baby. I ain't seen you in years," Pam said when she picked PYT up in front of the airport. I don't know how you been but you look the same," PYT said. They hugged and hopped in Pam's white C-class Benz. Pam was thirty-five, beautiful, smart, thick, successful, and about her money. She owned a chain of salons all over Atlanta, thanks to Naya who had given her the startup money some years ago.

"I'm sorry to hear what happened but I told you and Naya about that crazy gang life. Me and Naya were talking about you last night. What happened to your modeling career a few years ago you came to the states?" Pam asked, driving on the highway to get attention from the other drivers like she always did. She was Black and Arabian and she had a beautiful face with perfect chinky eyes, long hair, long eye lashes, and pierced dimples.

"That was years ago. I'm a college graduate and I didn't get shot for gang banging, Aunty. I was at the wrong place at the wrong time," PYT stated, looking out of the window at the nice, hot summer weather.

"Well, your sister doing okay. She got two lawyers now. I hope they come in handy," Pam said, as they entered the Buckhead area. There were big houses with pearl gates."

"They will. That's what we pay them for, but I'm getting married soon," PYT said blushing.

"Damn, girl. He got you like that? I thought I'd never see the day. I thought you would grow up gay," Pam said with a laugh.

"Whatever. How long you been down here anyway?" she asked.

"Years. Ever since I left New York. And I love it. But what your family in Africa gonna say about you getting married? Have you heard from them?" Pam asked, and noticed the uneasy look appear on her face.

"I haven't been home in years and I don't give a fuck what they think," she replied.

"I never knew Brazy had a brother. Him and Naya were like glue. They used to always follow each other around. That' so sad how the police killed that handsome boy," Pam said driving down her block in a gated area.

Pam was always out of the loop. She knew nothing of the empire or their crazy lives. She had been a hard worker ever since she was a kid. Her and their mom, and her older sister, all had a rough life living in the Middle East India and the states.

PYT started to think about Branden and how he had to move to Ruger's Safe House in Albany while Monica, the nanny, watched over him until shit died down.

Once in the large mansion, PYT admired the place and its six rooms, three bedrooms, a game room, basement, and a living room the size of a gym. The place was amazing and Pam showed her around.

***

Rugar sat outside of Lil C's estate waiting on his arrival but it was a no show and his patience was running short.

The lights in the house were and on he could see Mona walking around with a baby in her arms, catering to her seed. Something he would never know the feeling of since Lil C killed his. He know Lil C was responsible for shooting PYT. Nobody else would have the balls to do that.

It was midnight and Rugar had just seen Mona put her child to sleep through the bedroom window. He made up his mind. He hopped out of his Chrysler Pacifica van dressed in all black, speed walking through the front yard to the back, to make his entrance.

***

Mona was tired. Taking care of a child was a full time job. She needed some alone time now so she put baby Garbiel to sleep.

She got undressed and looked at her body in the mirror. She still had it but her breasts had got a little saggy from breastfeeding. But she knew a boob lift would do the job. She turned around and started clapping her ass as her ass moved everywhere, like a stripper shaking her money maker.

"Still got it," she said throwing on a Versace robe. She walked out of her room wondering if Lil C was gonna come home that night. She wanted to fuck and suck the life out of him.

The past week, Lil C had been in and out. They never had time for each other but she could tell he was very nervous and stressed.

She walked into the kitchen then to the bar in the living room to pour herself some wine. She wasn't heavy on alcohol.

"Damn, I had no clue you was this beautiful up close. This ain't the life you hoped for, is it?" Rugar said stepping out of the darkness. He scared the shit out of her and made her drop her glass of wine when she saw the big gun.

"Oh shit, please don't hurt me. I have a child," Mona yelled with tears in her eyes.

"Bitch, shut the fuck up it's too late!" Rugar said and shot her six times with the silencer on to muffle the loud gunshots. Mona fell on the floor slowly as blood spilled out of her mouth. Then her body went into shock.

Next, he went upstairs to the baby's room and found the baby asleep. He saw Mona's phone on the floor lighting up. He picked it up and it was Lil C's name that popped up across the screen. He answered.

"Baby, I'ma be out late tonight ,okay?" Lil C asked when Rugar answered. "Baby, you there?" he asked as the phone went silent.

"Well, well, well... wifey gone, baby boy. Checkmate. How many moves can you make with a pawn?" Rugar asked.

"Ima fucking kill you! I fucking swear!"

Rugar moved the phone from his ear as Lil C yelled into it. "You ain't in no position to be calling shots but I want you to heard this... *PSST! PSST!*

He let off two shots into the baby's head with no remorse at all.

"What was that? No please!" Lil C cried, hoping it wasn't who he thought it was.

"Wifey gone, son gone, now let's focus and play for keeps," Rugar said. He hung up the phone and walked out of the house regretting nothing he'd done.

Lil C knew it was over. He just prayed it wasn't. He was on the highway, rushing home with tears flowing down his face. His goons were in the truck behind him.

CHAPTER 41
MONTHS LATER
HARLEM

Loco stood in the apartment complex in Polo Grounds discussing the hit on Poo Bear. Tonight was the night he would meet his maker. There were five goons with pistols and rifles ready to shoot up the white house if Loco pushed the button.

For months, Loco had been trying to find a location on Poo but he kept coming up short. It just so happened he met a chick from Peekskill, the next town over, and she was talking about Poo having the town on lock.

When Loco asked Abbey about Poo, she'd told him he was a made nigga getting money all through Ossining and Peekskill. Abbey gave him everything he needed to know about Poo just from gossip.

Since Lil C's family had been murdered, he skipped out of town leaving Loco on his own. But he was holding it down. He's found a new Mexican connect in Yonkers. The work was good but nothing like Jumbo's. It was sellable and it was a good price.

Loco was still on the hunt for Rugar but word was he rolled around like the president did in Iraq, but he knew he couldn't hide forever.

"Let's get outta here," Loco said to the five goons tailing him out of the apartment. They were strapped up on their way to Westchester.

Ossining, NY

"Damn, Poo, you always save me the shake, fam," Rell said, looking at the 92 grams he had in his hands. The shit looked like rocky powder instead of crack.

"Nigga, you always complaining. That's 92 grams of fire you just copped," Poo said loud enough, so the tape recorder in his stereo could hear him clearly.

"You right. I'm out. Good looks, son," Rell said. He handed Poo the money not knowing he'd just signed his name on an indictment.

Poo pulled off in his Lexus headed to his new apartment across town. He lived with Simone who had become a full-blooded gold digger. She even dropped out of school to focus on her new career, and not to mention, she was four months pregnant.

He was working for the FEDS lining local drug dealers up by selling them work the FEDS provided. This was his new life, an official rat.

Once he'd made it back home, he cursed himself for not picking up the salad Simone had been craving. He knew she'd live without it. He walked up the stairs where it was pitch black because the lights were out on this end of the large complex.

"Gotcha, rat-ass nigga," Loco said as Poo bent a corner leading to his crib. Loco and two other goons were holding him at gunpoint. Poo was about to turn around and run until two short niggas creeped up behind him with their pistols out. "Loco, come on man. We go way back," Poo said. He was scared to death too.

"I almost didn't recognize you, nigga. You gaining weight on me. You eating good, dreads," Loco said laughing. Then he slapped him with the pistol and made him fall flat. The goons attacked him with their pistols as he yelled for help, and the police.

Loco saw people peeking out of there curtains. When they saw it was Poo, they went back to minding their own business as if nothing was happening. He had got a little minor pregnant and the neighborhood hated him. Plus, he was slinging poison in and out the complex all hours of the night.

"See you in hell," Loco said before shooting him nine times. His crew put two bullets a piece in his frame, killing him in seconds as blood spilled down the stairs.

California, Long Beach

Since the death of his son and Mona, Lil C had been hiding out in Cali with some of his Crip homies who had moved out there to the LBC area.

He had gained a lot of weight, grew a big Freeway beard, and his dreads were dirty looking. He had all but given up on life. He moved to Cali the same night his family was killed. It was too much for him to bare. He was still in touch with Loco and he sent him money every Friday through Western Union.

Rugar had been on his mind heavily the last couple of months and he wanted him. He knew with time his dreams would fall into place.

"Aye cuz, come here and get a plate of this shit, cuz," JBOC told Lil C. They were throwing a big get-together in a big park. It was full of Crips enjoying themselves, blasting Nipsey and YG, Crip-walking.

Lil C was sitting down watching the scene in his all blue Dickie suit and Chucks. This was Cali's style of dressing. He walked over to JBOC, who was on the grill cooking, showing his big prison muscles and tats.

"You see all these bitches out here, cuz? Lil Kimmy just asked about you, cuz. Hop on that. Her head-game fire fool," JBOC said. He handed him a plate of grilled chicken, hot dogs, and hamburgers.

The two had been close ever since JBOC was a big homie in New York in the Polo Grounds. He brought Lil C home with his Uncle Lo. JBOC had raised Lil C and Loco before he moved out to Cali with his wife and brothers, who were born and raised in the LBC.

"I'm good right now, cuz," Lil C said. He took a sip of a 40 OE. They spent the rest of the day with the Crips and the female Crips. The females were turned up and drunk, trying to fuck the New York Crips.

The night was shortly lived due to a drive-by killing of two Crips.

Harlem, NY

251

Loco pulled up to his projects ready to slide in some pussy from Tia. She lived on the fourth floor and she was a petite, brown skinned cutie who had that snap-back, even after having five kids.

"That shit was crazy, cuz. We shut that shit down," Lil 50 said, recalling the strip club scene. It was 4 a.m. so the hood was empty as they walked into the back of building 55.

Out of nowhere, twenty something Bloods surrounded the four Crips with guns already trained on all of them.

"How the fuck!" Loco shouted in the hallway. They were ambushed by so many niggas, there was no way they could even move a muscle

"Don't look so surprised now. We been waiting a whole hour for you," Rugar said. as he walked through the crowd with half smirk on his face.

"Loco laughed trying to hide his fear but he almost pissed himself.

"Glad you find it funny," Rugar said and smiled back. Then he shot Loco in the face seven times before walking off. "Kill the rest of them niggas and get out of here. Somebody gonna call the police," he told his crew. He heard so many shots it sounded like the fourth of July in mid-May.

Rugar had one nigga on his mind, Lil C. The beef could never be over until Lil C was dead. And unfortunately, he was MIA which made Rugar nervous because he was deadly.

CHAPTER 42
ATLANTA, GA

PYT was laying by the poolside in her Chanel bikini. She was tanning in the back of Pam's mansion and the Atlanta heat was perfect for it. She loved it. Yesterday was her birthday and she had enjoyed herself at the spa, a nice dinner with Pam, and then they both got dolled up and went to a big party down town.

The party was packed with rappers, NFL players, and ballers. PYT was the talk of the party. Almost every nigga there had tried their hand. Of course, she respectfully curved them.

Dirty South niggas wasn't her type. She liked clean-cut niggas with white teeth, tall, muscles, waves or braids, tattoos, and she preferred them to be smart and classy. The south niggas were just thirsty with no shame, and they didn't know how to speak to a woman, which was a turn-off.

Rugar was all she wanted. She thought about him all day, every day. Whenever she did, her pussy became instantly soaked. They had stayed on facetime the night before for three hours. Rugar assured her she could come back home in two or three months. After talking for hours, they had phone sex until they both reached a climax then they went to sleep.

Her phone ringing took her out of her train of thought. She took off her Gucci shades and looked at the block number. She already knew who it was.

"Hi. Sis. How you doing? I was waiting on your call," PYT told Naya.

"Happy belated birthday, Sis. I had a visit from Remell yesterday. Then, my dumb ass lawyers came talking about my all my motions had been denied," she said somberly.

"Damn. Try not to stress. I know it's easier said than done but we gotta stay positive, Sis. You hear me?" PYT reminded her. But I miss you, girl. I spoke to lil Brazy this morning and he having fun in Albany with Monica," she said, hoping the news would lift Naya's spirits. She got up from her folding chair and she walked into the house barefooted. She looked down at her six pack and the small war wounds that had healed quickly and nicely.

"I been reading the New York newspaper, and girl shit is crazy! Police getting killed, niggas' bodies getting chopped up on some Hannibal shit," Naya said, glad PYT was in the A.

"I heard. Umph, fuck that," PYT said. She grabbed a banana and a protein bar so she could eat it after she was done with her afternoon work-out session.

"You know I start trial next week, right? Me and only ten of my co-defendants are taking it all the way," Naya informed her. "Marcus is too. I love that kid. He a real stand-up nigga, but I got Allah on my side," Naya stated, surprising PYT.

"When you start believing in Allah?" she asked. Waiting to hear Naya's answer, she walked to the guest room to get dressed for her exercise circuit.

"To be honest," Naya said, "I was always interest in Islam and its form of self-disciple, self-control, and self-respect. As a woman that's very important," she said. "Plus, Brazy and Remell are both Muslims. I'm seriously thinking about becoming one too," she informed her sister.

"That's good if it's in your heart. You know my family back home in the motherland are all Muslims," she said. As she bent down to tie up her Nike track shoes she wore to train in.

"Thanks for looking out for my son. Monica said there's at least eight niggas protecting him at all times. That's crazy but thanks," Naya said. She knew Rugar was overprotective when it came to family.

"You know my boo, but I just heard the beep so call me later. Love you and don't stress," PYT said. Naya quickly told her she loved her before the phone shut off.

PYT went in the basement gym and lifted weights, jump ropes, did cardio treadmill, and punched on the punching bag. She also did a few sprints and some yoga in her work-out. When she was finally done, her work-out had lasted for three hours.

Harlem

It was a beautiful evening outside and kids and teens ran through Fosta projects looking for shit to get into. Rugar posted up in front of the hood at the ice-cream truck handing out free ice cream to kids, while his goons posted up near the entrance of the building.

"Rugar, I want this one," one said.

"Rugar, I want the cone please, Rugar!" another hollered out.

"Okay, tell the guy in the window." he said. Two little girls had their lips poked out because the ice-cream man wasn't moving fast enough.

Rugar had already paid him two hundred thousand dollars to give all sixty something kids ice-cream. It was something he did every time he came back to the hood.

Today, he had to meet with Bullet to discuss a new connect. He made his way to the parking lot to climb in his new Aston Martin. Six of his shooters were all dressed in jeans, shirts, and hats. They tailed him like always and usual they stayed ten to twenty behind him, just to give him a little space.

Rugar was dressed like the business he was in an all-white Michael Kors suit. He looked like money because after his meeting he planned to visit Montonta's grave after he went to Naya's court date at 1 p.m.

He heard a motorcycle roaring through the parking lot and it made him remember when he and Montonta used to play on sport bikes. A gray sport's bike Honda sped past Rugar's goons and before Rugar could even turn around to see who it was speeding through the lot, it was already too late.

Tat-Tat Tat-Tat Tat-Tat Tat-Tat! The bullets from the Mack 11 hit Rugar six times in his chest but the bullet to his skull made him drop to the pavement where he lay dead.

His team shot towards the bike but the gunman switched gears and popped the clutch hitting 90 mph out of the parking lot, digging a trail surrounding Rugar. The one man the whole hood loved had been shot. People were yelling, crying, and screaming.

Blood poured on the pavement as Rugar's eyes rolled in the back of his head.

"He's dead, help!" a civilian yelled, as an ambulance sped in to the lot.

The two Latino men hopped out and threw him on a stretcher with an oxygen mask pumping his heart. They tossed him in the truck and rushed off. People were left crying and upset knowing they had just lost a good life.

New York Federal Court

"United States of American versus Naya Jamison is now in order," Judge Lopez informed the court. He hit the gravel and got comfortable in his leather chair as his eyes scanned over the courtroom.

"I assume both parties have everything ready for trial today?" the Judge asked. He looked toward the Chinese, DA Mr. Chew Lu, a rookie on his sixth case.

Naya looked around the courtroom and saw Remell there but no Rugar. She wondered where he was since he'd told her he would show up. Dressed stylishly in a Valentino suit, high heels, and Valentino glasses, her hair was done up in a long ponytail and she looked very professional.

The Judge went over every count and charge she had as well as her background. Then the DA showed all the evidence he had on her impressing the 12-person jury to listen to his every word.

Once they started to call out witnesses shit got ugly. People Naya had grown up with took the stand on her, telling the jury she was a killer who was suppling New Jersey with drugs. There was seventeen witnesses called after the DA was done. After four hours, the jury was ready to choose her fate.

A white woman announced her verdict:

"We the jury have come to a 12 and 0 verdict and we've concluded that Naya Jamison is guilty of all charges and we agree that she should get the maximum time prescribed by judge. Thank you," the juror said. She sat down without a care in the world. She just wanted to go home and feed her cats.

Naya tried to hold her emotions back. Her heart felt like shattered bricks.

"Based on all of the foregoing circumstances, I'm going to impose a sentence of 4 life sentences of imprisonment and a two million dollar special assessment fine on the defendant. Does the defendant or her counsel have any objections to the proposed sentence and the same goes for the government?" the judge asked with his head down smirking.

"No, Sir. We're good," Mr. Chow stated.

"We would like to file a timely appeal today," Mr. Chow stated on Naya's behalf as the clerk and typist typed every word.

Naya had tears rolling down her face after the judge banged the gavel and the US marshals came out to cuff her up.

Remell was pissed and his eyes were glossy. But he knew Naya would be strong. She was very strong minded.

Everybody left the courtroom with saddened hearts. Naya was a loveable person and she did a lot for the people in New Jersey and New York.

CHAPTER 43
ATLANTA AIRPORT

PYT had just got seated on the plane headed back to New York. Never had she cried as much in her life as much as she had in the past 24/7 hours.

Red Hot called her minutes after Rugar was killed in his projects and informed her of every detail about what happened. The only thing that didn't make sense to her was when she called every hospital in New York City, Rugar was nowhere to be found.

There were no death reports in that time frame in New York expect for in a town called Newbury, but it was a Spanish kid who murdered there.

She had a lot on her mind. The news of Rugar getting shot in the head the way he was, left a 0-10 chance he would be alive. She only hoped it was somebody else instead of her baby. To add fire to the fuel, she saw Naya on the headline news blowing trial for four life sentences, and that crushed her.

PYT texted a close friend a photo of Lil C when she was in the air and able to get service. Two minutes later, she received a couple of addresses and phone numbers from her mysterious hacker. Rugar was the only person she loved more than herself. Without him, she was empty and heartless. She prayed this was only a dream and that she'd wake up soon.

Harlem

Lil C stood over Mona's and Garbiel's gravesites which were next to each other in the graveyard. He cried wishing he could just go back to New York because he was homesick. He had cut his dreads and rocked a big Philly beard, and he'd gained weight so he didn't look the same at all.

He felt like a new man after he killed Rugar days ago. He knew the bike would be a perfect decoy but he knew the headshot he gave Rugar had took him out of the game. Now he could live at peace with himself. He had tailed Rugar for two days, and the parking lot in broad daylight was perfect. He ended up getting shot in the upper back twice but luckily he'd worn a thick leather biker coat, so he was only grazed.

His job was done here. He planned to go visit his mom then go back to the West Coast and live his new life working as a plumber.

He hopped in his rented Nissan and left the gravesite thinking that the city of NY really was the rotten apple.

FBI Headquarters

"Ain't no fucking way we got all these murders and no arrests," Agent Pelzer told Agent Patterson and Madison.

"It's like everybody we get, leaves or dies, boss. I don't fucking know. But I'ma stay on these gangbangers' neck because somebody knows something," Agent Patterson said.

"What about them two detectives, Thomas and Wilson? I know they got some shit we can use. I want theses Crips and Bloods off my streets. I don't care if you arrest their grandmothers. They're fucking up my gold and yoga sessions. Fix this! Now get the fuck out," Agent Pelzer, the chief of police yelled.

Peekskill, NY

Lil C and Michelle walked in her home upstate from doing a little food shopping so she could cook him a big Rasta meal. She was mad he'd cut his dreads. For a Rasta that represented his or her strength as a person.

"Put them bags in the kitchen," she said, following him so she could stack the food in her cabinets.

"How's work? You need to get you a man," Lil C said laughing.

"Boy, please. Come upstairs, I got a surprise for you. I been holding it for some weeks. Your father won his appeal but he might get deported," she said walking upstairs.

"Wow," Lil C said happily. He respected his pops. They talked on the phone here and there, but he didn't really know him. He only knew what Michelle told him.

"I'm so happy you here," she said, walking into her bedroom. "Oh my Godddd," she yelled when she saw the beautiful woman standing in the middle of her room floor. The woman was in a red dress with heels. She had two pistols, one in each hand.

"You fucking bitch!" Lil C said. He'd forgotten all about Rugar's chick but he had never considered her a threat, just Naya because he really didn't know anything about PYT.

"I heard it all before. Put your fucking hands on your head. You too, old bitch," PYT said sternly, with a serious look on her face. She looked as if she was in a different zone.

"Okay, don't shoot," Michelle said scared to death.

"It's okay, Ma," Lil C stated. He thought if he could get to his gun in his back, he could shoot her before she shot him.

"You killed Rugar," she said, getting closer to see him. Then she smirked deviously.

"He killed my family now they can rest in peace," Lil C said, as Michelle looked on confused. She had no clue what was going on.

"I feel the same way." PYT shot him seven times in the head. Even when his body dropped and Michelle yelled out of fear, she continued shooting.

"For future references, please don't yell right in my ear," she said before shooting her three times in her saggy large deformed breasts.

Bronx, NY

PYT parked in front of her old condo. She still had it and it was paid for. She had stopped by to pick up some documents and money she had in her safe.

She walked in her lobby and there were no security guards which was odd since the building was always full of them. Since she hadn't been there in months shit might've changed since it changed every other day.

When she walked into her condo, she hit the lights but they weren't working.

"Man, what the fuck yo," she said, walking into her kitchen. Then, all of a sudden she heard swift feet sneaking up from behind her and someone started choking her. She grabbed the masked man's arm but he was too powerful to move. So she leaned over as much as possible and smashed her left elbow into his rib cage, making him grit in pain and loosen up. She tossed his body over her and came down on one knee, snapping his neck in two, and swiftly grabbed her pistol from her ankle.

Two more masked men jumped over her kitchen counter to attack her but she sent a bullet in both of their necks. She knew there was more niggas so she took off one of their masks and saw a dead Spanish man. She could tell he wasn't American.

Out of nowhere, the closet burst open and two more masked men hopped out with no guns. One of them kicked the gun out of her hand. PYT knew these were trained assassins so she smiled and got in her stance, going toe to toe with both men.

One of them attacked her with a double roundhouse kick, backing her into the wall. But he made a fatal mistake when he tried it again. She grabbed his leg and tossed him to the floor, then broke his left leg as he screamed out in pain.

"Come on," she said, as she raced to the other masked man hitting him with a five piece, knocking him to the floor. She was as fast as lightning. Two more came out from the bathroom and she knocked both men out on the hallway floor asleep.

Six more masked men ran out of her bedroom with red beans on assault rifles aimed at her, making her look like she had chicken pocks.

"Who the fuck are you?" she asked, surrounded and ready to fight. But she knew without a gun she was done.

The gunmen said something in Spanish and when she heard it she was confused by what they said. "Don't kill her or we're dead" After she heard that, two shots went off and she realized she was hit but it wasn't with a bullet it was two large needles filled with blue liquid.

"What the fuck was that? I'ma kil—"

Her words faded as well as her vision. Then she hit the floor in slow motion. Night, night, night.

***

PYT woke up chained and cuffed to a bed in a huge beautiful room with fancy curtains. Her head was spinning and her body was aching. Once she got her vision back, she saw coconut trees outside her window with baby monkeys swinging from tree to tree.

She realized she had on a clean all white, Saint Laurent dress and her hair was done neatly in a bun. She heard voices outside her door. It was in Spanish. She knew sixteen different languages. She couldn't make out what they were saying as she tried to listen.

The doors slowly opened and she saw a beautiful female who looked like Shirkia and J-Lo put together. They walked in with a tray of food.

"We're so sorry for the cuffs and chains but we have to be cautious with you Jasmine. I'm a fan of your work," the Latina woman said in a strong South American accent.

"Who are you and what's going on?" PYT asked the older man who had stepped in the room in a gray suit smoking a cigar.

"We're not your enemy, love. We're here to help you and you're in good hands. We're like family," the man said in an accent she knew all too well, New York.

"I'm not for the games, so where am I?" PYT asked.

"Cuba, you killed a couple of my well-trained men. They weren't there to kill you," he said.

"Fuck all that. Who are you? If you gonna kill me, please do it."

The woman laughed. "No wonder he likes you," she said as PYT's mind began to race.

"I'm Jumbo and this is my beautiful wife, Hager. We run the Cuban Cartel Family," Jumbo said. PYT was more confused because she couldn't tell if this was a hit or a game.

"You were Rugar's connect," she said, remembering the name.

"Yes, that's why you're here, love. We will talk more soon. Get some rest," Jumbo said as Hager stood to leave with them.

"Hold on. Wait. What happened to him?" she said with tears in her eyes.

Jumbo stopped and turned to her. "He's in a critical coma. There's a 50/50 chance he could live or die," Jumbo said. He walked out as PYT sat confused and shocked with her mind racing. She said a prayer to Allah and that was the first time she'd ever prayed.

To Be Continued...
Gangland Cartel 2
Coming Soon

Submission Guideline

Submit the first three chapters of your completed manuscript to ldpsubmissions@gmail.com, subject line: Your book's title. The manuscript must be in a .doc file and sent as an attachment. Document should be in Times New Roman, double spaced and in size 12 font. Also, provide your synopsis and full contact information. If sending multiple submissions, they must each be in a separate email.

Have a story but no way to send it electronically? You can still submit to LDP/Ca$h Presents. Send in the first three chapters, written or typed, of your completed manuscript to:

LDP: Submissions Dept
Po Box 944
Stockbridge, Ga 30281

DO NOT send original manuscript. Must be a duplicate.

Provide your synopsis and a cover letter containing your full contact information.

Thanks for considering LDP and Ca$h Presents.

Gangland Cartel

By **Aryanna**
COKE KINGS V
KING OF THE TRAP II
By **T.J. Edwards**
GORILLAZ IN THE BAY V
De'Kari
THE STREETS ARE CALLING II
Duquie Wilson
KINGPIN KILLAZ IV
STREET KINGS III
PAID IN BLOOD III
CARTEL KILLAZ IV
DOPE GODS III
Hood Rich
SINS OF A HUSTLA II
ASAD
KINGZ OF THE GAME V
Playa Ray
SLAUGHTER GANG IV
RUTHLESS HEART IV
By Willie Slaughter
THE HEART OF A SAVAGE III
By Jibril Williams
FUK SHYT II
By Blakk Diamond
THE REALEST KILLAZ II
By Tranay Adams
TRAP GOD III
By Troublesome
YAYO IV

A SHOOTER'S AMBITION III

By S. Allen

GHOST MOB

Stilloan Robinson

KINGPIN DREAMS III

By Paper Boi Rari

CREAM

By Yolanda Moore

SON OF A DOPE FIEND III

By Renta

FOREVER GANGSTA II

GLOCKS ON SATIN SHEETS III

By Adrian Dulan

LOYALTY AIN'T PROMISED II

By Keith Williams

THE PRICE YOU PAY FOR LOVE II

DOPE GIRL MAGIC III

By Destiny Skai

CONFESSIONS OF A GANGSTA II

By Nicholas Lock

I'M NOTHING WITHOUT HIS LOVE II

By Monet Dragun

LIFE OF A SAVAGE IV

A GANGSTA'S QUR'AN II

MURDA SEASON II

GANGLAND CARTEL II

By **Romell Tukes**

QUIET MONEY III

THUG LIFE II

By **Trai'Quan**

THE STREETS MADE ME III
By **Larry D. Wright**
THE ULTIMATE SACRIFICE VI
IF YOU CROSS ME ONCE II
ANGEL III
By **Anthony Fields**
THE LIFE OF A HOOD STAR
By Ca$h & Rashia Wilson
FRIEND OR FOE II
By **Mimi**
SAVAGE STORMS II
By **Meesha**
BLOOD ON THE MONEY II
By J-Blunt

Available Now

RESTRAINING ORDER **I & II**
By **CA$H & Coffee**
LOVE KNOWS NO BOUNDARIES **I II & III**
By **Coffee**
RAISED AS A GOON I, II, III & IV
BRED BY THE SLUMS I, II, III
BLAST FOR ME I & II
ROTTEN TO THE CORE I II III
A BRONX TALE I, II, III

Romell Tukes

DUFFEL BAG CARTEL I II III IV

HEARTLESS GOON I II III IV

A SAVAGE DOPEBOY I II

HEARTLESS GOON I II III

DRUG LORDS I II III

CUTTHROAT MAFIA I II

By **Ghost**

LAY IT DOWN **I & II**

LAST OF A DYING BREED

BLOOD STAINS OF A SHOTTA I & II III

By **Jamaica**

LOYAL TO THE GAME I II III

LIFE OF SIN I, II III

By **TJ & Jelissa**

BLOODY COMMAS I & II

SKI MASK CARTEL I II & III

KING OF NEW YORK I II,III IV V

RISE TO POWER I II III

COKE KINGS I II III IV

BORN HEARTLESS I II III IV

KING OF THE TRAP

By **T.J. Edwards**

IF LOVING HIM IS WRONG…I & II

LOVE ME EVEN WHEN IT HURTS I II III

By **Jelissa**

WHEN THE STREETS CLAP BACK I & II III

THE HEART OF A SAVAGE I II

By **Jibril Williams**

A DISTINGUISHED THUG STOLE MY HEART I II & III

LOVE SHOULDN'T HURT I II III IV

270

Gangland Cartel

RENEGADE BOYS I II III IV

PAID IN KARMA I II III

SAVAGE STORMS

By **Meesha**

A GANGSTER'S CODE I &, II III

A GANGSTER'S SYN I II III

THE SAVAGE LIFE I II III

CHAINED TO THE STREETS I II III

BLOOD ON THE MONEY

By J-Blunt

PUSH IT TO THE LIMIT

By **Bre' Hayes**

BLOOD OF A BOSS **I, II, III, IV, V**

SHADOWS OF THE GAME

By **Askari**

THE STREETS BLEED MURDER **I, II & III**

THE HEART OF A GANGSTA I II& III

By **Jerry Jackson**

CUM FOR ME I II III IV V

An **LDP Erotica Collaboration**

BRIDE OF A HUSTLA **I II & II**

THE FETTI GIRLS **I, II& III**

CORRUPTED BY A GANGSTA I, II III, IV

BLINDED BY HIS LOVE

THE PRICE YOU PAY FOR LOVE

DOPE GIRL MAGIC I II

By **Destiny Skai**

WHEN A GOOD GIRL GOES BAD

By **Adrienne**

THE COST OF LOYALTY I II III

Romell Tukes

By Kweli

A GANGSTER'S REVENGE **I II III & IV**

THE BOSS MAN'S DAUGHTERS I II III IV V

A SAVAGE LOVE **I & II**

BAE BELONGS TO ME I II

A HUSTLER'S DECEIT I, II, III

WHAT BAD BITCHES DO I, II, III

SOUL OF A MONSTER I II III

KILL ZONE

A DOPE BOY'S QUEEN I II

By **Aryanna**

A KINGPIN'S AMBITON

A KINGPIN'S AMBITION **II**

I MURDER FOR THE DOUGH

By **Ambitious**

TRUE SAVAGE I II III IV V VI

DOPE BOY MAGIC I, II, III

MIDNIGHT CARTEL I II

CITY OF KINGZ

By **Chris Green**

A DOPEBOY'S PRAYER

By **Eddie "Wolf" Lee**

THE KING CARTEL **I, II & III**

By **Frank Gresham**

THESE NIGGAS AIN'T LOYAL **I, II & III**

By **Nikki Tee**

GANGSTA SHYT **I II &III**

By **CATO**

THE ULTIMATE BETRAYAL

By **Phoenix**

Gangland Cartel

BOSS'N UP **I , II & III**

By **Royal Nicole**

I LOVE YOU TO DEATH

By Destiny J

I RIDE FOR MY HITTA

I STILL RIDE FOR MY HITTA

By **Misty Holt**

LOVE & CHASIN' PAPER

By **Qay Crockett**

TO DIE IN VAIN

SINS OF A HUSTLA

By **ASAD**

BROOKLYN HUSTLAZ

By **Boogsy Morina**

BROOKLYN ON LOCK I & II

By **Sonovia**

GANGSTA CITY

By **Teddy Duke**

A DRUG KING AND HIS DIAMOND I & II III

A DOPEMAN'S RICHES

HER MAN, MINE'S TOO I, II

CASH MONEY HO'S

By Nicole Goosby

TRAPHOUSE KING **I II & III**

KINGPIN KILLAZ I II III

STREET KINGS I II

PAID IN BLOOD **I II**

CARTEL KILLAZ I II III

DOPE GODS I II

By **Hood Rich**

Romell Tukes

LIPSTICK KILLAH **I, II, III**
CRIME OF PASSION I II & III
FRIEND OR FOE
By **Mimi**
STEADY MOBBN' **I, II, III**
THE STREETS STAINED MY SOUL
By **Marcellus Allen**
WHO SHOT YA **I, II, III**
SON OF A DOPE FIEND I II
Renta
GORILLAZ IN THE BAY **I II III IV**
TEARS OF A GANGSTA I II
DE'KARI
TRIGGADALE I II III
Elijah R. Freeman
GOD BLESS THE TRAPPERS I, II, III
THESE SCANDALOUS STREETS I, II, III
FEAR MY GANGSTA I, II, III IV, V
THESE STREETS DON'T LOVE NOBODY I, II
BURY ME A G I, II, III, IV, V
A GANGSTA'S EMPIRE I, II, III, IV
THE DOPEMAN'S BODYGAURD I II
THE REALEST KILLAZ
Tranay Adams
THE STREETS ARE CALLING
Duquie Wilson
MARRIED TO A BOSS… I II III
By Destiny Skai & Chris Green
KINGZ OF THE GAME I II III IV
Playa Ray

274

Gangland Cartel

SLAUGHTER GANG I II III
RUTHLESS HEART I II III
By Willie Slaughter
FUK SHYT
By Blakk Diamond
DON'T F#CK WITH MY HEART I II
By Linnea
ADDICTED TO THE DRAMA I II III
By Jamila
YAYO I II III
A SHOOTER'S AMBITION I II
By S. Allen
TRAP GOD I II
By Troublesome
FOREVER GANGSTA
GLOCKS ON SATIN SHEETS I II
By Adrian Dulan
TOE TAGZ I II III
By Ah'Million
KINGPIN DREAMS I II
By Paper Boi Rari
CONFESSIONS OF A GANGSTA
By Nicholas Lock
I'M NOTHING WITHOUT HIS LOVE
By Monet Dragun
CAUGHT UP IN THE LIFE I II III
By Robert Baptiste
NEW TO THE GAME I II III
By **Malik D. Rice**
LIFE OF A SAVAGE I II III

Romell Tukes

A GANGSTA'S QUR'AN

MURDA SEASON

GANGLAND CARTEL

By **Romell Tukes**

LOYALTY AIN'T PROMISED

By Keith Williams

QUIET MONEY I II

THUG LIFE

By **Trai'Quan**

THE STREETS MADE ME I II

By **Larry D. Wright**

THE ULTIMATE SACRIFICE I, II, III, IV, V

KHADIFI

IF YOU CROSS ME ONCE

ANGEL I II

By **Anthony Fields**

THE LIFE OF A HOOD STAR

By Ca$h & Rashia Wilson

Gangland Cartel

BOOKS BY LDP'S CEO, CA$H

TRUST IN NO MAN

TRUST IN NO MAN 2

TRUST IN NO MAN 3

BONDED BY BLOOD

SHORTY GOT A THUG

THUGS CRY

THUGS CRY 2

THUGS CRY 3

TRUST NO BITCH

TRUST NO BITCH 2

TRUST NO BITCH 3

TIL MY CASKET DROPS

RESTRAINING ORDER

RESTRAINING ORDER 2

IN LOVE WITH A CONVICT

LIFE OF A HOOD STAR

Coming Soon

BONDED BY BLOOD 2

BOW DOWN TO MY GANGSTA

Romell Tukes

CPSIA information can be obtained
at www.ICGtesting.com
Printed in the USA
BVHW040222291221
625121BV00013B/657